ESCORTING THE ACTRESS

THE ESCORT COLLECTION BOOK FOUR

LEIGH JAMES

CMG PUBLISHING, LLC

PROLOGUE

Eleven Years Earlier

"Don't you dare do it, Kyle Richards," I said, my tone a warning. It was a fake warning, of course. I felt tears like pinpricks in my eyes, burning, threatening to come out and humiliate me even further.

"Why? Will the little-wittle bookworm cry?" he asked. My stepbrother's arrogant, handsome face mocked mine.

"No," I said, my voice getting thick. "Just give it back."

Kyle looked at the heavy textbook he was holding, the one he'd ripped out of my hands only moments earlier. He grinned wickedly as he bent over it and read in a fake-clinical voice, "'First menstruation, also known as *menarche*, can start as early as age ten.'"

"Y'all don't have any manners," I said, my voice shaking. I only let my Texas out when I was livid—I hoped he recognized it as a warning sign and backed off.

"*Y'all?*" Kyle asked, raising his eyebrows. "There's only one of me here, Lo. See, this is why people think Texans are dumb."

Absolute fury bubbled inside my chest.

"'Female maturation begins at age nine,'" he continued. "'Many girls will start to experience breast development at this time.'" He peered at me from over the book. "Present company excluded, of course."

Don't you dare cry, Lowell Barton. I dug my nails into my palms. *Don't you dare let that boy see you cry.*

He went back to reading aloud. "'If you're self-conscious, you might want to start wearing what's called a *training bra*,' which is another word for a bra for girls with absolutely no boobs." He laughed at his own joke, little snorts erupting from the back of his throat.

"Give. It. *BACK!*" I roared, and lunged at him. I grabbed the heavy book from his hands and started beating him with it. "And this is *not* a training bra, I'll have you know!"

There was a look of shock on his handsome face. I wasn't sure if that was because he really thought I wore a training bra—or if he was surprised that I was hitting him with a thick textbook. It was entitled *Human Devel-*

opment and Human Sexuality, and I'd smuggled it out of the local library without checking it out.

I smuggled it out because I was embarrassed. That was the last thing I thought before Kyle tried to swat the book out of my hands and I whacked him in the face with it. Bright red blood spurted from his nose.

I watched for a second, frozen, as blood ran in rivulets down his face. Still looking stunned, he dabbed his fingers in it. "Did you just break my *nose?*"

"I don't know," I said, my chest heaving. "But for the record, *y'all* can be used in the singular. *That* I know for sure."

Kyle opened his mouth and then, maybe thinking better of it for once in his life, closed it.

And before he could come after me, I ran and ran.

LOWELL

"WHAT DO YOU MEAN, 'tighten things up?'" I asked. I stared at my director in horror.

I was pretty sure I knew exactly what he meant, and I didn't like it one bit.

"What I *mean* is, you're too...*cherubic*...right now. At this juncture, your character needs to be more...emaciated." Lucas Dresden, one of Hollywood's hottest directors, had the decency to look at his *iWatch* instead of my face as he delivered the news.

"Emaciated as in...*starving?*" I asked.

He sighed. "Your character's been out in the desert. She's been fighting bad guys. She can't look like she just sucked down her fifth *Frappucino* of the week."

"I beg your pardon—"

"You can beg for all sorts of things," Lucas said, his

calm, grey-eyed gaze finally meeting mine. "But the producers said you need to tighten things up—which is code for hit the gym and stop eating, *today*—otherwise, they're going to exercise, no pun intended, the option in your contract. The one that lets them replace you if you fail to perform per the agreed-upon terms."

I could feel myself getting hot as an angry, all-out blush heated my skin. "I don't remember my lawyer or my agent saying I had to starve myself when I took this role."

"That's because you were thinner when you signed it, and your ass was smaller." Lucas pursed his lips. "I'm sorry, I know this is harsh, but this is Hollywood, and this is how it works. You know that. So no more carbs, no more sugars, no more extras at craft services. Go on a cleanse and start hitting the gym twice a day. We start shooting again in two weeks. And we never had this conversation."

I nodded silently. I was stuck somewhere between mortified and enraged, but I didn't argue. I kept my mouth shut. Angry tears threatened but I held them back—there was no crying in Hollywood.

Apparently, there wasn't going to be any eating, either.

KYLE

A few years ago, if someone had told me that I'd be a male escort someday, I would have had a one-word response: *Awesome.*

Now that I was an actual escort and hustling to earn every dollar I made, I had a different response: *H to the E to the L-L no.*

I loved the ladies and the ladies loved me, but I'd been playing Hide the Salami non-stop, and my salami was *tired.* That was depressing for a number of reasons, not the least of which was that I hadn't known it was even capable of getting tired. But Big Dude was exhausted. And now something I'd always been good at and enjoyed—casual sex—was making me feel sad.

Sad was new low for me. I didn't like sad.

When I'd started out working for the service, I'd thought I was so clever. Desperate for money, sure, but also clever. My father would *freak* if he knew how I was paying the bills since he'd disinherited me. That had seemed like a great idea at the time, but the more "dates" I had, the more I started to doubt myself. Why was I doing this with my life? If my main motivation was spiting my father, didn't that mean I was still just a big, belligerent adolescent?

I didn't want to keep turning tricks, but as I didn't have any other job prospects, I was still taking assignments. Today I was with one of my regular clients, Dallas. She was young and gorgeous, not the type you might picture to hire a male escort. But now that I'd been doing this a while, I realized there was no one "type" of client.

Dallas was a second-year med student. She said she didn't have time to look for a relationship. A string of one-night stands didn't interest her, and neither did a 'fuck-buddy.' She said she liked me because this was a business transaction and that I was tested for STDs regularly.

I liked her because she was (a) gorgeous, (b) appreciated Big Dude and (c) seemed pretty normal.

"Oh baby," she said breathlessly as I nuzzled her clit with my mouth. I nipped at her a little and put two fingers inside her wet pussy, which spasmed around me.

"I want to fuck you from behind," I said, sliding my fingers in and out of her purposefully. I'd been with her enough times to know exactly what she wanted and exactly when she wanted it.

"I love it when say that," she said. She immediately got up and got onto all fours, spreading herself open for me. Dallas liked to get to the point.

Not wasting any time—I was only here for an hour—I smacked her on the ass, rolled on a condom and entered her. She was so wet for me. I ran my hand down her chest, fondling her breasts, rolling her nipples between my fingers just the way she liked.

She moaned beneath me, throwing her head back and grinding herself against my shaft. I thrust into her harder and harder and fingered her clit until I could feel her body tighten and spasm around me, her cries increasing with each stroke.

That's when I faked my orgasm, timing it perfectly with hers so that she'd never guess a thing. I tugged on her pretty hair and called her name, thrusting and groaning like all get out.

Afterward, we lay in a sweaty heap together. Thank God Big Dude had gone back down. Dallas never guessed a thing.

None of them ever did.

"Hey," I said, getting up and buttoning my jeans. "Do you want to go get something to eat?"

"Oh, you're sweet," Dallas said, pulling her bra on, "But I have to study. See you next week?"

"Sure," I said, forcing myself to smile at her. "See you next week."

I TOOK A PRETTY long shower that afternoon, scrubbing every inch of me. I couldn't even have an orgasm any more, and I hadn't been able to for some time. *For fuck's sake.*

And I'd asked Dallas to go out to eat with me. *For double fuck's sake.*

I turned off the water, toweled myself off and padded out of the bathroom. Then I flopped across the bed. The worst thing about living in a hotel was that there was no refrigerator. Oh, how I missed the refrigerator in my old condo. It had been huge, and my housekeeper always kept it stocked with all the good stuff from Whole Foods. Smoothies, grapes, sushi, Indian food…my mouth watered at the thought.

And now I was at The Standard. With cheap towels, a stapled-on fabric headboard, bottled water that sold for seven dollars a pop, and no freaking refrigerator.

I turned over onto my back and regarded the ceiling. The refrigerator wasn't the worst part, and neither was the fact that Dallas had said no to me. It was that I was lonely. I, Kyle Richards, who'd spent my entire trust-funded young-adult life partying, surrounded my pussy, surfboards and beer, without a care in the world, was *lonely.*

And I hadn't the faintest idea what to do about it.

LOWELL

"I SHOULDN'T BE DRINKING THIS," I said through a mouthful of delicious tequila and salt. "Too many calories."

"Do *not* let those assholes get to you," my best friend, Tori, said. She pushed one of her dark-brown curls off her face, fuming. "You're not fat. I don't care what the stupid director said."

"He didn't say I was fat—he said my ass looked like it might weigh too much. And that I needed to be more emaciated and less cherubic." I took another rebellious gulp of my drink.

"Because *that* makes so much sense," Tori said under her breath.

"And he's not just a stupid director. He's a stupid *successful* director. Lucas Dresden is a Hollywood god.

And he told me that I need to stop eating before we start shooting those scenes on the beach. So that's what I'm going to do."

"That's just great." Tori looked as if smoke was about to pour out of her ears. It was good that we were in a crowded bar in Venice or she would probably have started yelling a litany of obscenities about my director. "What did you *say* to him? That you hope various body parts of his rot off and die? I hope?"

"Ugh...*no.* I said okay. I can't afford to lose this job." I didn't tell her that I'd gone into my trailer and cried afterward. I was worried I was going to get fired from this film, and then my career would be over.

I couldn't let that happen.

I grimaced and took another sip of my margarita. "The thing is, my ass is my ass. It likes to be a certain size. Starving myself for the next two weeks won't make it a whole lot smaller."

"Your bum is perfect," Tori said. "I'm so tired of the people you work with. And the press? It's sick, the things they say about you. If I thought you would, I'd tell you to quit."

"I'm not quitting." I'd dug my claws onto the Hollywood ladder and I wasn't leaving until they pried off my dead, cold hands. Still, after the past few weeks, I would have taken a long vacation to Cabo if I could've. Just the other day, my photo had been on one of the gossip websites. In it, I was heading into the gym with a scowl and a big bag thrown over my shoulder. The headline read: *Lowell B Takes Fight Against Fat to LA Gym.*

Oh, how I loathed the press. Let me count the ways.

My agent, Shirley, kept saying: "Just *smile* at them, for the love of God! You're starting to look like that girl from *Twilight* in these pictures!"

I also had a new movie, *Hearts Wide Open,* coming out at the end of the summer. With the recurring pictures of me looking...cherubic-cheeked...and heading to the gym, the producers had reached out. They wanted me to "slim down, tighten up, and dress appropriately sexy" for our upcoming promotional events. I'd had a few things to say about that. Then the producers had a few things to say back, which included phrases such as "breach of contract" and "never work with this studio again."

I'd called Shirley, who'd advised me to shut my mouth immediately. When I'd called her today and told her what Lucas had said, she told me that if I wanted to keep the role, I had to hit the gym. With a smile. And go on a cleanse. "I'm pretty sure the concepts of smiling and cleansing are mutually exclusive," I'd wailed.

"Nobody's forcing you to be an actress," she'd said. "So if you're in, you have to be all in. And make sure you smile when the paparazzi takes your picture! Not like that girl from *Twilight!* She makes it harder on herself, I swear. She needs me for an agent."

I wished that the girl from *Twilight* was having a drink with me now. I had a feeling she'd have some good advice on how to deal with both the press and Lucas Dresden, and that said advice might include the words *stuff* (used as a verb) and *it* (used as the object of the verb).

"It's been a rough couple of weeks," I admitted to Tori.

Tori pushed another margarita toward me.

"I really shouldn't," I mumbled. After a nanosecond of hesitation, I changed my mind and chugged some of it.

"I'm driving," Tori said, holding up her seltzer in salute. "Drink up, girl."

I did as I was told. I was working on that, and I needed all the practice I could get.

"OH, FUCK ME," Tori said an hour later. She pulled the car over.

I was completely hammered at that point, but I was

alert enough to notice the blue flashing lights all around us.

"Huh? Whad'd you do?" My voice came out thick and foamy, tequila and a sudden burst of adrenaline roiling in my stomach.

"I think I might have forgotten to update my registration," she squeaked.

"Oh, for fuck's sake," I said, annoyed that we were being pulled over. "Are you *sure* you went to Stanford? Y'all need to keep up with things." *Oh shit.* I was drunker than I thought—my Texas was showing.

"Just be quiet," Tori begged.

I snorted at her and gripped my seat. I wasn't sure, but it seemed as if maybe the car was spinning a little.

An officer came up beside us, peering into the car with a flashlight. "License and registration, please."

Tori fumbled in the glove compartment and shakily handed him her papers. The officer looked at them briefly then shined the flashlight directly in my face.

"Stop it!"

"Oh, sorry." He moved the flashlight away. "I thought I recognized you. You're that actress, right?"

"Right." I tossed my hair, a vague idea of getting Tori out of her ticket motivating my muddled brain. "*Hiya,* Ossifer"

"Um...hi." He peered at me for a beat. "I just saw a

picture of you online. Didn't do you justice. You're much prettier in person."

The tequila in me turned immediately ugly and I glared at him. "Am I s'pposed to say thank you? For thass ass-backward compliment?" I sounded slurry and mean. The car was definitely spinning now. I heard him sigh, like an already long night had just gotten longer.

Fucking margaritas. But my mind, ugly with booze and still reeling from the events of the day, couldn't be reasoned with.

"I didn't mean any disrespect, miss," the officer said contritely.

I snorted. "Coulda fooled me!"

Tori froze. "Lo"—her voice was a warning—"he didn't say anything wrong. He was actually being nice. Just be cool."

"Don't you tell me what to do!" I yelled at her.

She looked at me with wide eyes, shaking her head as if to say *Oh shit* or *Please stop, you crazy bitch!* Or both. Probably both.

"I'm outta here." I unbuckled my seat belt and heard the police officer sigh again.

Tori sucked in a breath next to me. I rarely drank too much, but when I did, I got belligerent. I should have known better. *Shoulda woulda coulda,* I sing-songed inside my dizzy head.

It was too late now. I opened the car door.

"Miss, I need you to stay restrained and inside the vehicle," the officer said.

"Why y'all always telling me what to do?" My voice was twisted and thick.

"I'm not. I'm asking you—no, you're right, I'm telling you—to stay buckled in the car. Your friend's registration is expired. I'll just give her a warning, and you two can be on your way." He sounded professional and almost apologetic, which just made me feel more confused and angry.

"Don't you try to make this all okay. Like you're a *dad* or something. And we're a couple of Girl Scouts. Are you *mansplaining*? Are you a mansplainer, Ossifer?" I yelled.

I was too drunk to be sure, but he might have groaned. "No, miss, I'm just trying to get you girls home safe." He probably wished he'd never pulled us over.

I was going to make sure of that. Because I was too cherubic, I hadn't eaten for seven hours, and I was on a tequila rage-spiral. I climbed out of the car and marched toward the officer. "I'm so tired of this. I got too many mansplainers in my life."

"Lo, no!" Tori yelled. "Just get back in the car!"

The officer watched me with a mixture of regret, annoyance, and mild amusement as I stopped and swayed in front of him. I noticed another officer with him, still in the cruiser—a woman in her forties. She got out and came toward me warily, as if I was a dog who might either bite or pee on her, her hand on the handle of the firearm in her belt.

"You okay, Scott?" she asked.

"I think so," Officer Scott said. "I think I upset this young lady. She's an actress, and I made a comment about her appearance. I apologized, but I think she's feeling a little...belligerent."

"I'm not belligerent," I corrected him. "I'm tired of mansplainers!"

He said to me, "I'm sorry, miss. But I recognized you and was trying to say something nice. Sometimes those pictures don't show how pretty you are. You've always got this scowl on your face."

I scowled at him, and he coughed.

"Right. I'm not making this any better, am I? Deborah, please take over for me." He gave me one last look. "You should go home and sleep it off, miss." He took Tori's papers back to the cruiser to check them.

Officer Deborah scowled at me. "You need to get back in the car." Her tone was no-bullshit, firm.

"No," I said stubbornly. I felt the world spinning around me. "This is a protest. I'm tired of the way this town operates. Every. Little. Thing. Y'all gotta give me a hard time." When I was really drunk and really angry, that Texas twang I'd worked so hard to rid myself of came back.

"Your friend's registration isn't up to date," Officer Deborah said, looking at me as if I had three heads. "This has nothing to do with giving *you* a hard time. In fact, you're the only one who's giving anyone a hard time around here."

"Do you know who I am?" I pointed at my chest so hard that I knocked myself back a little. "The whole world's givin' me a hard time right now. You know why? Because I'm a *woman*. And every single mansplainer out there wants to tell me not to scowl. What type of dress to wear. What size my ass should be. And I'm tired of it, you hear?" I stepped closer and almost fell over. Regaining my balance, I leaned toward her conspiratorially. "You understand what I'm sayin', donchoo?"

"Are you asking me if I understand what you're saying because I'm a woman?" she asked.

"That's right," I said, wobbling. "That's absofucking-lutely what I'm asking you."

Then I leaned over and threw up all over the road.

Officer Deborah took a careful step back and watched as I retched again. "Of course I understand. I've been a cop for twenty years. I've worked with every mansplainer on the force, and I've arrested my fair share of them too."

I looked up at her, and suddenly all the belligerence went out of me, along with the toxic tequila I was spewing all over the road. Now all I felt was morbidly embarrassed and in desperate need of my toothbrush.

"You want to deal with the mansplainers? Start by keeping your shit together," she said. "Last time I checked, getting drunk and hysterical was the opposite of helpful. And please don't puke on my shoes. I just polished them."

LOWELL

"IT'S VIRAL. It's absofuckinglutely—to borrow your word —viral," my agent, Shirley, said. She was sitting on one edge of my bed while Tori, fidgeting and holding a mug, sat unhappily on the other. Between them was a laptop, a bottle of Advil, and a box of Kleenex.

I peered at them through one squinting eye, thoroughly confused. "What's that?" My tongue felt thick and dry. I had no idea what day it was or what time.

"Your incident with the police last night. The video's gone viral," Shirley said, louder than was either necessary or nice.

I squinted at her through both eyes now. Scenes from last night came back to me through a deep, insidious fog.

"Coffee?" Tori sounded miserable as she nervously

handed me the mug. She watched my face. "I'm so sorry. I royally fucked up last night."

I sat up and took the coffee from her, wincing at the pain in my head, sharp and jagged. "If I remember correctly, you told me to stay in the car."

I reached for the painkillers and took one. Looking as though she disapproved of my very existence, Shirley handed me a bottle of water to wash the pill down.

"Who posted the video—one of the officers?" I asked. The specifics of last night were coming back to me in jagged, ugly pieces.

"No," Tori said. "They were actually really nice about the whole thing. They just gave me a warning. It was… someone else. Just some random person on the sidewalk. They heard you yelling, so they filmed it. When they realized you were Lowell Barton, they sold it to *XYZ*."

I groaned. *XYZ* was a gossip website that seemed continuously out to get me. They were the ones who had posted that most recent picture of me, scowling in my gym clothes, getting ready to fight off my fat.

"Show it to me," I snapped. I swallowed another Advil and chased it with coffee.

Shirley pushed the laptop toward me, and I watched myself in the video, horrified. I was wobbling and shouting and slurring. My carefully hidden Southern accent kept popping out like a flasher opening his coat.

I even said *y'all.*

I even said *mansplainer.*

At least they'd bleeped it out when I said *absofucking-lutely.* Still, I had a sinking feeling that the Disney role I'd been called about was no longer on the table.

I closed the screen and buried my face in my hands. "Fuck me. Stupid margaritas. And I totally puked on her shoes."

"It's all my fault," Tori wailed, throwing herself across the bed. "I made you get drunk. You never drink that much."

"S'okay. This isn't your fault, Tor." I patted my best friend's head. "My issues obviously run a little deeper than a couple of margaritas. But do you mind sending Officer Deborah some new shoes from me? And some flowers with a thank-you card?" I needed to apologize to both of the officers. A trip to their precinct, with a large amount of cupcakes and coffee and humility, was in order.

Tori nodded and tapped something into her phone while Shirley glared at me.

"What the hell is a *mansplainer?*" my high-powered agent spat. Her frosted, multi-layered bob was fluffed out in odd spiky clumps, as though she'd been running her hands through it in frustration.

"It's a man who thinks he can explain everything," I mumbled. "Because he's a man."

"Well, that's just fucking brilliant," she said, getting up and pacing. "I'm sure Lucas Dresden and all six of the producers on your movie will love that little term. Since they're all men."

"And they're all totally mansplainers," I said under my breath.

Shirley stopped pacing and turned to me, her hands on her hips. "I don't know what you want from me, Lowell. You tell me you want to work. I help get you jobs. You tell me you want to be a star. I worked hard to get you your last two parts, and now you're on the verge of becoming a headlining actress. An A-lister. Then you go and pull a stunt like this."

I looked up at her pleadingly. "I made a mistake. You know how much I want this."

She just shook her head and closed her eyes.

"Shirley, I'm sorry. I got drunk because Lucas told me I need to lose weight." It sounded ridiculous and childish, but there it was. "And when that cop told me I was prettier in person than he expected, I just lost it."

"But *why*?" Shirley looked flabbergasted. "You knew going into this movie that Lucas wanted you in great shape. You also know that people see your pictures online and will be critical about how you look. It's part of this life. What's the big deal?"

"The big deal is that all anyone in this town cares about is what my ass or my face looks like!" The words tumbled out angrily before I could rein them in.

"Lowell, you sound like a child who isn't getting her way," Shirley said, her tone a warning.

"This isn't a temper tantrum." I got up and paced even though moving hurt my head. "All I'm saying is— I'm an *actor*. I take my work seriously. I'm not just a face that may or may not scowl too much, attached to an ass that may or may not look like it weighs too much. There are more important things to worry about, but that's all I ever hear about. It's frustrating, and it's demeaning. Is that too difficult to understand?"

Shirley glowered at me while Tori pretended to read texts on her phone and not listen.

"Yes, that *is* too difficult to understand," Shirley said. "This is Hollywood. This is the deal. If you want to be paid millions of dollars for your 'craft,' or whatever you want to call it, you have to live with the way things are. You have to deal with people commenting on your face, your weight, your dating status. That's the trade-off."

"You're right." I sat back down on the bed and all of

the fight drained out of me. "Of course. I know you're right."

"If you want to keep the role you've got right now and ever have the chance of getting another one, you have some serious damage control to do. I'm hiring a PR team to take over from here. I should have done it sooner—I can see that now. You're just about to get to that next level, and I'm not going to kiss all my hard work with you good-bye. We're going to get your image whipped back into shape ASAP."

I felt Shirley studying my face, which I was struggling to keep neutral. I didn't want to cry. I also didn't really want a PR team—I didn't want to admit that my image was out of my control.

I can fix this. I have to fix this. "What do I do?"

"You need to rehabilitate your public image. Immediately," she snapped, grabbing her cell phone and car keys. "You have Lucas to worry about, and you have the premiere for *Hearts Wide Open* coming up. You need to pull a rabbit out of a hat, Lo. Today. I'm calling my people. They'll figure something out."

"Like what? And where are you going?" I wailed. I needed her help, and she was heading toward the door.

"This business is for the hungry. I'm hungry, Lo. So I'm going back to my office to do some work for clients who don't take me for granted by throwing up all over their careers in public," she called over her shoulder. "The PR team will take care of everything. I'll set up a meeting, and we'll be in touch later today. In the interim, don't do anything stupid."

She slammed the front door, and I just sat there, opening and closing my mouth as if I were a stunned guppy.

"She's a little harsh, huh?" Tori asked.

She got up and started organizing my closet, a nervous habit of hers. She was my best friend, but right now, she was doubling as my personal assistant. She was on break from the series where she worked as an apprentice lighting technician. Now that I was paying her to answer my emails, sort through my schedule, and help me keep on top of my finances, she felt the need to constantly be doing *something* instead of just hanging out. I'd hired her because I trusted her with my life and because she was hyper-organized, but sometimes I just wanted her to sit still. Instead, she was color-coding my closet.

"Shirley's all about tough love," I said.

I could just picture my agent white-knuckling the steering wheel of her Mercedes sedan, barking at another client on her Bluetooth on the way back to her office. She was angry and disappointed, and I couldn't blame her.

I blew out a deep breath. "Wow. I'm really managing to fuck this all up, aren't I?"

"No. You made a mistake. Everybody makes mistakes." Tori continued herding all of my black pants together. "But we need to think of something, stat. Shirley's mean, but she's got a point."

"I know she does," I said, "but I have no idea how to fix this. I don't want to leave my life up to some PR team I've never worked with. That makes me nervous. I have no idea what they'll make me do."

"You could also just admit that you're a control freak," Tori offered.

I arched my eyebrow at her as she refolded a pair of skinny jeans and carefully hung them up. "Uh, takes one to know one." I continued to pace while Tori continued to organize. Finally, I turned to her. "I'm just going to call Lucas. I'm going to be direct and just say that I'm sorry, that I messed up."

Tori nodded at me, her face pale. "And I'm going to go clean your kitchen. To give you some privacy."

I nodded grimly and watched her flee from my room. I took a deep breath and called his cell.

"You have got to be fucking kidding me, Lowell," he answered.

My heart sank. "Hey, Lucas." I felt sweat forming on my brow.

"I hired you because you were a good girl, okay? Because I thought you were a hard worker. Because you weren't the type to go out and snort coke and dance on tables. I fought for you—and then you fuck me like this? The producers called me last night and woke me up. They are *furious.* They want to fire you, and I can't even come up with a good reason why they shouldn't."

"Please don't fire me," I begged. My mind, still fuzzy, tried to remember the terms of the contract and all of the scenes we'd already shot. If the producers wanted to fire me at this stage of production, they must really be livid. It would cost them a small fortune to redo the work we'd already completed. That meant they thought this movie would lose money now, big time—because of me. And they were just trying to cut their losses.

Lucas sighed. "Give me a reason not to, Lowell."

I took a deep breath. "I'll make it right—I promise. Can you give me another chance?"

"I don't know," Lucas said. "I really don't know."

Tori peeked through my door a little while later, after my sniffling had subsided.

"You okay?" she asked.

"I'm fucked. I have a catastrophic PR problem and a

director who now officially hates my guts. My ass is genetically designed to stay its size, my agent's about to cut me loose, and I have a raging hangover. Not to mention that little video that everyone's one-clicking. So no, I'm not so good." I blew my nose loudly.

She sat next to me on the bed. "What did Lucas say?"

"That the producers want to fire me and I have to come up with a viable reason why they shouldn't. By the time we shoot next." I rolled over and put a pillow over my face. As if that could block out the ugly truth of how fucked I was.

Tori was quiet for a second. "Shirley said you need to pull a rabbit out of a hat. Right?"

"I know, I was here."

Tori hopped up, meeting her threshold of sitting time. I peered around my pillow and watched as she tore through the jeans in my closet. She appeared to be organizing them by wash.

"I think it means you need to do something drastic to distract the press and the public," she said, her brow furrowed as she inspected my denim. "It has to be something bigger than how drunk you were last night. And everything you said."

"That's a pretty tall order. It would have to be some huge news—like I'm pregnant or getting married."

Tori looked at me and smiled enthusiastically. "The press loves marriage and/or a baby bump! Let's do that!"

I scrunched up my face at her. At this rate, I was going to need another Advil. Or possibly another margarita. "I can't be pregnant or get married! Because I'm *not* pregnant, and I don't even have a boyfriend to marry!"

"So how about a hot *new* boyfriend?" she asked. "That you might eventually marry? And get pregnant with? That'd keep the press happy."

"That would be great. For all sorts of reasons." I winced as I thought of how long it had been since I'd been with a guy. "But there's one problem: I don't have a hot boyfriend. Or a new boyfriend. Or any boyfriend. Or any *prospect* of a boyfriend, for that matter."

"Well, we could get you one," Tori said. "What about Troy?"

"Troy?" I practically spit out his name. "He dumped me, remember? Right after I told him I was serious about him and brought him to all those premieres? Troy is out."

Tori nodded. "Sorry, that's right. In all the excitement, I forgot he was a douche." She scrunched up her face in thought. "How about Kevin? That hot agent?"

"Engaged. Recently."

"Bummer."

I rolled over and sighed. "Besides, it couldn't just be *any* guy. I'd need someone who seemed crazy about me, someone so totally hot that the press would go nuts over him. I need Charlie Hunnam. Or Joe Mangiello. Or Channing Tatum. And I need them to fawn all over me."

"Yes!" Tori squealed, clapping and jumping up and down with excitement. "Yes, yes, and yes! This is awesome! Let's do it! Oh my God, I'm finally going to meet Channing Tatum!"

"You're crazy, you know that?" I asked, sitting up and staring at her in disbelief. "That's not going to happen. Charlie's taken. Joe's engaged. Channing's married—and plus, I don't know any of them!" I groaned and sank back down on the bed. "Even if I did...I need someone to commit to me. To be in love with me and flaunt it. *Today.* That's not going to happen. No one owes me a favor that big."

My situation was dire. I was imagining how many hits the video was getting on *XYZ* as I sat there, spinning my wheels. The enormity of the trouble I'd gotten myself into was sinking in. The press, my director, the producers, and the people putting together the new film I was up for would want nothing to do with me from here on out. I had the premiere and press junket coming up for *Hearts Wide Open,* and I was sure everyone associated with that movie wanted to kill me. Even with the impending arrival of Shirley's PR team, I was toxic for the near future. They wouldn't be able to save me. The paparazzi would be ruthless, following me everywhere, taunting me. I knew myself too well—I would snap under that sort of scrutiny.

Then it would all be over. Everything I'd worked for. Everything I wanted so badly.

I wish I did have a new boyfriend to throw at them. Then I sat up again. "Hey…huh. I just thought of something."

"What?"

"Something my mom always says. Whenever she has a problem, she says she just throws some money at it. Like it'll magically make the problem disappear."

"That's because she's throwing *your* money, and lots of it."

"But what if *I* did that? What if I threw some money at this?" I paced again. "What if I threw enough money at this that I could make it go away? Or at least obfuscate it?"

"Huh?" Tori looked at me as if I was crazy. And she had every right.

If I was attempting to apply my mother's "logic" to my problem, I was in deep, deep trouble. "What if I hired someone to act like my boyfriend and paid him enough so that he kept his mouth shut?"

"Who would you even ask? George Clooney? *Chris*

Pratt?" She looked so excited, I was worried she was going to hyperventilate.

"I wish. But they're both married. I don't know...I don't know anybody I could ask." My mind racing a hundred miles a minute, I stared out the window at the tiny, pretty backyard of the house I'd saved and planned for.

What I needed was a body. A hot, handsome, strapping male body. I needed a showstopper of a guy to redirect the press. A super-hot guy who would do exactly what I said. I was pretty sure that didn't exist in real life, but this was Hollywood, and sometimes illusions seemed real here.

Huh.

I had a crazy idea about what I could do. Not only was it crazy, it was risky. Although I wasn't normally a risk-taker, I wasn't a quitter either. I'd clawed my way up over the past five years, doing a mindless sitcom and a string of pseudo-brooding indie movies, to get to where I was today—on the verge of real commercial success. I refused to watch my career crumble without putting up some sort of fight.

"I could always hire someone, I guess..." *Maybe that would be easier than an actual boyfriend. Less messy. Less emotional. More of a business transaction.*

"What?" Tori asked. "I'm not following you."

"Just give me a minute." I threw myself onto the bed and fired up my laptop.

I exited out of the *XYZ* screen so I wouldn't have to see that image of myself, hair plastered against my forehead as I looked belligerently at the officer. Then I did a quick internet search and found exactly what I was looking for.

What I couldn't believe I was looking for.

"Bingo," I said, finding a site for a service located in LA. "Tori, can you throw me my phone?"

KYLE

I WAS HEADING out for a burrito when my phone buzzed. It was Elena, the owner-operator of AccommoDating, Inc., the "dating" service where I was currently employed.

I picked up immediately. "Elena, talk dirty to me."

"Kyle, knock it off," Elena said briskly.

As usual, she was all business. I could just picture her in an impeccable suit, her short hair spiky with mousse. I wasn't sure how she'd gotten involved in the escort business; she always seemed so proper.

"I just had a call come in from a first-time client. Someone who could be very valuable as a source for future referrals. Are you available for a long-term assignment?"

"How long?" My voice was neutral, but I cringed. I was looking for a way out, but I hadn't found it yet.

"It could run for a few weeks," Elena said, "depending on the circumstances."

Well, that was a new one. "Who needs an escort for a few weeks?"

"It's not that uncommon actually. My girls are often hired to take vacations with a client. In this case, it's more of an undercover assignment than a straight-up date."

"I'm totally lost right now," I said, raking my hand through my hair.

"The client is a young woman—a pretty famous actress, actually—who needs a fake boyfriend. The press has been giving her a hard time, and she has a premiere coming up. She needs a distraction in the form of a hot, new, completely devoted boyfriend."

I sat there, trying to understand what she was getting at.

Elena sighed in exasperation. "That would be *you*, Kyle. Come on, connect the dots with me."

"*I* would be the completely devoted boyfriend?" I said.

"Correct. If it works out, she might keep you on for a while longer, until things calm down. Does that sound like something you'd be interested in? Your earnings would be significant."

"I'm in," I said immediately. Significant earnings might just be my ticket out of the escort business.

"Excellent," Elena said. "Come on in, get your health status verified, and sign the paperwork. You have to get your things together too. She's moving you into her house. Today."

"What if she doesn't like me?" I asked, but it was a purely rhetorical question. Getting women to like me had never been a problem.

I had a lot of problems, but that wasn't one of them.

Elena snorted. "She'll like you just fine. They always do."

"So...who is it?" I asked later.

Elena and I were in the bright, immaculate, and minimalist Los Angeles branch of AccommoDating. She had started the escort service back on the East Coast, in Boston; she'd done so well that she expanded her operations out here.

"I'm not going to tell you right now, because I want you to meet her without any preconceived ideas about what she's like." Elena smoothed the button-down shirt she'd picked out for me and held up different ties next to it. "Just treat her like the nice, gorgeous, successful starlet that she is."

"What's wrong with her?" I asked. Elena shot me a dirty look, and I scoffed. "There's got to be something wrong with her. Why's she hiring me?"

"I told you"—she frowned and held up another tie— "she's had some trouble with the paparazzi lately. She needs to feed them a story starring her new love interest. That's where you come in."

"Right, I get that—but why doesn't she actually *have* a love interest?"

"I think she's been busy with work," she said and shrugged dismissively. "It doesn't matter why. You don't actually have to *be* her boyfriend. You just have to *act* like her boyfriend. And follow any other rules she might throw at you. She sounded pretty Type-A, so I have a feeling there might be a few."

That a Type-A, gorgeous starlet had hired a male escort to help her out with the press seemed a little strange. "So I'm just going to drive to her house, meet her, move in with her, and pretend that I'm in love with her. In front of the paparazzi," I said, watching Elena warily.

"That's right—in front of the paparazzi and everyone else. And she said she doesn't want to sleep with you. So think of it as a vacation from your real job."

"What the hell? She doesn't want to sleep with her hot male escort? That's what I'm *for*. That's what I *do*." I looked down at myself. "Seems like a waste." Secretly, I was pleased. A break from sex-for-hire would be a real vacation for me right now.

Me *and* Big Dude.

"This is an *emergency* hire." Elena selected one of the ties and continued packing for me. "She couldn't find an actor to do it on such short notice. Besides, we have all the appropriate paperwork at the ready: a criminal background check, confidentiality agreement, clean bill of health, non-disclosure agreement, and I have insurance for you. She's in a tough spot, but she's a bright young woman. She knows what she's doing."

"If she's in so much trouble that she's hiring an escort to be her insta-boyfriend, it sounds like she might not know *exactly* what she's doing. Just saying."

Elena frowned at me. "You are advised to keep that, and any other hypotheses you might have, to yourself."

I sighed. "So what am I going to do? Rattle around her house and do exactly what she says?"

Elena beamed at me. "Young man, that might be the smartest thing you've said to me yet." She zipped up my suitcase and stepped back to look at me. "You look good,

Kyle. Healthy, muscular—a strapping, red-blooded American. The press will love you two together. I hope." She considered me for a moment. "And if she eventually decides she wants to sleep with you, count your blessings. You could do a lot worse."

I grinned at the madam, feeling some of my old swagger. "Elena, baby, so could she."

LOWELL

WHILE I WAS WAITING for the escort to arrive, I paced around the house.

Just when I was absolutely sure my day couldn't get any worse, my mother called from the latest stop on her spiritual junket—somewhere deep in Japan.

"I'm in *Kobe*, Lowell. I told you I was coming here!" she said, her voice crackling through my cell phone. "It's the Paris of Japan—very fashionable! It's exotic, darling. Hot springs and street fairs. All of the men are very short, of course, so I haven't met anyone—"

"Mother!" I desperately reached for my Advil. "Don't be so racist!"

"I'm not being racist, darling, I'm being honest, which is one of the things I'm supposed to focus on during this trip. It's a spiritual journey, I told you. I'm drinking the tea and doing the poses, and I'm going to come back totally clear!"

She rattled on for what seemed like forever about the weather and the food and her yoga practice while I paced and counted backward from one thousand so that I wouldn't snap.

"So how are you? How's it going?" she finally asked.

I took a deep breath. I'd been hoping we'd lose our connection so that I wouldn't have to tell her, but apparently this wasn't my lucky day. Again.

"Mom, there's something I need to tell you. I...sort of got into trouble last night. I got drunk and there was... there were...some pictures. And now I'm in trouble with my agent. And my director." I couldn't bear to tell her it was a video and that I might be fired.

"What?" she shrieked. Apparently all the yoga in the world couldn't keep her from losing it. "You got *drunk?* What did you do? What *pictures?*"

"Lucas told me I needed to go on a diet or I'd lose my contract. I freaked. And then I drank too much," I admitted.

"I told you to stop eating carbs," my mother warned. "I am sending my trainer over to you, and my chef. You have got to get control of this. We *need* this role. Everyone who works with Lucas Dresden gets nominated for a Golden Globe. It's your *turn,* darling."

I rolled my eyes. *We need this role.* My mother never failed to include herself in my career. With no current husband to focus on, she made my successes and failures her own.

She rattled off a list of things I should stop eating, and who she was going to hire to help me, and how where there was a will, there was a way. The only person who wanted my success as much as me, or maybe more, was my mother.

She was like the cheerleader from hell.

Finally, I couldn't take it anymore. "Mom, you're breaking up!" I yelled for effect. "I'm hanging up. Don't send anyone over here! Shirley's all over this, and so am I. I'm taking care of everything—I promise to hit the gym every day—I love you!" I tossed the phone down and leaned against my front door, shaking and completely drained. I loved her, but my mother often had that effect on me.

The doorbell rang and I jumped about a foot. I looked through the window pane beside the door and saw a guy outside; he must be the escort. He was young, maybe in his mid-twenties, and tall, dark, and handsome. He had thickly muscled arms and a hulking chest.

He turned toward me, his eyes catching mine, and I stared at his face. His handsome, familiar face. It was as though I recognized him...but I couldn't have recognized him. He was a male escort, for fuck's sake.

I kept staring, and he slowly smiled—a large, shit-eating grin. Then it hit me. Who he was.

I recognized his face within his face.

"Are you fucking kidding me?" I yelled and ducked under the window. I pressed myself against the door, my chest heaving. *No no no no.*

It couldn't be. I must be hallucinating. Because my worst nightmare was standing in broad daylight right out in front of my house. I turned around and peered through the peephole, barely breathing. It was him. It couldn't be him, but it was him.

Kyle Richards was on my doorstep, looking amused, muscular, and very sexy.

Kyle. Fucking. Richards.

I'd always known I would pay for every bad thing I ever did, and here, on my doorstep, was living proof of that.

"Open the door, Lo," he called. "I think there's a photographer out here in the bushes. You don't want to leave me out here. I could tell him some good stories—about you. Before you were hot." I heard the shit-eating grin in his voice.

I stood, opened the door, and angrily motioned him in, my face flaming. "What're you doing here, Kyle?" I struggled to keep my voice even. "You looking for someone to suck money off of, besides your dad?"

"Ha-ha," he said. He proceeded to look me up and down. "You know, I would say you haven't changed, but…you have. You've really grown into yourself." He gave me a wide, predatory smile as he pushed past me into the house, his eyes still raking up and down my body hungrily. I closed the door then crossed my arms over my chest. Then I crossed my legs, just for good measure.

Heat was rushing through me. Heat from embarrassment and disbelief. Heat caused by examining the thick, ropy muscles that covered Kyle Richard's arms and legs and the width of his massive, powerful chest. I couldn't believe he looked so good. But of course he did. This was just another life lesson—that in no way, shape, or form was life fair.

I watched helplessly as he flopped onto the bench in my front hall, looking far too much at ease for my liking. He settled his thick frame down comfortably, as if he belonged in my house. As if he were staying.

No. No fucking way.

"What're you doing here, Kyle?" I asked again, panic mounting inside me.

"You sent for me." Now he looked as smug as an alligator that had just swallowed a baby hippo. A sexy alligator.

But I was no baby hippo.

"What are you talking about?" I asked through gritted teeth, even though I had a sinking feeling I knew exactly what he was talking about.

"Elena sent me. From AccommoDating—you remember her, right?" He grinned, his eyes sparkling. "Surprise! I'm your friendly neighborhood escort, sent here from the Valley just to make your day. Or your week. And I'll tell you, Lo, I'm worth every penny. I've aged like a fine wine."

I didn't doubt him. Even though I desperately wanted to. I hadn't seen Kyle in almost eight years, but he'd only gotten better-looking, which was a predictably cruel twist of fate. His wavy dark hair and wide-set green eyes were the same, as was his handsome, arrogant face.

"You've got to be fucking kidding me," I said.

"Nah," Kyle said, looking pleased as punch. "I'm not."

He stood and walked over to me slowly, his eyes taking in every square inch of my body, and he shook his head as if he couldn't believe what he saw. The last time I'd seen Kyle, I was a pasty, brace-faced fourteen-year-old, saved from being ugly only by the stubborn plainness of my face and the light-blond color of my hair.

I still felt like that girl. When I looked in the mirror now, I was always pleasantly surprised that she wasn't staring back at me. But I still knew she was in there.

He leaned over toward me, and I felt his breath in my ear. I shivered.

"This is what you call karma," he said, "coming back to bite you in your holier-than-thou ass. Which is looking pretty good, by the way. I don't care what all those mansplainers say about it."

I glared at him, a hot blush creeping up my neck. So he knew. He'd seen my video, and he knew I was hiring an escort to try to save myself. Bitterness rose within me, overtaking every other feeling.

"I'm not holier-than-thou, Kyle. And if I am, that's at least better than being a stoned, trust-funded loser," I said, putting my hands on my hips and straightening my spine.

He beamed at me. "There she is. That's the Lo I remember—Little Miss Perfect. Except that now you're smokin' hot. Those braces really paid off."

My blush deepened—either in anger, or because of his ass-backward compliments, or both—but I kept my game face on. "How can you remember anything? You were too busy sneaking around with your friends, stealing your dad's cars and doing bong hits."

He snorted and stepped back. "Oh, and you were watching all of it—taking notes, I'm sure." Suddenly the sexy twenty-something was gone, replaced by the accusatory and exasperated teenager I remembered. "You were always ratting me out."

"I did it for your own good," I said, my chin jutting out.

Actually, I'd done it because I wanted to get him into trouble. He and his friends were always taunting me. His favorite name for me during my mother's four-year marriage to his father was either "bookworm" or "jerknerd." Thank the Lord he'd never heard my thoughts, in which I referred to him as "scrotumhead" and "loserface" on a semi-regular basis.

He'd always been handsome though. That'd just made everything worse.

Back when we were kids, Kyle had been really reckless. So yes, I'd told on him—in part because I didn't want to see him and his stupid friends get hurt. Well, I didn't care so much about his stupid friends. But I didn't want Kyle getting hurt, no matter how many times he slammed my books shut without their bookmarks in them, just to bug me. No matter how much he tortured me...when he actually was bored enough to notice me.

"Well, bookworm, you've made quite a name for yourself," Kyle said. "I guess you couldn't keep that mouth of yours in check though. I saw you on *XYZ* last night. You totally puked on that officer's shoes, you know."

"I know. I was there," I snapped, even though I didn't actually remember that part too well.

I glared at him. As bad of a predicament as I'd been in this morning, it now seemed like a cakewalk compared to what I'd gotten myself into this afternoon. I'd hired an escort. To act as my boyfriend. So I could rehabilitate my image.

And now I had an event to go to—in Santa Monica, later this afternoon—and Tori had already leaked to the paparazzi that I'd be there. With my new, hot, completely devoted boyfriend.

My new, hot, completely devoted boyfriend who was actually my escort.

My escort who actually was my stepbrother.

My hot stepbrother.

My hot *ex*-stepbrother, but still.

But still.

I was so fucked.

We just looked at each other for a beat.

"You want a drink?" I asked finally. In spite of my lingering hangover, I desperately needed some alcohol.

"Hell yeah," Kyle said under his breath and followed me to the kitchen. "You know I never say no to a drink."

"That hasn't changed?" I asked, looking through my liquor cabinet. I bypassed the tequila, vowing to pour it down the drain later.

"That hasn't changed." Kyle sat on one of my barstools and looked around my orderly, thoroughly updated kitchen. "Looks like you've done well for yourself. Maybe having your nose stuck in a book for so many years was a good idea after all."

I sighed and leaned back against the counter. I was exhausted. First the video, then my mother, and now Kyle. I felt as if someone had let all the air out of my tires.

"Does this look like a happy ending to you?" I asked, motioning to him and me and the bottle of Belvedere between us. "It's four o'clock. We're drinking hard liquor. I have to go to a designer sneaker event in two hours because I puked on a police officer last night. And someone filmed it. And it went viral. And I have to fix it somehow."

I opened the bottle and made two very tall vodka and tonics. "And you're my escort. I hired you to help rehabilitate my downward-spiraling image. *And* you're my stepbrother." I cackled uncontrollably and took a big swig of my drink. "So I don't think I've actually done that well for myself."

"Well, when you put it that way..." Kyle watched me from across the marble island. "Drinks seem like a great idea."

"But what about you?" I asked. "How'd you end up in southern California, working as a male escort?" I grimaced. I didn't mean to be so blunt—it just slipped out.

"I moved down here last year. The surfing's better. And I ended up being an escort—a *high-end* escort, mind you," he said, "about two months ago. My father cut me off, and I couldn't pay my bills anymore."

I watched his face. "You couldn't do something else? Like wait tables? Or be an office assistant or something?"

"Unfortunately, I'm not in possession of that many transferable skills," Kyle said, the cocky look leaving his face. "I never went to college. I barely finished high school, if you remember. And as for work...it's not like I have an extensive resume. And without my father's contacts, I only had a whole lot of nothing to fall back on."

"Oh. Wow." I didn't know what to say.

"So my only transferable skills really are this"—he motioned to his face—"and this." He motioned to the rest of his body. "I was giving this lady a surfing lesson and she told me about AccommoDating. She said they wanted to recruit men for the business. I said I was interested, and Elena—she's the owner—came out to the beach that day and hired me on the spot. Apparently male escorts are a growing sector of the industry. I get paid pretty well." He shrugged.

"And all you have to do is have sex?" I asked.

He took a sip of his drink. "Sometimes it's more than that. Sometimes I go to dinner with my client, or we go hiking...sometimes they like to talk. Some of the women are just lonely. But yeah, once they see me, they usually want to have sex with me." He stared at me. "Okay, they *always* want to have sex with me."

And who could blame them? I wondered, looking at his bulging biceps and massive chest. The worst was his face. He was just so handsome, he looked as if he might almost be...nice. In any event, he was so handsome a person would definitely wish he was nice, so that he could be her real-life boyfriend. Forever.

Ugh Lo—stop!

"And do you... like your job?"

Kyle shook his head. "Of course not. It's uncomfortable. But I'm hoping to make enough money off this assignment with you that I can quit. Then I can maybe go back to school."

I took another sip of my drink. "Kyle, this assignment's not going to happen. You cannot be my pretend boyfriend. You're my stepbrother."

"I'm your *ex*-stepbrother. And besides, nobody but you and I know that."

"They'll find out. Your dad's a Silicon Valley executive. I'm a Hollywood actress. You're a bad-boy-surfer-trust-funder escort. They'll find out everything. This"—I pointed at him then back at me—"is a no-go."

"I think I'm the best chance you've got," Kyle said.

My phone beeped. It was a text from Shirley: *PR on its way.*

I cursed under my breath.

"You have a press event, right?" Kyle asked, checking his watch. "You puked on a police officer's shoes last night, and as Elena explained it, you're on the verge of getting fired from your movie. You might not ever work in this town again if that happens. I'm the only option you've got, Lo."

"No," I said firmly.

"No one knows who I am. Only my friends and my dad, and none of them will say a thing. My friends won't because they're loyal, and my dad won't because he's wrapped up in his latest project in Boston. He's completely clueless. *No one will know.* There're no pictures of us together—we lived together back before

54

anybody had an iPhone. We only ever lived in Orange County. That's practically the other side of the world to most of the people around here." He looked at me pleadingly. "I need this. Please. Nobody has any idea who I am or who I am to you. And they won't find out."

"How can you say that?" I asked.

"I'll use a fake name. Kyle Jordan." He reached out to shake my hand and smiled, revealing his dimples. I gave him my limp hand, and he pumped it enthusiastically. "Pleased to meet you."

I finished my drink, clutching the glass in my spare hand. The hand that wasn't making a deal with the devil himself.

"Kyle Jordan." I sucked on an ice cube and resigned myself to the fact that I was making the stupidest decision of my life. "It's nice to meet you."

The doorbell rang, and I cursed again. "That's my new PR agent. Stay here."

I hustled to the door and checked the window. A stunning blonde was on my doorstep.

"It's Gigi," she called through the door. "Your agent sent me. I'm your new PR team."

I begrudgingly opened the door, and she sailed through, all legs and clicking high heels, her sleek ponytail swinging, and thrust herself squarely in my living room.

"Lowell! It's such a pleasure! That video doesn't do you justice." She air-kissed my cheeks and beamed at me, but I could tell she was inspecting me head to toe.

"Um...thanks," I mumbled. "I told Shirley I was all set..."

"But you know Shirley, right? It's not like she's going to leave you alone after that stunt you pulled last night. Now, I understand you've agreed to attend an event tonight—smart move. No sense in hiding. I would caution you strongly, however, to not drink a thing and to try to avoid direct questions. We want you to be seen looking gorgeous, sober, and contrite, but we don't want you to say too much. Not yet. You're going to do an exclusive later. It'll be a very controlled message, very tight."

"Did someone say tight?" Kyle asked and strode into the room, grinning mischievously.

I clenched my fists. First of all, he was being crude. Second of all, I'd told him to wait in the other room. My hired boyfriend and I already needed a serious heart-to-heart.

"Well, *hello*," Gigi said. "I'm Gigi, Lowell's new PR agent. And you are?"

"Lowell's boyfriend. Kyle Jordan." Kyle threw his arm around me, the grin never leaving his face.

Gigi looked a little disappointed, and I wanted to tell

the lanky PR socialite that she was more than welcome to my so-called boyfriend. Instead, I smiled, pretending that I was thrilled to have him beside me.

"Shirley didn't tell me you had a boyfriend," Gigi said, her thought process ticking almost audibly.

"Shirley doesn't know."

"I'm Lowell's secret weapon." Kyle changed his posture so, I swear to God, he was sticking out his dick at her.

"Well, *bang bang*. I like it." Gigi smiled at him appreciatively, either completely undeterred by his dick or approving of it. "I assume you're attending the event tonight too?"

He pressed himself firmly against me. "Absolutely."

"Well, I must admit—I'm impressed," she said to me. "The debut of a new boyfriend—especially one like Kyle —will do wonders for you after last night."

"I know, right? That's exactly what I told her." Kyle sounded smug.

I would have elbowed him in the ribs, but he was holding me too tight. *Grr.*

"Let me just bring Shirley in on this." Before I could protest, Gigi was already on her phone, FaceTiming my agent. "Shirley, it's me. I'm with Lowell and her *fabulous* boyfriend, Kyle."

"Since when does she have a boyfriend?" Shirley screeched.

She always wanted to know every little detail about my life, and now I'd hidden something from her. Except not really. Well, sort of—ugh, I was still too freaking hungover to think this whole thing through.

"Give me the phone," I snapped. Shirley scowled at me from the screen, and I smiled at her, my face a lying mask of calm. "I have a boyfriend. His name's Kyle. Tori set us up." That was the story I decided on, in all of its lackluster detail, right on the spot.

"Why am I just hearing about him?"

"Because I wanted to keep it private. I didn't want the press hounding us."

"And now?" She arched her carefully waxed eyebrow.

"The press is already hounding me. I want to give them"—I looked at Kyle—"a nice, juicy piece of meat to gnaw on."

"Aw, you flatter me." He squeezed me again.

"Let me see him."

I held up the phone so she could examine Kyle. I heard her clucking in approval as he beamed at her. I practically threw the phone back to Gigi.

"He's perfect, right?" she asked Shirley, her voice all sparkly approval.

"He'll do nicely. I hope. Tell them this is do or die, Gigi."

Gigi hung up and looked at us. "Right. Like Shirley said, this is an important night. Get out there and show your best side." She beamed at Kyle. "Not that you have a bad side."

"Bye, Gigi," I said and hustled her out the door while she eye-fucked Kyle. "I'm pretty sure we've got this." I slammed the door and leaned against it, breathing hard. I felt as though the walls were closing in on me. I looked at Kyle. "We absolutely do *not* have this."

"But you have me, your secret weapon. Everything'll be fine. *Bang bang.*" Kyle grinned, looking completely at ease.

"*Bang bang,*" I agreed weakly. All I wanted to do was bang my head on the door.

But since this was my show and I was about to go on, I went and got dressed.

For better or, most likely, for worse.

KYLE

I'D NEVER THOUGHT that my geeky stepsister would grow up to be a hot Hollywood actress, but over time, I'd gotten used to the idea. But never in my wildest dreams did I imagine that Lowell would hire an escort. She'd always been a good girl—annoyingly good when we were growing up. Her public image had been squeaky clean, aside from the occasional scowl at the paparazzi. That was why that video of her drunk and surly was so shocking—she was America's up-and-coming sweetheart.

And now she needed help. My help. I just had to convince her that I was the right person for the job, our past notwithstanding.

When I'd pulled up to her Mission-style house, my mind had been racing, trying to figure out who the actress who'd hired me could be. Elena had been clear it was someone who needed to stir up positive press, but I never would've guessed that it was my uptight ex-stepsister, trying to recover from going off about body shaming and sexism in Hollywood then tossing her cookies all over YouTube.

But now I was here and I wanted to earn my keep, to show Lowell that I was worth the money. I wanted to show her I was worth keeping around.

I wanted to *be* worth keeping around...

"Let's get changed," she said, dismissing me. "This is a casual event. I'm wearing a sundress, and you can wear whatever you want. There'll be press at the entrance. They'll be taking pictures and...asking questions." She looked grim at the prospect.

I went outside and grabbed my suitcase, then I put my things in the room Lo showed me. I picked out my clothing with care. The cameras weren't the only thing I was dressing up for. *Holy shit. She looks even better in person than she does on the big screen. How is that even possible? And where's the little twerp she used to be?*

She didn't look like the puffy, pasty fourteen-year-old I remembered. Of course, I'd seen all of her movies, but she looked even prettier in person.

I looked at myself in the mirror and adjusted the collar of my shirt. At least I looked good. That was one thing we had in common. I tucked my white shirt into my jeans and ran my hands through my hair. Satisfied, I went out and met her.

"You look...good." It sounded as if the statement had to be extracted from her like an abscessed tooth.

Lowell looked good too, but I didn't tell her that. I didn't want to make her any more uncomfortable than she already was.

"I called for a car," she said as we headed out the door. "I didn't want to drive after having that drink. I'm in enough trouble as it is."

"You always were responsible," I said.

"Except for last night," she muttered as we headed outside. The driver opened the door for her, and I caught a flash of her tanned thigh as she climbed in.

Down boy, I thought. "We'll make everyone forget about it."

"*I'm* not going to forget about it. My guilty conscience isn't going to pardon me any time soon," she said.

She moved to the other side of the car, as far from me as she could, and looked out the window. I didn't know if she was lost in her thoughts or just trying to ignore me. I couldn't believe that they'd told her to lose weight. That shit was crazy—she was *perfect.* She looked strong and vibrant, unlike so many other actresses, who were so skeletal they looked as if they lived on nonfat Starbucks and Diet Red Bull.

She turned to me with her brows scrunched up. "What?"

"Nothing," I said and quickly looked away. I heard the guilt in my voice. *Busted.*

She put the privacy pane up between us and the driver. "This is insane, Kyle. I can't believe we're in this car together right now."

"I can't either."

"It's been eight years, right?" she asked. "I was thinking about it when I was getting ready…"

Eight years ago, our parents had stood on opposite sides of a courtroom, listening to the judge recite the terms of their divorce. Lo had sat across the aisle, never looking at me. When I heard how much money her mother was getting in a lump sum settlement, I'd snorted loud enough for Lo and everyone else to hear. Our parents had only been married for four miserable years. When it was over, her mother had grabbed Lo's hand and led her out. Neither one of them said good-bye. That was fine by me. All I was thinking was *good riddance.*

"I never thought I'd see you again," I admitted. "Even though we were both in LA, I didn't think we'd run into each other."

Lowell raised her eyebrows. "Probably not." *Since you're an escort,* she kindly left out.

"I saw all your movies. You're a really good actress—it surprised me."

She raised her eyebrows. "Thanks. I think."

"I didn't mean that in a bad way," I scrambled. "I just don't remember you having an interest in acting when we were growing up."

"I don't remember you ever actually paying attention to me. Except to torture me."

That was certainly true. I had been so busy with my friends, partying and being popular, that I rarely noticed her. Except to occasionally torture her or swat her away like an annoying gnat.

"A lot's changed in eight years," I said. Understatement of the year.

"Everything's different," she agreed. "My mother's divorced from Husband Number Four. I'm an actress—that is, if I still have a job. You're…employed. Your father's moved on too." She turned and gave me a rueful smile. "This is beyond awkward, right? I'm sure you don't want to be here as much as I don't want you to be here."

"I don't know about that. I'm pretty happy to have a job—even though it's with you." I smiled at her, teasing.

"I'm not that bad anymore."

"You got that right," I said under my breath.

"Ha," she said, choosing to ignore that I'd intended it as a compliment. "You should talk. You weren't exactly a pleasure to be around."

"You still followed me around though. I couldn't have been *that* bad."

"Oh, you were that bad, all right." Her cheeks were getting red. "I used to follow you around to make sure you didn't break your neck. Seriously, you were always doing stupid things. I felt like no one was watching you."

That's because no one *was* watching me. My mother had passed away, and after that, my father struggled to make time for me while running his technology empire. I'd had nannies then a stepmother, but no one could keep me in line. I remembered my teenage years as a red period. I'd felt out of control and angry all the time, which I masked by getting smashed.

"Lo, I didn't know you cared." My tone was sarcastic, but I was actually curious.

She shot me a look, her brow furrowed. "I cared. I mean, I didn't want you to end up dead." She jutted out her chin. "That's all."

"Well, if *that's* all." I smiled at her. "Sorry I closed all your books on you without your bookmarks." I laughed at the memory, but Lowell looked as if she was trying to practice yoga breathing while scrunching her hands into fists.

"Let's just concentrate on what we're doing," she snapped, back to business. "We have this one event. We're here to ogle designer sneakers and have our pictures taken. It's good press for the designer and the celebrities who show up. All the proceeds from the event go to the local animal shelter."

"This'll be a piece of cake. I look great in photos."

She sighed, her brow still furrowed. "They're going to ask us questions too." She sounded as if she was talking to a first-grader. "You're going to say you're Kyle Jordan. That's the *only* thing you're going to say. I'll do the rest of the talking."

She was insulting me, but for some reason, I wasn't offended. I was only amused. The idea of what we were actually about to do was sinking in, and I realized how crazy it was.

"What else are you going to tell them?" I asked.

"That you're my boyfriend…that you're from New York…and that we're madly in love." The last part came out so muffled, I almost couldn't hear her.

"Huh? What was that?"

She groaned. "We have to play this up. *All* the way up. We have to act like we're nuts about each other. It has to be a big deal." She turned to me. "By the way, no one knows you're an escort except for my best friend, Tori. She's also my personal assistant. She's the one who let the press know we're going to be here tonight."

"I got it." I sat up and straightened the collar on my shirt. "We're a big deal."

"That's right. And no talking."

I pretended to zip my lips but then immediately said, "What sort of work should Kyle Jordan do? I'm guessing being an escort's not going to cut it."

She fidgeted. Nervous energy rolled off her in waves. "I don't know. Any ideas? It shouldn't be flashy. It has to be under the radar so no one can find out you don't exist."

"I'll just say I'm in consulting. SEO or something." I shrugged. "Nobody knows how to talk about that." *Including me.* But I had faith in my ability to bullshit.

"That works." Lowell sounded mildly impressed.

"So"—I threw my arm around her shoulder—"if we're in love, we better act like it."

"Knock it off!" Lo ducked out from under my arm and pressed herself against the opposite side of the car.

I fake-pouted. "Well, are we in love or aren't we?"

She grimaced and adjusted her dress, making sure that not an ounce of cleavage was showing. "We're in love, all right. And you can put your arm around me—*at* the event. I'm an actress, remember? I can put on a show when I *have* to. Not until then."

"Fine. Your rules, your show."

"That's right," Lo said, and her voice wobbled a little.

I looked out the window; we were almost there. "Are you nervous? You seem a little anxious."

Lo adjusted and fidgeted some more. "I'm nervous. Last night was really, really bad. But tonight's going to be worse."

"What happened, anyway?"

"I drank too much tequila." She pursed her lips.

"That part was pretty obvious. But what made you do that? And what was that about mansplainers? Something bad must have happened. Getting that hammered really doesn't seem like a nerdface kind of move."

She stiffened. "I'm not that nerdy girl I was when we were kids."

I held up my hands in surrender. "I know. That's pretty obvious too."

Lo shot me a look. "My director told me yesterday that I needed to go on a diet. He said my ass is too big and that I needed to do something about it before we start filming our next set of scenes."

"Seriously?" From what I'd seen of it, her ass was perfect—round and firm and luscious.

"Nope, I'm not," she said, her voice flat. "So I made

the mistake of letting Tori take me out and buy me an endless supply of margaritas. Then we got pulled over because her registration was expired, and then the police officer told me I was prettier in person than I was in my scowling photos, and then I lost it. I got out of the car and started arguing."

"I heard you say *y'all*, and that's when I knew you must be really shit-faced."

Growing up, Lo had fought against her accent, which was courtesy of her early childhood in Texas. She controlled it fiercely; you only ever knew she was Southern when she was really pissed. One night, our parents had dragged us to dinner. In the car, Lo told her mother that I'd been lighting firecrackers under bottles to see if they'd explode. In retaliation, I took the book she was reading and chucked it out the window. I heard a lot of her Texas drawl after that, yelled right into my face.

"Yeah…I was completely drunk and showing my Texas. Then I threw up on that cop. After I said a bunch of bad things about mansplainers and the movie industry."

She shrugged as if she didn't care, but I knew she did. For her to be in this car with me, headed to an event, less than twenty-four hours after it had happened, her life must have depended on fixing this.

She looked at me again. She was still fidgeting with nervous energy, but her eyes looked tired. "I knew I had to come up with a brilliant plan to save my career. So here we are."

"I'm the brilliant plan? I feel so special."

"*You* are not supposed to be here. My hot escort is supposed to be here. Not my *ex-stepbrother* escort."

"I might be your ex-stepbrother, but I'm still hot. And because we go back so far, I have a vested interest in helping you. I'll pull out all the stops." I adjusted my shirt again, making sure it was tucked snugly into my jeans. "I'm sure no one will be looking at your ass tonight anyway."

"Why's that?" Lo asked, a mixture of amusement and general disbelief on her face.

"Because they'll only be looking at mine." I made sure to flash my dimples.

"Great," she said, sounding both resigned and appalled.

We pulled up at the curb, and I saw at least fifty photographers, cameras flashing at all the beautiful people spilling toward the event.

Lo looked as if she was about to walk the plank. "This is all just great."

LOWELL

I TOOK a deep breath and waited for our turn to get out of the car. A nervous pit formed in my stomach as I looked at Kyle. His brown hair was thick and artfully messy; his green eyes were sparkling, and his tanned and rugged chest peeked out from underneath the dress shirt he'd changed into. He was good-looking enough to be an actor, honestly. He would fit right in.

That was just fucking perfect.

I had no plans to let him stay for long. We were going to walk in together and preen for the press, but after that, I would show Kyle the door. His father had been married to my mother. We'd lived under the same roof from the time I was ten to the time I was fourteen. If the press got a hold of *that* story, I might as well pack my bags, sell my Prius, and buy a bus ticket back to

Texas, where I could live out my life in twang-filled obscurity.

I looked at him as he watched the crowd outside. He didn't seem nervous, but that didn't surprise me. Kyle had always been cocky as hell.

I'd told on him constantly when we were kids, but deep down, I'd always wanted him to like me. Partly because I was a pleaser and wanted everyone to like me. Mostly because he was handsome. But then he'd do something mean, like throw my book out of the car or call me a brace-face, and I would just want to wind my fingers around his pencil-neck and squeeze. And squeeze and squeeze and—

Kyle squeezed my hand. "You ready, princess?"

"Do we have to hold hands?" I asked, jerking my hand away from him uncomfortably. "And don't call me princess."

"I meant it as a term of endearment," Kyle said, calmly grabbing my hand again. He motioned to the throng of reporters lined up, elbowing each other and looking at our car excitedly. "Calm down, Lo, and hold my damn hand. We've got this. We've brought a cake for these people. We need to let them eat it."

I looked at him for a moment, confused. He almost sounded smart.

"Okay." I felt defeated. I couldn't believe I was

listening to Kyle's logic after I'd rationalized hiring him based on my mother's logic.

There was no way this would end well.

I twined my fingers back through his. "Then let's let them eat cake."

FOR BETTER OR FOR WORSE, the press absolutely loved Kyle. We stopped and posed for every single photographer on our way in.

"Lowell, over here!" they yelled, flashes going off wildly.

"How's your head?" another one called.

"Who's this?" everyone wanted to know.

We smiled and preened and held each other. I was suddenly glad Kyle was there, which both surprised and annoyed me. I felt myself starting to sweat from the constant flashes going off all around me and all the questions being hollered, one on top of another. I'd grown accustomed to the attention of the press, but this had an urgency I wasn't used to.

Kyle, however, seemed completely in his element. He kept his arms wrapped tightly around me, and his smile glittered in every direction as we made our way down the carpet. I felt his strong, muscular body next to mine.

I could tell that he could pick me up and throw me over his shoulder if he wanted to. If I wanted him to. If I let him. If…*oh hell, I really needed to knock it off.*

He stopped halfway down the carpet. "Hey"—he flashed a brilliant smile at a female reporter—"you're looking sharp this evening. Love the jacket."

"Aw, thanks." She grinned at him in a way she would never have at me. "It's vintage."

"That's Katie from *XYZ,*" I whispered to him through gritted teeth.

"I know," he whispered back. "I've seen her on TV." He pulled me closer and asked me, loud enough for the press to hear, "It's a lovely jacket, isn't it, babe?"

"Yes," I said, awkwardly letting him hold me and inwardly cringing. I saw the *XYZ* reporter watching me. "You look great." I flashed her a megawatt smile.

"Good girl," Kyle said under his breath. "Let's give 'em a show." He called to her, "Don't you think my girlfriend's looking lovely this evening as well?"

"Who *are* you?" Katie asked, her eyes widening in excitement. She could sense the opportunity for a scoop.

He kept his arm protectively around me. "I'm Kyle Jordan. Dedicated boyfriend of the one and only Lowell Barton." He smiled while a thousand flashes went off. "And I asked *you* if you agreed that my girlfriend is looking lovely this evening." He sounded as if he was challenging her.

Wait, I wanted to yell at Kyle, *you're not supposed to be talking!* But he was on a roll. I couldn't have stopped him even if I dared to try.

"Lowell always looks beautiful," Katie said quickly, "even when she's puking."

"Aw thanks, I think so too," Kyle said, ignoring her taunt. He planted his hand firmly on my ass, and I had to literally bite my tongue so I didn't bite off his head instead. "She's gorgeous no matter what."

He turned to me and nuzzled his nose against mine. I could later blame my high-quality thespian skills for kicking in, but I pressed my chest against his and gazed at him adoringly, playing along.

I turned back to Katie. "It's great that I have such a wonderful boyfriend to support me during this difficult time."

"Do you want to comment further about last night?" she asked me, barely containing the glee in her voice.

"Lowell would love to tell her side of the story about last night's incident, but I'm afraid that's going to be an exclusive," Kyle answered immediately. He made a phone motion and winked. "Call us. You might be the lucky reporter who lands that interview."

She hastily got out her cell phone, scrambling to add Kyle's information. "How can I get in touch with you?"

But Kyle had already moved on to the next journalist, a crocodile smile on his face and his hand fastened securely to my ass.

"Lowell!" the next reporter called. "How're you feeling today?"

"I have a headache," I called back and laughed shakily.

"Do you have any comment? About why you have a headache?"

"I do." I took a deep breath and nodded at him. We stopped on the carpet, and I tried to gather my courage. "I just want to say thank you to all law enforcement who serve the wonderful city of Los Angeles, and all of the police officers in this great country. They keep us safe and protect us. No matter how poorly I acted last night, I'm always grateful for what they risk and all they do to keep us safe."

"How do you feel about what happened, Lowell?" another reporter called.

"I feel ashamed. And hungover," I admitted. Kyle hugged me tightly, and I was relieved to have him to hold on to. "I'm so lucky I have such a supportive boyfriend to see me through this difficult time."

This is my story, and I'm sticking to it.

Kyle beamed and leaned over me. "You're doing *very* well," he said, brushing his lips across my cheek. "Let's give them a kiss. A real one. Go big or go home, and all."

"No," I insisted, mortified. I'd never kissed a guy in front of cameras before.

He didn't listen. He put his mouth over mine and gently kissed me. Then he got less gentle.

And then I started kissing him back.

Heat coursed through me as he pressed his lips against mine. My knees wobbled, and a thousand flashes went off around us. Then just as quickly as he'd started, he stopped. He pulled back and smiled at me devilishly.

"Now that wasn't so bad, was it?" he whispered.

My head was swimming as I looked at him. Then I remembered where I was. And who he was. "I've had worse."

I pulled back from him and turned to smile sheepishly at the press. "I'm a lucky girl. Unconditional love is exactly what I need right now. Kyle's giving me the strength I need to face this."

"You *are* lucky," one of the female reporters said, eyeing Kyle appreciatively. "How long have you two been together?"

"Just long enough to know we're meant for each other," Kyle said immediately. About a thousand more flashes went off. "Now if you'll excuse us, we have sneakers to try on."

"Kyle!" they called, more flashes popping. They were worked up into a frenzy.

"Kyle, are you a mansplainer?" one of the reporters called.

He stopped. "Absolutely not. I believe in listening first." He kept that smile on his face and that hand on my ass as we headed into the event.

"I see *you* don't have a problem with Lowell's behind!" one of the male photographers called.

Kyle beamed at him over his shoulder and smacked me playfully on the bum. "That's because it's perfect!"

I tried very hard to keep my head high as we walked into the event and die neither from embarrassment nor from my secret, sick joy at his compliment.

THE EVENING FLEW by in a whirl of champagne, glittery sneakers, hand-holding, and about a million questions about my new boyfriend. Only one person mentioned the events of the night before to me, which was a testament to how much of a splash Kyle was making.

"Sorry that happened to you," said Tracy Ross,

another young actress. She had a bleached cropped bob and skin as white as porcelain.

"Let me be a lesson to you," I said.

"To not get drunk?" she asked.

"That, and to just in general keep your mouth shut. It's safer that way."

She nodded toward Kyle, who was examining a pair of platform high-tops. "He seems to be a hit tonight."

"He's holding up nicely," I admitted.

"Well then, you *will* be a lesson to me. Next event I have, I'm bringing man candy. Quality man candy."

"Quality helps," I agreed. I watched him for a minute.

He was chatting easily with some of the other guests while checking out the shoes. Letting him come tonight had been a mistake. A mistake in a long line of mistakes, I lamented. The press loved him, which meant I wouldn't be able to get rid of him easily. Shirley and Gigi had already sent me about ten text messages saying what a great job he was doing and how impressed they were.

And he needed this job. He wanted to quit turning tricks.

Tonight was going surprisingly well. Everything was heading in the direction I wanted so badly—to clean up the mess I'd made last night. To make the press happy with a new story and win back my director's approval.

Still, I couldn't help feeling as though I was making a terrible mistake.

Stop it, Lo. You need this. You have to make it work.

I went to fetch Kyle. I had a headache, and I wanted to intercept him before he went back to the press and started trying to sell an interview with me to the highest bidder.

"Are you ready to leave?" I asked hopefully.

"I'm at your command, princess," he said, flashing his dimples.

Heat pooled in my belly as I remembered his kiss. I made myself shake it off, or at least try to disguise it to myself as righteous indignation. He shouldn't have kissed me in the first place. "I'm hardly a princess." Still, I reached for his hand when he offered it.

"I just want you to feel special," he said.

"That's a first from you," I said lowly, so no one else could hear. I needed to take him down a peg or two.

"I've grown up," he said, sounding hurt but keeping his grin intact for the public. "It would be lovely if you did too."

I wanted to frown at him, but we had to walk by the press. Being the fine actress I was, I beamed at him instead.

He took the opportunity to put one hand on my ass

again as he waved at the press with his free one. "Call us! We'd love to go on the record!"

By the time we finally made it back to the safety of the car, my righteous indignation was bubbling over. "You weren't supposed to talk. You weren't supposed to grab my ass. You're a loose cannon, Kyle. I should fire you. You don't have the right to speak on my behalf like that."

Control freak, Tori's voice sing-songed in my head.

"Now, Lowell," he said, sitting back calmly, "you don't strike me as the reactionary type. Except, of course, for when you hired an escort to clean up the proverbial mess you left all over the internet."

"I can't do this," I said, my chest heaving.

"Of course you can. They loved me. Admit it."

I glared at him, but he was right. They *had* loved him. "You look good. They like that."

"That's awfully objectifying." Kyle *tsked* under his breath. "That doesn't seem like part of your brand."

I rolled my eyes and counted backward from ten, trying to calm down.

"Lowell, I need this." He was looking at me earnestly, and the shit-eating grin had completely evaporated from his face. "And so do you."

"You weren't supposed to talk," I said stubbornly. "And no one said you could kiss me. *Or* grab my ass."

"But grabbing your ass was brilliant, and you know it."

It was brilliant, and I did know it. I had, however, absolutely no intention of admitting it.

"You need to remember that you work for *me*." I tried to sound authoritative, but I still felt like a bratty kid next to Kyle. It was as if I was trapped in another dimension of myself.

Kyle held up his hands in mock surrender. "I promise. You're the boss, Lo. You always have been."

The truth was, as many lines as he'd crossed, he'd earned his keep just now. A good boss never takes the hired help for granted. Not everyone was replaceable.

But it would be a lot more convenient if he was.

KYLE

WE WERE both quiet on the rest of the ride home. I didn't know what she was thinking—aside from her obvious annoyance at some portions of my commanding performance—but I was processing what felt like a triumph. The press had eaten us up. *XYZ* had taken a particular liking to me.

Lo was a smart girl. She'd said she didn't want me to stay, but she'd backed off. She knew we'd been successful in obfuscating the ugly, vomit-filled truth about last night with the sexy, promising glory of today.

And when I'd kissed her—it was brief but...*wow.* Just wow. It was as if her whole body had lit up beneath me.

When I'd cupped her fine ass—I shouldn't have just put my hand on her like that, but Jesus. It was so firm and curved, just begging to be squeezed. My hand still felt hot from touching her. I felt the stirrings of an erection, but I willed it to go away. When the time came, maybe I could try. If she'd felt what I'd felt back there, she wouldn't say no to me.

They never said no to me.

Don't get too far ahead of yourself, Big Dude. This was Lowell Barton I was dealing with. She wasn't someone who gave in to her baser instincts. I'd tried many times to get her to drink her first beer at one of my parties— mostly as insurance that she wouldn't rat me out for having said party—but she'd always said no. I was sure she was curious, but her caution and sense of responsibility had won out every time. She'd only gone on a bender last night because she'd had a damned good reason.

I shoved the thoughts about my dick aside and checked the gossip sites on my phone as we drove home. *XYZ* already had tons of pictures of us posted, laughing and smiling, our arms wrapped around each other. The headline read: *Lowell B Debuts Secret Boyfriend.* Not a word in any of the headlines about her run-in with the cops, which was pretty amazing. I examined the pictures more closely. We looked excellent together, all muscles and white teeth and perfect grooming.

We looked as if we belonged together, which, at one point, we sort of had—but not in the same way. I remembered the one picture I had from when our parents were married. In it, I was tall, reedy, and sulking, my arms crossed. Lo was smiling earnestly, braces glaring, her puffy face yearning to be pretty.

The new pictures were a solid improvement.

"Look," I said, showing the phone to her, "they love us. Even *XYZ* loves us."

She took the phone, her brow furrowed as she looked at the screen. "That's because you were flirting with their reporter, and you told her we'd give her an exclusive."

"It *was* a nice jacket," I said. "Vintage. And I never promised her a thing. It's all a part of my master plan."

"Excuse me," Lo said, shoving the phone back into my hand, "but it's *my* master plan."

I was going to argue, just for the fun of it, but my phone vibrated. It was a text message from Eric, my father's personal assistant. *Call me immediately.* My stomach dropped. The last time I'd received a message from Eric, it was because my father had frozen my bank accounts and cancelled all of my credit cards. I'd gone to the bank and tried to get money from my trust, but I was informed that the provisions had been changed and I wouldn't be seeing a dime of it in this lifetime.

Can't talk now, I texted back.

As soon as you can, Eric responded immediately.

Great. Just fucking great. Just when I thought things might finally be looking up.

AFTER LO HAD AGREED that I could stay—for now—and shown me to the guest room, I took a deep breath and called Eric.

"Kyle," he said, picking up before the phone even had a chance to ring, "your father's very unhappy with you right now."

"What else is new?" I flopped down on the bed and tried to sound more casual than I felt.

"Your girlfriend, apparently," Eric said.

"I don't know what you're talking about."

"Yes, you do. I have an alert set up online—any time your name is mentioned or your image is posted, I get a text."

"Great," I said.

"So you know exactly who I'm talking about—that actress," he said. "Lowell Barton."

"What about her?"

"She's your *stepsister*," Eric said.

I didn't know Eric personally, but I heard what clearly sounded like contempt in his voice. "My ex-step-sister. Emphasis on the *ex*."

"You can't date your stepsister." Eric's voice was flat, non-negotiable.

"I'm not dating her," I said, finally thinking of a way out. I was going to one-up my father for once.

"What does that mean?" Eric asked.

"Tell my father to ask me that himself," I snapped and hung up.

I sat there and fumed for a minute until Lowell poked her head in. "You want a snack?"

"And a drink," I said.

"Okay," she said.

"Okay." I followed her out of my room.

She'd changed from her cocktail dress into a pair of sweats and an old Cal Tech sweatshirt. She'd scrubbed off her makeup and was barefoot. I could almost see the girl I'd known underneath the current-day babe. Almost.

"What's the plan?" I asked, settling in on the couch. I gratefully accepted the glass of red wine she handed me. Thinking about my father could give me a headache like nobody's business.

"Well… I had every intention of firing you when we got back here," Lo said, adjusting her feet on the coffee table.

"That's not good."

"It actually would have suited me fine." She yawned.

"But then I looked online again. It isn't just *XYZ* gushing over you—it's all the sites. We got picked up by everyone. They loved you. In some of the articles, they were even being nicer about my puke-formance. Gigi and Shirley are in their glory."

"And you think that's because of *me*? Because of my brilliant work earlier?" I asked, allowing myself to feel an echo of my former smugness.

"I think it's because of *me*. Because of *my* brilliant plan, in which you are a mere pawn."

"But I'm an awesome mere pawn. Admit it," I said.

"I admit nothing."

"That's not surprising." I swirled the wine around in my glass. "After all, you never admitted that you bashed in my face with that textbook." I laughed until I saw her face, which looked both ashamed and livid.

"You just had to bring that up, didn't you?" She sat up straighter and took what looked like an aggressive sip of her wine. "I knew it wouldn't be long. But you know the truth—you deserved it. You actually deserved a lot worse. For a lot of things. You were lucky that I had proper Southern manners. And that I was a chicken shit most of the time."

I bit my tongue. I wanted to argue with her. I wanted to make her feel bad about almost breaking my nose all those years ago. But the thing was, she'd been right to do it. The things I'd said to her that day came back to me in a rush.

"I'm sorry I brought that book up," I said stiffly.

She looked at me for a bit, and I saw her anger bubbling just below the surface. I wasn't sure if it was just because she was around me, but she seemed angry sort of a lot.

I blew out a deep breath and decided it was time to be a big boy. "I was pretty awful back then."

Lowell's hand wobbled her drink a little. "You *were* pretty mean." She was quiet for a second, seeming to think it through. But when she looked back at me, the anger was gone from her face. "But all kids are—they're cruel. Teenagers are even worse. You weren't any different."

"I know. But I shouldn't have teased you about being from Texas. Or that training bra."

She laughed then clapped a hand over her mouth. "I can't believe you remember that. And by the way—it was *not* a training bra."

"That's what you said." I felt the anxiety drain out of me. "But I still want to say I'm sorry. You were, like, eleven."

"Thank you for the apology." She was quiet for a second, taking another hefty gulp of wine. "You got what you deserved anyway." She giggled. "I did not expect to ever have this conversation with you, especially under these circumstances."

"Me either. Not in my wildest dreams."

We were both lost in our thoughts for a little while after that.

"So you were saying," I said. "About the paparazzi."

She nodded. "They loved you. My agent and my so-called PR team loves you. So you're in."

I beamed at her. "I guess you're stuck with me. I *am* a bit of a keeper, you know."

"We'll see." She put her half-full glass of wine on the table and stood. "I gotta go to bed. Early work at the studio tomorrow—that is, if I still have a job."

"Want me to come with you?" I asked.

She raised her eyebrows and backed away. "Um...*no.*"

I laughed. "I meant tomorrow, not to your room right now. Unless that's an option. That *is* what you're paying me for, after all."

Lo's face flamed. "No to tonight. As in no way, no how, no sir. You can come with me tomorrow if you want, but you'll just be sitting in my trailer all day. If I'm lucky enough to still have my job."

"Sounds good. It'll be just another opportunity to express my undying devotion for my sexy, talented, remorseful girlfriend."

She nodded, the blush still hot on her cheeks. "Okay.

You're good at this, you know that, Kyle? You might want to think about a major in marketing when you finally go back to school. I think you have a real future in PR."

"Thanks for your vote of confidence," I said, feeling simultaneously flattered and patronized.

"Anytime." She smiled at me uncomfortably. "Goodnight, Kyle. Thanks for saving my ass." I smiled, but she frowned at me. "Not grabbing it. *Saving* it."

"You know you liked it," I called after her as she backed toward her room. "At least more than you thought you would."

I LAY in my bed that night—Lo's posh guest bed—and thought about the day. It had been most unexpected. I'd never imagined Lowell Barton would get herself into this kind of trouble. I certainly never imagined I would be the one to help her out of it.

Especially not as her male escort.

Not in a million years.

But now that I was there, in her home, with our pictures splashed all over the internet, I smiled.

It was the most awkward family reunion of all time.

But that was okay. This job could save both of us. I

couldn't turn tricks anymore. I'd gotten into hooking for the reasons I'd told Lo—I needed the money. When I told her about meeting Elena and getting hired on the spot, that was also true. But I'd left out what had happened right before that. The thing that had made me desperate enough to become a prostitute.

My phone buzzed. I warily picked it up from the nightstand.

I understand you want to talk to me, it read. *Tomorrow.*

I turned my phone off and scrunched my eyes closed, wishing that tomorrow would never come.

LOWELL

I LOCKED the door to my room that night. I wasn't sure if I was locking Kyle out...or locking myself in.

I was being silly. He would never come in unless I invited him. And I knew that I would *never* invite him.

But he was here, in my house, just a few rooms away. Sleeping. Probably in his *underwear.* I clapped my hand over my eyes as if that could block out the picture in my head.

The picture in my head looked good. Too good. I could just imagine his abs, rippled and defined from all of his years surfing and lifting weights. *So yummy...*

I suddenly realized that I was ravenous. For all sorts of things.

And I was going to have to starve myself for the foreseeable future.

At least I'd make my director happy.

I CHECKED my phone first thing in the morning, like always.

Nice work, read a text from Shirley. *Keep it up.*

Almost as good as Channing Tatum! Tori's text read. *Call me when you can—I want details!*

I could just picture her, heading out on her run first thing this morning, a bundle of nervous excitement and optimism. I needed to call her and let her know the truth about Kyle and who he was to me. Besides just being my escort.

I groaned inwardly and kept reading.

The producers have decided that you can come to the set today for a meeting, Lucas texted. *But I'm not promising anything.*

I sighed and put my phone back down. The good news was, I got to go back to work. The bad news was, it was because of a lie.

Coffee. I pushed everything else aside. *Must. Get. Coffee.*

I dragged myself out of bed and rummaged around in the kitchen. Kyle padded out a few minutes later in nothing but his boxer briefs, looking just the way I'd imagined.

"Hey, Lo," he said, the shit-eating grin back on his face.

"Hey." My voice was dazed because the sight of his gorgeous, half-naked body was singeing my brain. His pectoral muscles were large and carved over his six-pack...or was it a twelve-pack? I looked at it quizzically, pondering this important question, while I examined the chiseled lines of his abdomen and simultaneously tried to count the packs. My mouth pooled with saliva. I was literally a Pavlovian dog, salivating over the hot man in my kitchen.

Starving. I'm starving, and I can't have anything I want. Not a croissant, not a bagel with cream cheese, not a...Kyle.

"Kyle!" I yelped, coming to my senses. I spun toward my coffee machine so I couldn't look at him anymore. "Good morning. Please go put some clothes on."

I heard him yawn, and it sounded as though he was stretching all of those packs. Good lord.

"Can I have some coffee first?" he asked, sounding chipper.

Great. Not only was he hot and half-naked, he was also a morning person. I punched the start button on my Keurig, but I wanted to punch myself instead.

"Aw, come on, Lo," he said. "It's not like you've never seen me like this before."

I handed him the coffee without turning around. *I'm pretty sure you didn't look like that the last time I saw you.*

"Clothes," I insisted, starting a cup for myself.

"Fine," he said. I heard him shuffle out.

I hurried into my room, gulping my coffee. I had bigger problems than Kyle's abs to deal with. I had to go face the firing squad today—my director, my producers, and all the other men connected with the film I was working on. Who were the very mansplainers I'd complained about…in that little video that had been viewed all over the internet.

Closely followed by the video of me oversharing my personal problems and bodily fluids, there were the *new* pictures of me. Making out with my mysterious, sexy boyfriend who came out of nowhere. *Who was secretly my escort. Who was also my stepbrother.*

Shit. I was going to need another cup of coffee. Stat.

Usually I dressed for work in sweats and an over-sized grey T-shirt; I rarely, if ever, wore makeup because the makeup artists plastered so much on when I got there. Today I pulled on a pair of capri leggings and a pretty pink tank top, and I put on just a little makeup. Just a dab, along with some mascara. For the producers, of course.

A few minutes later, I poured two more cups of coffee in to-go mugs and found Kyle waiting for me by the door. He was dressed in a tight-fitting T-shirt (which I refused to think about), sexy cargo shorts (and I refused to think about why they were sexy, because I was pretty sure I had no idea), and leather thong flip-flops (the words *leather thong* throbbed in my brain, and I wished that I could punch myself so hard that I would shut up for a long, long time).

"You ready?" I asked, trying to pretend I was normal.

"Is that coffee for me?" I handed it to him and he smiled. "Then I'm absolutely ready." I went to open the door, and he stopped me. "There are at least ten different photographers out there." He smoothed down my hair and turned my face into the light, inspecting it. "You look good."

"Thanks," I said, pulling back from his scrutiny. I pushed by him to get to the window.

Kyle was right. I saw four plainly visible photographers on the sidewalk, looking bored. My neighbors couldn't be happy with me. There were other actors living on the street, and they guarded their privacy jealously. Our little neighborhood was for up-and-comers —we didn't have a gated community or security to keep out the paparazzi. We only had our best behavior for that.

My best behavior had gone rogue. "Ugh."

"Look at it as an opportunity," Kyle said. "We can show them that we're a legitimate, well-behaved couple that leaves for work early in the morning. Not an angry, tequila-swilling starlet and her disinherited escort." He grinned at me.

"When you put it that way," I said, staring out the window, "I just want to throw up."

"You're a good actress, Lo," he said. "You can do this."

I blew out a deep breath. "Thank you." I grabbed his hand, annoyed that part of me felt excited by his touch. "Let's do this."

We pulled our sunglasses down at the same time, simultaneously balancing our coffees. Then we clasped hands again. If I'd been in a different frame of mind, I might have thought we looked cute.

"Good morning," Kyle called to the photographers. "Nice to see us all up and at it so early. Must mean good things for the economy."

"Good morning, Kyle. You were a big hit last night!" one of the photographers called. "Quick question—what do you do for work?"

Kyle nodded at him. "I'm in SEO consulting. In New York."

"Where'd you two meet?" called another one.

Before I could even try to answer, Kyle was flashing

his blinding-white teeth at them. "I gave her a surfing lesson. I surf in my spare time."

"Cool!" one of the other guys called.

"It was totally cool. She was wearing a bikini," Kyle said, his teeth glinting mesmerizingly in the early-morning sun.

"Smile, Lowell!" one of the photographers called. "No reason to scowl when you have a man who loves you like that! No matter who you threw up on earlier this week!"

I smiled at the photographer even though I would have been thrilled to just dump my coffee over his head. We posed for more pictures then got into the safety of my car before I let the scowl settle onto my face.

"Asshole," I said.

"Well, he complimented *me*," Kyle said. "Which by extension—as I'm your better half—is a compliment to you too."

I gave him a grim look. "No more talking. Coffee. Just coffee."

"But we have so much to catch up on," Kyle said, showing no intention of being silent. "How's Caroline, by the way? What's she up to these days?"

I sighed, turned onto the freeway, and settled into the traffic. "You don't want to know how she is, Kyle. Remember? You hate my mother."

"I don't hate her now. When she waltzed into my life when I was a teenager, throwing my dead mother's furniture out of the house and trying to ground me all the time, *then* I hated her. Now that she's nowhere near me, I can confidently say I only mildly despise her."

My mother despised Kyle, too. When she'd replaced the draperies in Kyle's dad's house, he sneered at her. "My mother had those custom-made in Paris," he'd said. "But I guess being from Texas, you couldn't appreciate that."

My mother had burned the curtains in a bonfire out back that night. Then she made Pierce buy her a newer, bigger house. With custom-made drapes. From Italy.

He said, "So. What's the evil old gold-digger been up to?"

I shot him a dirty look, although he sort of had a point. "She got married again. And divorced again." Talking about my mother made me feel exhausted. Because she was exhausting. "Now she's traveling across Asia. She called me from someplace in Japan yesterday. She's on a spiritual journey. Or something. They aren't supposed to have any screens. They're just drinking kombucha and chanting their way across the continent."

"Hopefully she's busy finding inner peace over there. I don't think she'd like to see you online, mouthing off to the police one night and lip-locked with me the next."

"I told her I'd gotten into some trouble. She threatened to send over her personal trainer." I gripped the steering wheel, my knuckles turning white. I hoped my mother would honor the no-screens rule. She would have a heart attack if she knew about Kyle or saw the video. "But thanks—way to point out the upside."

"She must be thrilled that you're so successful."

"She's so thrilled, she's downright scary. It was her idea, you know. After she and your dad got divorced, she thought *she* might try acting—but she tried out for a couple of roles and didn't get anything. So she enrolled me in acting classes." *And got my hair colored and straightened, got me a posture coach, took me to the dermatologist, and consulted with a plastic surgeon to see if I should have my nose done. And had my teeth bleached.* "She was pretty happy when my teacher said I was gifted."

"Why am I not surprised?"

I shrugged. "It turns out that I love it. I've finally found my 'thing.' Then I started auditioning and getting parts pretty quickly. I *do* have to thank my mother for that." *Even though she's been living through me vicariously and draining my bank account like a rabid vampire ever since.* "But my ultimate goal is to start my own production company someday. I'd like to produce movies that are more female-oriented. With roles you don't have to take your shirt off or starve yourself for."

"You should totally still take your shirt off in your movies," Kyle said, grinning. I glowered at him, and his face turned serious. "When it's artistically appropriate, I mean."

"How's your dad?" I asked, desperate to change the subject from both my mother and from me being topless.

"He's fine. He's working on some super-secret app up in Cambridge. He says he's never getting married again."

"My mom said the same thing."

"Is she still supporting herself with her divorce settlement from my dad?" Kyle asked, and I heard the bitterness in his voice. "Or has she moved on to the next one?"

"She…spent your dad's money. Then, like I said, she got married again and divorced again. That's all gone too."

As soon she'd cashed the check from husband number four, she'd gotten a full facelift and breast lift. She said she needed to feel "refreshed." So she bought a luxury condominium with closet after closet stuffed with designer clothes, then she had the plastic surgery, then she took the spiritual journey to the East, where she intended to "cleanse" herself. She had unplugged from electronics, was only eating fresh, whole foods, and was spending a large chunk of money to do yoga in ancient temples she knew nothing about.

I was the one financing her adventures now. She'd shown me all of the clothes she'd bought for the trip. Thousands upon thousands of dollars' worth of yoga pants and organic cotton tank tops. I'd felt sick when I looked at them all, the tags still on, spread all over her room.

"She's not a bad person, you know," I said defensively. "After my father left her—with a newborn baby, no job, no education, and no family to lean on—she did what she felt she had to do. She got married to someone who'd take care of us. *That* was her job. She's not perfect, but she did her best."

"Are you saying that for my benefit? Or yours?" Kyle asked.

In response, I had another sip of my coffee.

"Sorry. Your mother's always managed to push my buttons," Kyle said, looking out the window. "But let's switch gears. Are you nervous about going in this morning?"

I didn't take my eyes off the road. "It's more like I'm overwhelmed with dread."

"It's going to be okay. You didn't say anything too horrible in the video. You didn't name names."

I kept my death-grip on the steering wheel. "I didn't

have to name names—I'm sure everyone involved in this film knows who I was talking about. And so does half of Hollywood." I blew out a deep breath. "I'm just going to have to apologize. And tell them that the movie's really important to me."

"Is it? Do you love the movie?" he asked.

"No," I said too quickly. Then I felt bad, as if I was being mean to my movie, which it didn't deserve. "It's not like it's a *bad* movie. It's just not a *good* movie. You know what I mean?"

"Of course," Kyle said. "Most movies are like that."

"But I *need* this movie. If I get fired, I'll never get another job in this town. That's how it works. Hence the overwhelming feeling of dread."

Kyle put his hand on my knee and squeezed. Before I had the chance to bite his head off, he released me.

"You can make this okay," he said. "No matter what you feel. Just give them a show. You can do it. I've seen all your movies. You're a star for a reason."

I looked at him for a second then quickly brought my eyes back to the road. "You've seen all my movies?"

I didn't understand why, but my face flamed at the thought. I knew people saw my movies. I just didn't know *Kyle* had seen my movies. All of them. That fact unnerved me more than I cared to admit. I'd taken off my top in one of those movies. You couldn't see anything, but I'd still taken it off.

"Of course I saw them all," he said, his voice casual. "When you have a famous relative, it's totally okay to stalk their movies. Plus, I liked them. Most of them, anyway."

"Oh, I didn't know."

"*The Family Pride* was my favorite," he said and grinned at me.

I cringed. *The Family Pride* was the movie where I'd played the misunderstood nerd who later became a famous actress. It was also the movie featuring my naked shoulders.

"It seemed so…natural, that role. Like it was written for you. I especially liked the part when you took your shirt off. It was very cinematic."

"Ha-ha, Kyle." I tried to focus on driving. "That movie was hard for me. Obviously it hit close to home."

I'd played the main character, who was seriously dorky in high school and decided that the only way she could escape her controlling mother was to become successful in her own right. Meredith Striper, a famous actress, had played my mother in the movie; my own mother hadn't been impressed.

"What did Caroline have to say about that one?" Kyle asked.

"She didn't care for it," I admitted.

Kyle snorted. "Oh, I bet she didn't."

"Not for the reasons you might think," I said, inwardly cringing. "She didn't actually *understand* the movie. She thought it was too slow. And she thought Meredith Striper was too old to play my mother."

Kyle practically spit out his coffee. "That's all she had to say about it?"

Now it was my turn to grin. "She also said my hair looked bad."

"You've got to be fucking kidding me," Kyle said. "Except I know you're not."

"No, I'm not," I said. Suddenly we were both laughing.

"Between your mom and my dad, really, it's no wonder that we ended up in this car together." Kyle was laughing so hard he was snorting. "They put the 'fun' in dysfunction."

"Right? It's so messed up, but it makes perfect sense. I mean, it would make perfect sense to our therapists. I almost think they deserve each other—Caroline and Pierce."

Kyle raised his eyebrow and looked at me. "They just might."

"I wouldn't wish Caroline on anybody though. Maybe not even your dad. You thought she was bad before? Now she's bad and gluten-free, wearing sancti-monious organic cotton yoga pants." It was my turn to snort. "You don't know what bad is."

"I think I have a pretty good idea," Kyle said, sounding as if he meant it.

KYLE

WE PULLED into the studio lot, and Lowell got out of the car. Even though she'd been laughing only moments earlier, she now looked a little pale.

"You okay?" I asked.

She shrugged. "It's not like I can do anything about it if I'm not."

"Well, while I'm here," I said, throwing my arm around her shoulders, "you can lean on me. You should get your money's worth."

"You really need to think about a career in PR," she mumbled. "I know people. Hell, the way you're doing with the press, *you* know people."

A young woman wearing a headset over her frizzy hair bustled toward us, clutching a clipboard. She nearly fell over when she saw me with Lo. "G-g-good morning, Ms. Barton." She tore her eyes away from me to Lowell.

Lo's face softened. "Ellie, for the millionth time, call me Lo. And this is…this is my boyfriend, Kyle."

Ellie tried to smile at me and failed. She just nodded and tapped her pencil. She seemed as though she'd had about ten cups of coffee already. "They're waiting for you."

"Oh, I'm sure they are," Lo said, sounding braver than she probably felt. "Ellie, will you take Kyle to my trailer?"

"Of course." The girl's face was ashen. "But they called a big meeting, and they've already been in there for an hour—"

"Don't worry about it," Lo interrupted. "I can handle Lucas and the rest of them. It'll be okay. Go get a doughnut from craft services. And an orange juice. You look like you're going to pass out."

I leaned toward Lowell and whispered, "Good luck. I'm rooting for you."

She nodded and pulled her sunglasses down enough so that I could see her eyes, which looked resigned. "Be good. Don't make Ellie work too hard. She's got me for that."

She walked off, and I mentally crossed my fingers for her. I also watched her fine ass and cursed the stupid director for ever telling her it was too big. I turned to find Ellie watching me, a frown wrinkling her brow. "She's my girlfriend, not that it's any of your business. And a doughnut would be lovely." I used the same tone that I used to use on the staff when they caught me doing something in poor taste.

"Of course," Ellie said but didn't move. She looked forlornly at the building where Lo was heading. "They're *all* waiting for her. Even one of the producers who hasn't been on set before." She sounded as if she thought Lo were walking the plank and a bunch of crocodiles were waiting in the water below.

"She's a big girl," I said, even though I felt a small spark of anxiety on Lo's behalf. "She can handle them."

Ellie nodded, looking as if she might cry.

"Right. Come on." I nudged her shoulder. "Let me buy you a doughnut."

"They're free," she said, as if it were her sworn duty to tell the truth and always tell the truth.

I could see why Lo got along with her.

We headed to craft services, and I was waited on by a striking woman with long brown hair.

"Would you like some help?" she asked, leaning over just enough so I could look down her shirt.

"No, thanks," I said reflexively, not looking up at her —or down her shirt.

"I saw you on *XYZ* last night. I *loved* your shirt."

I wasn't looking at her face, but I was pretty sure she was batting her eyes at me. I finally looked up—all the way up, totally skipping her chest. "My girlfriend picked it out. She has excellent taste."

"I'll say," the girl said, tossing her hair and flashing her blinding teeth at me.

I nodded tightly and retreated with my doughnuts.

I handed Ellie hers. "Eat it," I said, my tone a warning. "Lo wanted you to."

She chewed on it listlessly as she took me to the trailer. "I hope she doesn't get fired."

"I hope they don't insist that she starve herself," I said.

Ellie stuffed another bite of doughnut into her mouth and talked through it. "It's ridiculous. She's the most beautiful person I've ever met. Inside and out."

"Aww, Ellie, that's sweet. No wonder why she says the nicest things about you."

"She does?" Ellie asked, hopeful and eager.

"Of course she does," I said, even though Lo had said nothing about her on-set assistant.

"This is hers." She motioned to the trailer. "It was nice to meet you, Kyle. I thought you wouldn't be nice, but you are."

"Why'd you think that?" I asked, baffled.

"I saw you on *XYZ* last night too. I thought you were too handsome to be nice."

"You've already been in the business too long," I called.

She hustled off, dusting the doughnut crumbs from her blouse before she put her headset back on. "I'm aware of that."

I went into the trailer and collapsed on the couch, grateful for the privacy and quiet. Lo's trailer was simple and spare, with nothing on the table but a bunch of tulips and only bottled water in the mini-fridge. I ate my second doughnut, wondering how Lowell was faring with the crocodiles who paid her millions of dollars then asked her to spend none of that money on food.

I felt a headache coming on, and I knew why. Thinking about Lowell wasn't going to make the why go away.

I had to call my father, and it was the last thing I wanted to do.

I finished chewing my doughnut and, desperately wishing it was a beer instead, picked up my phone.

"You have got to be fucking kidding me," he thundered as soon as his secretary got him on the line. "Lowell-fucking-*Barton*?"

"It's not what you think," I said. *It's worse.*

"When I cut you off from your trust, I was hoping you would start making better decisions. I didn't think you were going to make an even bigger ass out of yourself. Honestly, I didn't think that was possible."

"Gee, thanks, Dad." I got up and paced the trailer. "I forgot how belittling you are, but this is bringing it all back. Every little belittle."

"You need to grow up, Kyle." Pierce blew out a disgusted, angry huff. I could just picture his square face ruddy with frustration.

My father and I hadn't been on good terms for a long time. I wasn't sure exactly when I'd gone from his promising only son to the bane of his existence...but it *might* have been when I crashed his brand-new Lexus SUV into a ditch. When I was drunk. And then got arrested for it. And then tried to lie to him about it.

It didn't help that after he'd paid for my legal defense and somehow gotten me acquitted—even though I was clearly guilty—I continued to spend more of his money. I continued to drink and party and surf. Bottle service was a nightly event for me. I continued to refuse to get a job, even though he graciously offered me a job after all of the stupid and dangerous things I'd done.

It might have been somewhere around that time that his feelings changed. That he finally gave up.

"Dad, you need to listen to me—"

"I don't have time to discuss your feelings," Pierce said. "I don't care. I called because you can't *date* your stepsister. That's a new low, Kyle, and I know you're just doing it to get back at me. You know what her mother did to me."

"Actually, I'm not doing it to get back at you. Not at all. Although if it bothers you, I suppose that's a bonus."

"I don't know what I've done to make you hate me," he said, seemingly out of the blue.

I recoiled. "I don't hate you. I'm not thrilled that you took away all my money, but I don't hate you. My thing with Lowell isn't about you."

He didn't answer for a second. "You can't tell me you have feelings for this girl. You two couldn't stand each other growing up."

"She's nice now," I said. "And really pretty, in case you hadn't noticed. But it's actually a little more complicated than that."

Pierce sighed. "What the hell does that mean?"

"You don't want to know." Suddenly my headache

subsided. Because for the first time in a long time, I was telling my father the truth.

"Well, I'll make it simple," he snapped. "You break up with this girl, or I'll leak it to the press that you two are related. We'll see how you both like *that*. We'll see what happens to her little acting career then."

Anger flared within me. Pierce was demanding, difficult, and used to getting his way—but he wasn't going to run this show. I wouldn't let him.

"You might not want to do that," I said, my tone a warning. "There's actually more to the story. And trust me, you're not going to want anyone to know it."

LOWELL

MY STOMACH WAS PITTED with dread as I headed into the meeting. Cristina, Lucas's habitually unfriendly assistant, was waiting outside the conference room. She crossed her arms in disapproval when she saw me.

"Hey there," she said, as if I'd come all the way from Echo Park just to ruin her day. "They're waiting for you. They're totally pissed about what you did, obviously."

"Obviously," I said.

"Good luck," she said sourly.

"Gee...thanks."

My palms were slick with sweat as I went through the door, but I straightened my back and took a deep breath. I composed my face so that I looked calm and collected. I was a famous actress for a reason, dammit. I could look calm for a meeting. I wasn't going to let a little tequila—okay, a *lot* of tequila—come between my dreams and me.

But the little voice in the back of my head kept asking, *Am I on my way up? Or am I on my way back down?*

Eight men were sitting at the table, waiting. Eight of the mansplainers I'd been complaining about. They collectively frowned at me. Lucas was at the head of the table, wearing the biggest frown of all. His grey hair stood up in a wild, artfully crafted swirl. His tortoise-shell glasses made him look intelligent, which he was, and easy-going, which he was not.

"Lowell." He nodded curtly. "Take a seat."

I felt as though he was the principal and I was about to get a ruler across my knuckles. Or my ass.

"As you might imagine, we were all very surprised and displeased with your little performance on *XYZ*. None of us expected you to be a problem. Or a party girl, for that matter." Lucas rubbed his face. "That's one of the reasons why we hired you. We thought you were trustworthy and reliable. Instead, you've shown us that you're immature and capable of a wicked temper tantrum. Not what I was expecting, Lowell. Not what I was expecting, and nothing I find acceptable."

"Lucas, you've got to give me a chance to explain—"

"I have to do nothing of the kind." He looked at me

from across the table, and my heart sank. "You're lucky we've decided not to fire you. Not yet, anyway."

I looked around the table and saw nothing but blank or disapproving looks from the other producers. "What do I have to do?"

"First of all, you need to apologize the right way. Your behavior has been very damaging to this film's prospects. We want you to do a contrite sit-down interview with one of the major networks. Second of all, you need to keep this guy Kyle around," Lucas said.

I gulped. They had no idea what they were really asking. "Why is that?"

Lucas gave me a tight smile. "Because he's the only reason you still have a job right now. You're lucky the press is eating this story up. We ran some market tests, and your approval ratings are higher than they've ever been. Which is really saying something because you threw up on a cop. After spewing a feminist rant. You know the public doesn't like that shit."

"It wasn't a feminist rant," I said, desperately trying to control my anger. "I was upset about the fact that you said I needed to lose weight."

"I didn't tell you that you had to lose weight," Lucas said, his tone a warning. "I *told* you that you need to be in better shape for our upcoming action sequences. As per your contract. You knew what you were getting into, Lowell. We talked about this before you came on board. There's no room for excuses now. You're supposed to conduct yourself like a professional. You're being paid enough to do at least that."

My face flamed. "I'm sorry about what happened. I'll be on my best behavior for the rest of the shoot."

"That's a relief," Lucas said. "I need you to do some voice work for a few scenes this morning. Without any drama. After that, we need the following: You need to be in better shape for the action scenes. We're pushing the schedule back six weeks so you have more time to train, and also more time to put this incident behind us. Keep it up with the new boyfriend. Keep him in front of the press. Do the one-on-one interview. We want you to generate some excitement, some curiosity during film- ing. People want to see movies they're personally invested in, so if they feel like they know you and they know you were falling in love while we filmed *Renegades Forever,* we might have a chance to turn this thing around."

I nodded mutely. My head was spinning.

"I want exercise. A healthy diet. Lots of pictures of you with the boyfriend, smiling and holding hands. Do you copy?"

"Of course," I said, trying to be brave. I nodded calmly and met each producer's eyes. "I won't let you down. I want this movie, and I know it'll do very well at the box office." *It'll do well, and I'll make enough money to start my own company and never work with you mansplainers again.*

"I really hope so, Lowell," Lucas said.

"I really hope so too, Lucas," I said contritely. *You prick.*

Dismissed, I hustled through the door. Cristina jumped back as though she'd been eavesdropping.

"They're all yours, Cristina." I jerked my chin toward the conference room. "Good luck with that."

I CALLED Shirley before I went to production, and I told her everything that had happened in the meeting.

"That's the plan then," she agreed.

My heart sank. I was stuck with Kyle for the foreseeable future. No one knew the trouble that could cause me.

"I want to see lots of pictures of you two going to the gym. I'll have Gigi work on getting that exclusive interview scheduled." She was quiet for a moment. "You're doing a good job, Lo. You pulled a rabbit out of a hat, just like I said. I have to thank Tori for finding him—she might just get back in my good graces after all."

I winced. If Shirley knew the truth, I was the one who would never get back in her good graces.

"Hold his hand," she ordered. "Smile! Have fun!"

Just when I thought it couldn't get worse, my phone buzzed again. My mother was calling. I sighed and answered.

"Darling," she said, breathlessly, "I've been thinking about our talk. I think you need your mother. I'm cutting my trip short. I'll be home soon."

"No!" I wailed, then I tried to calm myself down. "I mean, please, don't cut your trip short for my sake! I'm fine. I talked to Lucas this morning—everything's *fine*."

"You aren't fired?" she asked hopefully.

"No! Everything's fine...I was just being silly," I lied. "Don't come home yet. Enjoy your trip. I'd feel so guilty if you came back just for me." *And trust me, you wouldn't like what you'd find.*

"Well...maybe I'll stay for a few more weeks then. We're supposed to visit some amazing temples..."

"Visit them!" I practically shrieked. "Please!"

"Are you sure everything's okay?" she asked.

"Yes. I promise," I said, steeling myself for the road ahead. "I want this job just as much as you want me to keep it, Mother. So I'm doing everything I need to do."

God help me.

KYLE

ELLIE KNOCKED on the trailer door later and told me they were doing voice work for the next six hours straight, so I just stayed inside and paced. When Lowell finally came in, her face was pale and drawn.

"Rough day at the office?" I asked, handing her a bottled water.

She nodded worriedly. "What about you? You sort of look...distressed."

I looked at myself in the small mirror on the wall. My hair was disheveled from running my hands through it, and my eyes were a little wild. I'd been replaying the conversation I'd had with my father over and over in my head.

She hired me, Dad. I'm working for her.

What the fuck does that mean? he'd asked. *Are you her*

assistant? Who kisses her in public?

I'm her escort. Her hired date.

What the fuck does that mean? he asked again, but that time, his voice was flat.

It means that when you cut me off, I had no money to eat or pay rent. So I went to work as a male escort. And Lowell Barton hired me.

He hadn't said too much after that. But I knew that he was thinking, and that was probably dangerous for me. And for Lowell.

"What is it?" she asked.

"I'll tell you later. Did it go okay? The meeting?"

She shrugged.

"Are you done for the day?"

She nodded. She obviously wasn't in the mood to chat, which suited me just fine.

"Good," I said, grabbing her hand. "Let's go to the beach."

She surprised me by not pulling away. "Okay. That actually sounds good."

We left the studio and drove in silence back toward her house so we could change. I wasn't ready to tell her about my talk with my dad, and she didn't seem ready to talk about her meeting.

She slowed as we got near her neighborhood— about a dozen cars were parked in front of her house.

Photographers, waiting for us. She sighed, and I turned to her.

"Just turn around," I said.

She drove away, frowning and lost in thought.

"There's a great beach in Santa Monica. Let's go there," I suggested, and she nodded. "You seem upset. What's up?"

She blew out a deep breath. "I just can't believe I did this to myself."

"Did you get fired? I was hoping everything was okay because you were gone all day."

"They didn't fire me," she said, then said nothing further.

"Do you want to talk about it?" I asked.

"Is there a bar near this beach?"

IN THE END, we bought beers and sat on the pier, drinking them out of paper bags.

"This is so...slummy," Lowell said before swigging her beer. "It's so slummy it's awesome."

I watched her face. "You don't relax much, do you?"

"All I do is work. For all the good it's done me." She stared at the water. "So...back to Lucas. He didn't fire me, but he said they'd talked about it. I'm basically on probation. I *have* to get in shape before the shoot. They pushed it back six weeks so I have enough time to starve myself." She read the calorie contents on the beer and groaned.

I shook my head. "That's ridiculous. Did they actually tell you to lose weight? I thought that was illegal."

"They didn't say 'lose weight'—they said come back in six weeks and weigh less." She shrugged. "It is what it is. They also said that I need to make this"—she motioned between us—"work. They appreciated that I've publicly rebounded in less than twenty-four hours. They said you've gotten me amazing approval ratings—better than before my, er...incident. So I need to keep you around and make the most of the press momentum."

"That's great," I said, grinning at her. "You keep getting paid; I keep getting paid."

"We can't let anyone find out about us." Worry creased her forehead. "If it gets out that we knew each other...that our parents were married...that you're my *escort*...I'm dead. Tori's the only one who can know. "

I swung my feet over the water, back and forth, nervous energy bubbling through me. "Tori's not the only one who knows."

She looked stricken. "Did you tell *Ellie*? Because she's really sheltered. She probably really can't handle that—"

"I didn't tell Ellie," I said. "I told my father."

She looked stunned. *"What?* Why?"

"So he wouldn't blackmail you into firing me, Lo."

She looked at me, surprise and anger playing out on her face. "You told him the *truth?* We have an agreement. A *non-disclosure* agreement."

She shifted her weight as though she was about to stand up, but I put my hand on her. "Wait. Please." I held my breath until she'd sat back down. "He'd already seen the pictures. I didn't know it, but he's had his assistant keeping track of me."

She looked at me, waiting.

When I was pretty sure she wasn't going to run, I continued. "He called me this morning. He threatened to call the press, to tell them that you're dating your ex-stepbrother—*if* I didn't break up with you immediately."

"Would he do that? To you?"

"I think my father has gotten into the habit of trying to protect me from my own bad judgment." I scrubbed my hands over my face. "I had to explain to him why it was in his best interest to keep his mouth shut. It wouldn't look too good for his latest business venture and his upcoming feature in *Forbes* if the press found out that his son's an escort."

"He didn't know?"

I shook my head.

"What did he say?" she asked quietly.

"At first, he didn't say anything. I think he was in shock. But when he came to, he said that he was glad he'd disowned me, that he'd rather give his fortune to a pet shelter or a distant third cousin than to me."

"I'm so sorry, Kyle."

"Don't be. I'm an adult. All the bad choices I made led to this."

"You lost all your money. You had no education. It's not like you had a lot of options," she said, trying to console me.

I snorted. "I was a drunk-driving party boy until my dad took my inheritance away. But you want to know how I ended up here? Doing this?"

Her eyes softened toward me. "Only if you want to tell me."

"I was giving surfing lessons, and a woman I was teaching asked me out. She was older, and I wasn't interested, but I *was* hungry. So I let her buy me dinner. No big deal, right?" I stopped and stared at my hands, feeling sick. "I slept with her afterward, because she seemed to expect it. And then she offered to buy me breakfast the next day. Are you getting the picture?"

She nodded.

"She asked me stay with her, so I did. For a weekend. That turned into a week. And then a month. I was like her little…pet. I ate her food and lived in her house and did what I was told. Because it was…easy."

"It doesn't sound easy," Lo said. She sounded as if she felt sorry for me.

"It was easy until I got so disgusted with myself that I couldn't stand it anymore. After I left and Elena asked me to come work for her, I didn't even hesitate. I knew it would be better than what I'd had with that woman. Cleaner. I have a contract with my clients. They pay me in exchange for my services. That's it. No one's pretending it's anything else."

"Just because you made bad choices doesn't make you a bad person." She patted my shoulder. "At least, I hope that's true—for my sake too."

"Thanks." I smiled at her. "But I made my own bed where my father's concerned. I lost his respect a long time ago, and I've only gone downhill from there."

"I'm sorry about your father," she said.

"It's okay."

"Did he say anything else?"

I sighed. "No. But I don't think he's done with this yet. He sounded like he was thinking about what options he had. Which is unfortunate, because he's a brilliant guy. So if he's thinking about ways to sabotage us, he'll probably come up with one sooner rather than later. And it'll probably be pretty good."

"Great," Lowell said. "That's just great." She took a swig of her beer. "Speaking of great, my mother called today too. She threatened to cut her trip short to come back and 'help' me. I talked her out of it, but I'm worried she's going to show up sooner rather than later."

"Great."

"You can say that again. And again," Lo mumbled.

ONLY A HANDFUL of photographers were left at her house when we got back.

"Lindsay Lohan just got back in town," one of them explained, shrugging. "But we thought we'd wait for you guys."

I pushed thoughts of our parents aside and flashed him a megawatt smile. "You have excellent taste." I threw my arm around Lo and beamed. "I approve."

"How about that exclusive interview?" the other photographer asked.

"We'll make an announcement soon," Lo said. I looked at her in surprise, and she shrugged. "I want to keep them on their toes."

We finally made it into the house, and I could tell Lo was tired. "Do you *want* to do an exclusive interview?" I asked. I couldn't really picture her sitting down with Katie from *XYZ* and, er, spilling her guts. Again.

"I have to eventually. Gigi's apparently working on it. Lucas said he has to approve everything I say though. He wants a representative from the movie to be there."

I looked at her skeptically. "Don't you think you'll scowl during the interview?"

She scowled at me. "No."

"Don't you think they'll bait you? About mansplainers and all?"

She jutted out her chin. "I'm perfectly capable of handling the press, Kyle Richards. *Kyle Richards* who's only been in the spotlight for twenty-four hours."

"Okay," I said, not wanting to fight.

"Okay." It sounded as though she was forcing herself to drop it. "It's been a long day. I'm going to take a shower. You want to watch TV afterward?" She almost sounded nervous, as if I might say no.

"Of course," I said. "Meet you on the couch in fifteen."

She came out a little while later in her sweats, with wet hair, and handed me a glass of wine. She sat on the couch, yawning. "I'm already bored. Nothing to do but starve."

"I refuse to let you starve. I know you don't want me to say it, but your body's perfect. Anyone who tells you otherwise should Photoshop themselves out of existence."

It looked as if her face was turning red, but I couldn't be sure.

"That's sweet," she said. "I just wish the rest of the world agreed with you."

"The rest of the world *does* agree with me—it's those freaking industry people who are insane. People love you because you're a great actress, and because you're funny and gorgeous."

She just looked at me, seeming confused. "That's...nice. I don't remember you being nice. You're kind of freaking me out."

"I can be nice," I said defensively. "I'm nice."

"You didn't use to be nice," she said.

I sighed and looked at her helplessly. "I already said I was sorry. And that I've grown up. Now let's just have some wine and relax."

She just looked at me. "Wine has too many empty calories."

"Fine. I'll drink wine and relax. You can sit there and scowl."

She scowled at me, and I rolled my eyes at her.

"Let's not worry about dieting right now—let's worry about the next couple of weeks. We should make plans," I said. "We should go to the gym together. Go to

Jamba Juice. Hit a different hot spot every night. Work the reporters into a frenzy and make your agent and director happy."

"I'd actually love to just get out of here for a while. I haven't had this much time off in forever," Lo said wistfully. "Can we pretend to go on an exotic vacation?"

"Can we just *go* on an exotic vacation? My favorite beach is in Hawaii. I'd offer to take you, but...I'd need you to front me some cash." I smiled at her, humbled. I'd had all the money in the world for so long, I thought nothing of jetting off to Hawaii for a weekend. I used to do it all the time.

Lo sat up straighter. "We should totally go to Hawaii. The magazines always have pictures of the stars vacationing there. You can teach me to surf. Perfect photo op."

The idea of her standing on the board in front of me, my hands around her waist as I showed her how to get her balance, made my cock twitch. *Down, boy.* The days when I answered to it were over.

But I would really like to have my hands around her waist.

"Hawaii is my favorite place in the world. Let's say if we turn this situation around and emerge victorious, we'll treat ourselves and go. When this is all over and you've paid me, so I don't have to borrow money from my hot Hollywood actress girlfriend," I said, winking at her. "But right now? I think we should stay here and work the press."

She nodded. "It's a deal. If we pull this off, I'm going to get back in Lucas's good graces. As long as your dad doesn't rat us out and the press doesn't find out anything."

"Crossing my fingers," I said. My father wasn't an easy man to evade, and the press was just as interested in us as we were hoping—which was both a blessing and a curse. "But do you promise? Hawaii? Someday?"

She smiled at me. "Sure. If we 'emerge victorious' like you said."

"We will." *We have to, if I'm going to finally turn my life around and you're going to stay in the game.* "Can I have some more wine? And will you please have some too?"

She grimaced. "I already ate dinner and had a beer. A *big* beer, remember? Do you know how many carbs that has?"

I sighed. "Do you think I give a fuck how many carbs it has? Do you need me to tell you how hot you are?"

"No," she said, that blush creeping up her cheeks again.

I grinned. "Are you sure? Because I really don't mind."

I TOOK his glass and headed to the kitchen, pretending I was giving in to him. The reality was, I wanted a glass of wine. The reality was, I'd like to drink a whole bottle of wine and have an excuse to throw myself at Kyle, to run my fingers along that strong jawline and finally know what those lips tasted like...just once.

Just once, and nobody ever had to know.

Mental slap, I told myself harshly and slammed the glass on the counter, almost breaking the stem. *Mental fucking slap.*

THE NEXT FEW weeks fell into a surprisingly easy routine. I supposed that was because we'd lived in the same house before. Strangely, I didn't remember ever being as comfortable around him while we were kids as I was now.

Like a lot of other things, I was choosing to ignore that.

Every morning, we had coffee in our pajamas. Kyle and I took turns going out and offering hot coffee and baked goodies to the paparazzi. There were always a bunch of them out there, even early in the morning.

Then we got dressed in our workout clothes and held hands as we walked to my car, smiling for the press. After a punishing two-hour workout—Kyle always made me post pictures to social media so Lucas knew we were working up a sweat—we headed over to Jamba Juice, always holding hands, followed by the press. We'd all gotten used to the routine—even the Jamba Juice attendants. They knew our regular orders and usually had our drinks waiting for us.

After that, we'd head home, shower, and eat lunch. Then I would read scripts and check email while Kyle checked social media sites for news about us.

Then we'd change and head out for our next public spectacle.

We went to Whole Foods. We went out for (fat-free) frozen yogurt. We hiked in the canyon. We went bowling. We went to dinner.

We held hands everywhere we went, and Kyle often kissed me in public. Just little kisses, but still.

But still. If I was being honest with myself, I would admit that I really looked forward to those outings….and those kisses.

Of course, I was being anything but honest with myself.

We'd come home after dinner, put on our sweats, and continue binge-watching the first season of *True Detective.* Kyle would have one glass of red wine while I had a seltzer.

Kyle's good behavior was impressive. He had comprehensively reformed—the Kyle I remembered would *never* have had just one glass of wine and gone to bed at a reasonable hour. When he was a teenager, he partied until dawn on a regular basis, sneaking back into the house while our parents slept in their own wing, oblivious to what was going on.

Having him around really was like having a live-in boyfriend, except we didn't kiss or hold hands when no cameras were around. And we didn't sleep in the same room, and never would.

Otherwise it was exactly like Kyle was my live-in boyfriend.

I still locked my door every night—to lock myself in.

Of course I knew that was ridiculous. Like I would *ever* go find him at night.

Caroline hadn't called, and neither had Pierce. It was eerily quiet on the parent front. I knew that couldn't last, but I was choosing not to think about them.

No one had run a story about Kyle being my stepbrother or my escort—or both, God forbid. But I felt as if I was holding my breath every day, waiting for the other shoe to drop.

I got multiple daily texts from Lucas, Shirley, Gigi and Tori. Everyone agreed that we were doing great. I even got a note from Officer Scott and Officer Deborah, thanking me for the gift cards, balloons, flowers, coffee, and doughnut bonanza Kyle and I had personally delivered to their precinct. I'd also given them a long-winded, teary, and heartfelt apology.

All in all, considering I'd hit rock bottom only a short time ago, things were looking immeasurably up.

So of course I knew it wouldn't last.

KYLE WAS WAITING for me to go to the gym. We were running late, which he hated. I got into the kitchen, and whatever he was about to say died on his lips as he inspected my lycra workout pants and snug-fitting tank top.

"Sweet baby Jesus," he said.

I laughed, blushing as he stared at me. "What?"

"Nothing," he said, his eyes raking over me hungrily.

I felt myself blush deeper, in pleasure and in anger at myself. I was playing a dangerous game, and I knew it. I craved his eyes on me. I craved more than that, but in my heart, I knew his eyes were all I could ever have.

"You look nice," he said, his voice strained.

"Thanks." I flashed him a grin in spite of knowing better.

He held out his hand for mine, and I took it, my eyes tracing the lines of his biceps, visible from beneath his T-shirt.

"Let's do this," he said, and my insides clenched.

"Okay. Let's do it." *It. All sorts of It.*

We went outside for the flashing cameras and the myriad questions, and I found, quite unexpectedly, that they no longer bothered me at all.

KYLE MADE ME DO WEIGHTS, which made me scowl, but he put his hands on my waist to help me, which made me smile.

Which made me scowl.

"You don't need to touch me like that," I whispered. "We're inside."

"You never know who's taking a picture," he said into my ear. "Like that guy? The one who keeps checking himself out in the mirror? He could totally be an *XYZ* informant."

I looked at the huge, fake-tanned man Kyle was talking about, and I giggled. He was watching his reflection in the mirror as he lifted enormous weights over his head; it seemed as though he only had eyes for himself.

"He doesn't look too interested in us," I said.

Kyle kept his hands on me. "Better safe than sorry."

Resigning myself to the garbled emotions running through me, I lifted the heavy weights again. He kept his hands on my waist, and heat rushed through me. For once, I just let myself enjoy it.

As we were leaving the gym, Kyle threw his arm around me.

"Ew, I'm all sweaty," I said, recoiling.

He gave me a wicked grin. "I know, and I don't mind

one bit. Besides, you know our friends are waiting outside."

I excused myself, running to the locker room to quickly wash up and put on a small amount of makeup. I told myself it was for the photographers, but the deodorant was definitely for Kyle.

He whispered in my ear before we went through the door, "You look gorgeous, and we're going to show them all that I love you even when you're post-workout. That I love you for better or for worse." He pulled me closer to him, and my breath hitched. I felt the heat blooming between us, and it wasn't because we were hot from the gym. "Although I'm not sure there's a worse here. You look great amazing when you're all hot and lycra-ed up."

I gave him a small, bewildered smile. "You *are* good at confidence building."

His gaze lingered on mine. "You shouldn't need it. You're perfect."

With that, we went through the doors to meet the press, all sorts of hot flashes going through me to match the flashes from their cameras.

"You guys look like you had quite the workout!" Rob, one of the regulars, called. "Is Kyle a good workout partner, Lowell?"

"He's the best," I said, giving the reporter a megawatt smile. "Looking at him's a good incentive."

"A good incentive to work on losing weight?"

I gritted my teeth and turned to find Katie, the annoying reporter from *XYZ,* looking at me expectantly. Of course it had been *her* question.

"A good incentive to work on having a healthy body." I'd decided, without telling anyone, that I wouldn't promote losing weight to be skinny. I didn't think that was a responsible example to set for young women, many of whom would never be model-thin. Just like me.

I inspected Katie. She was stick-thin, her collarbones jutting out beneath her patterned blouse. *No wonder you're such a miserable bitch. You need to go eat something.*

"I thought you were required, per your contract, to lose weight," Katie called, not giving up the point.

Anger bubbled up inside me, but I made sure I kept my face neutral. I'd learned the hard way that *XYZ* was not an entity to be messed with. "My contract requires me to be fit for my role in an action-adventure film. My *conscience* requires me to act as a healthy role model for young women around the world." What felt like a thousand flashes went off. I put my hands on my hips. "And now that I've had a great workout, I'm going to go have a Jamba Juice, if you don't mind. Feel free to check the nutrition information."

Kyle put his arm around me and led me to the car.

"Katie, that exclusive's not looking too good," he called back to her, grinning.

I saw the sour look on her face as she packed up her equipment and followed us with the rest of the reporters.

Trouble. Trouble was still following us.

Kyle threw his arm back around me. "I'm very proud of you, young lady."

I grimaced. "Lucas might not approve of what I just said. That might have been a mistake."

"It wasn't. Doing the right thing's never a mistake."

I gave him a nervous sideways glance. "Thanks."

He was becoming too indispensable. I *liked* him too much for my own good. I'd known from the beginning that this would end badly, but this added a whole new layer of bad.

"You're welcome. Now let's go get some overpriced juice. Overpriced juice makes everything better."

I CALLED Tori before I went to bed that night.

"Oh my God, Lowell! You've finally met the perfect guy! I am *dying* over these pictures of you two! It's too cute!" my best friend gushed.

I pinched the bridge of my nose and took a deep breath. I loved Tori, but she had an issue with looking at the bright side of everything—sometimes to the detriment of reality. "He's an *escort*. Remember?"

"I know," she said defensively. "Doesn't mean you two can't actually *like* each other. And it looks like you do—in the pictures anyway."

I sighed. "I'm an actress, remember? It's an *act*."

Tori hesitated for a second. "Don't you at least like him? A little?"

I looked at the picture of my mother and Pierce on my dresser and sighed. "I like him. A little."

"So why do you sound sad?" she asked. My best friend knew me too well.

"Because I *know* him. From before this." I was dying to tell her and wishing it wasn't true all at the same time. "You have to promise not to tell anyone."

"The fact that you already knew him can't be worse than the fact that he's an escort, and I'm already keeping *that* secret," she reminded me. She was silent for a second, as if thinking through her words. "Unless you mean you've *hired* him before—is that it? Do you have a history of hiring escorts? Oh my God, I never would have guessed—"

"Tori?" I waited while she continued babbling about

escorts, how you never really knew anyone, and how much she hated it when I kept secrets from her. "Tori!"

She finally stopped.

"Of course I've never hired him before. I *grew up* with him. His dad was married to my mom. His dad was Husband Number Three."

Tori made a couple of unintelligible noises, as if she was trying to speak but the words kept canceling each other out. "What? What the heck did you just say?"

"He's my stepbrother, Tor. He used to be anyway."

She took several deep breaths. "That is unfuckingbelievable. Of all the luck. Your hot escort is actually your *brother*. Gross!"

I felt my hackles rise. "*Stepbrother*. And actually, he's my ex-stepbrother, so it's even more removed than that."

"So it's not gross? Or is it just less gross?" Tori asked.

Sometimes, I wasn't sure she'd actually gone to Stanford.

"No, it's not gross! It's not even less gross—it's just *not* gross. I mean, I don't think it is anyway." I groaned. "It's *unfortunate*. But it's not like I've done anything with him, anyway."

"You kissed him at that shoe event," Tori reminded me. "And in every other picture of you two, he has his hand on your ass."

"It's an act," I said, trying to sound superior.

"I'm pretty sure he likes having his hand there," Tori said. I could just picture her twirling her curls and giving me a you-are-so-busted look. "He does it *all* the time."

"He does sort of do it a lot." I didn't want to agree with her, but I still sort of wished she was right.

"But you're *not* sleeping with him?" she asked, still sounding a little hopeful.

"Of course I'm not sleeping with him," I snapped. "Jesus. That's the last thing I need. Sleeping with my escort ex-stepbrother."

"But you're pretending, remember? That he's your boyfriend."

"Uh, yeah, I remember. It was my idea, wasn't it?" I asked, exasperated.

"So you *could* actually sleep with him. Like he's your boyfriend. It'd actually make your story tighter." She snickered. "Emphasis on *tighter.*"

"What does the word 'tighter' have to do with anything?"

"I don't know." She giggled. "It just sounds dirty."

I shook my head and snorted. "Tori, you're gross. And I know you're smart, but you make no sense. I have to go."

"So go! But try to have fun. Try to have sex! See if you remember how—it's just like riding a bike!"

I hung up on her, disgusted. Whether I was disgusted with her or with the fact that I was actually considering what she said, I wasn't sure.

And I couldn't afford to find out.

KYLE

"Do you want to do something different today?" I asked.

Lo peered at me over her coffee mug. "Like what?"

This was one of my favorite times of day. We were in her kitchen, having coffee, and her hair was pulled up in a messy bun, her face scrubbed clean of makeup. She was adorable, and I adored her, and it was becoming a real problem.

"Something…fun," I said, grinning. "The *most* fun. That doubles as a great photo opportunity."

She grinned back, even though I felt certain it was in spite of herself. "How can I say no to that?"

"You can't. So go get dressed. Wear something casual, with sneakers. I'll meet you at the front door in ten."

Ten minutes later, she came out in a tank top, baseball hat, and denim shorts, her long legs tanned and gleaming. I just stared.

"What?" she said, blushing underneath the brim of her hat.

"You're sort of cute," I admitted.

"Well, thank you. Sort of." She smiled and grabbed my hand; it had almost become automatic for us. "Where are we going?"

"Not telling." We went through the door and greeted the throng of photographers.

"Are we headed to the gym? The usual?" one of the photographers asked, scratching his head and yawning.

"Nope," I answered. "We're mixing it up today."

"Where are you going?"

I beamed as I hustled her to the car. "I can't tell you—I'm surprising Lowell. But so we don't lose you and end up causing an accident with some sort of high-speed chase, I *will* tell you that we're headed to Anaheim."

They perked up a little.

"Are you going to *you-know-where?*" one of them asked.

I grinned. "Exactly."

"Cool!"

"Awesome!"

"See ya there!"

I got into the car, and Lowell was scowling at me.

"Where the heck is *you-know-where?*" she asked. "And why does everybody besides me know where that is?"

"Because you don't get out much." I threw the car into drive.

"No way!" Lo exclaimed as we turned down Disneyland Drive. "No, sir!"

"Yes way. Yes, sir." I looked at her face as I got in line to pull into the quickly filling lot. She looked excited, looking up at the Tower of Terror in the distance as I parked the car. "Do you...*like* Disneyland?"

"I've never been here," she said breathlessly.

"Never?"

She shook her head. I would have been surprised, but I couldn't really picture Caroline Barton on a roller coaster, getting her hair messed up, or waiting in line with a bunch of tourists. That was surely beneath her.

"It's fun," I said. "We used to fly down here sometimes for the weekend when I was younger. My mom loved it." I felt Lo watching my face.

"What was your mom like?"

"She was awesome." I smiled from just thinking

about my mother. "She would be happy I'm here. I hadn't even thought of coming back, but it popped into my head this morning."

I grabbed Lo's hand, lacing our fingers, after we got out of the car and headed for the tram to take us into the park.

"Hey, Kyle, wait for us!" called Alex, one of the photographers.

I looked back at him, momentarily caught off guard. I'd been so excited about surprising Lo, I'd completely forgotten about them on the ride over here.

And yet, I'd already been holding her hand.

It wasn't just for show anymore, and I knew in my gut that spelled trouble for me. Big trouble. Still, I smiled at the photographers easily, then I decided to forget about them for the rest of the day. Today was about me and Lo.

For better or for worse.

WE WENT ON ALL the rides.

"Can we do it again?" she asked when we got off Space Mountain.

I grinned at her. "You *liked* that?"

She grinned back. "I loved it."

So we went again. And again. We stayed until the sky was dark. I kept my arm around her the whole day, and neither of us stopped smiling. In the back of my mind, I knew the paparazzi were taking pictures of us, but I didn't care. We posed with Goofy, and I took a selfie.

Because I wanted it. For me. For later, when I was alone again.

We watched the fireworks from a gondola on Mickey's Fun Wheel.

"The Ferris wheel kind of reminds me of my career," Lowell joked when we reached the top. "It goes up, up, up, then it goes down, down, down." She laughed.

"I don't think that's just your career—I think that's life in general." I pulled her to me and nestled her against my shoulder.

"No one's in here with us," she whispered. "Even if they have a zoom lens, they probably can't see us up here."

"So?" I asked.

"So"—she sat up and away from me—"we don't have to sit that close together."

I pulled her back, feeling hot and needy and confused. "Just because we don't have to doesn't mean that we shouldn't. Or that we can't."

She leaned into me and looked up at me, making my heart stop. "But we shouldn't. And we can't." She smiled sadly.

I kissed the top of her head and just held her. The jumble of feelings was replaced by a dull ache. I wasn't sure what it meant, but I had a bad feeling I was about to find out.

LATER, I walked Lo formally to her bedroom door.

"Goodnight," I said.

She smiled, but it was a tired smile. "Good night, Kyle. Thank you for today. It was awesome."

"It *was* awesome." I stood over her, wanting to put my arms around her, wishing the press was in here so I had an excuse to touch her. To kiss her.

She held my gaze. Just once, I wanted to run my hands down her whole body. Take her clothes off and press my face against her naked skin. Feel what it was like to see her light up underneath me. Make her moan in pleasure.

"Well, good night," she said again, seeming flustered. "See you in the morning." She pushed past me and closed the door immediately.

Fuck. Fuck, fuck, fuck. Or not. Sighing, I headed back to my room. *Ugh,* I thought, collapsing on my bed. *This is what having feelings is like.*

Frustrated, I padded back to Lo's room. She had to be feeling what I was feeling—at least some of it. When I got there, I promptly lost my nerve. I just stood outside her door, wanting to knock.

For an hour.

I had to respect her boundaries, even as I wanted to crash through them to take her in my arms. I gave up and went back to bed. I wanted to feel her next to me. Nothing else would satisfy me. I tossed and turned, cursing my attempts at being a responsible adult. Being a responsible adult was exhausting and lonely.

I was starting to lose hope, and that dull ache was back. If Disneyland wasn't going to work on her, what the hell was?

And what was I even thinking? What if I slept with her—then what?

I forced myself to fall into a fitful sleep, before I could figure out the answer. I had a feeling I wasn't going to like it.

THE NEXT MORNING, we were all business. *Gym, Jamba, lunch.* Neither of us spoke about the day before.

Lo wasn't looking at me, and I was too ashamed to look at her. It was as if we'd crossed some sort of line, and although there was no going back, there no going forward, either.

After lunch, we set up camp in her living room. She was checking email, and I was catching up on the *XYZ* site when my phone buzzed. It was a text from my father.

I want you to come up and meet with me, he wrote. *I have an offer for you.*

I can't, I wrote back.

Find a way to make it work. Charge the tickets to my account. I'll see you tomorrow, he wrote. He texted me his credit card numbers, which was an act so out of character that I sat there, stunned. I hadn't seen him in so long. I felt as though this was an offer I couldn't refuse. Sighing, I looked up to find Lo watching my face.

"What's the matter?" she asked.

I held up my phone. "My father wants to talk to me. In person. Tomorrow. In Boston."

She blew out a deep breath, looking worried. "What does he want?"

"He says he has an offer for me. I think I should hear

him out, but I don't know how that's going to work right now..."

"I'll go with you," Lowell said. "I mean, if that's okay."

I smiled at her. "Of course it's okay." I didn't want to be away from her for a minute.

"We can make it look like a sexy getaway. Which hopefully won't push your father over the edge."

I grinned, trying to make light of the heaviness between us. "You had me at *sexy*."

"Stop," she said, looking back at her screen. "I'll have Tori take care of the tickets and the hotel. How many nights should we go for?"

"Three?" I asked. "I've never been to Boston."

"Me either."

"Then let's be tourists while we're there. The photographers probably won't follow us, so we'll have to take a ton of selfies to keep everybody happy."

"I'll let Lucas and Shirley know what's going on," Lowell said.

I nodded. "And I think we should go out tonight. Yesterday was a huge success. If we're going to be out of town for a couple of days, we need to leave them with plenty of material."

"You mean go to dinner?"

"I mean go to dinner then go *out*. Get all dressed up and go to a nightclub."

Lowell wrinkled her nose at me. "I don't go to nightclubs."

"I know. Which is why we should."

Lowell shook her head. "I don't want to project a party-girl image after what I did."

"That makes sense, but I think the press needs to see you out at night, looking hot." I watched her face. "You can be a good role model by enjoying yourself responsibly."

She looked as though she was struggling with the idea of the club, but then she nodded. "While people still care."

Not caring about her seemed impossible.

"Works for me," I said and started counting the minutes until I could hold her tight little body on the dance floor.

SHE CAME OUT IN A SHORT, skin-tight black dress and black booties. I almost passed out.

"Is this okay? Or is it too slutty?" she asked.

"It's perfect."

She looked tentatively pleased. "Really? You'd tell me, right? I'm used to having my stylist do all this. Okay, my stylist is Tori, but still."

"Skype her," I said, pointing at her laptop. "She'll approve, I swear it."

Lowell went over to her computer and fired it up. After clicking away for a few seconds, she smiled at the screen. "Tori? How are you? I miss you!"

In spite of my protests, Lowell hadn't allowed a single person from her inner circle to meet me. Not Tori, not Shirley, and I hadn't even glimpsed that Gigi with the long legs again. Lowell had been working with them all from her laptop at home. She was protecting me like Fort Knox. I wasn't sure if she was keeping me away from everyone because she wanted to shield me, or because she was embarrassed by me, or because she thought somehow one of them would be able to tell that I used to be her stepbrother—just by looking at me in person.

But Tori knew who I was. And yet Lowell still wouldn't let me meet her.

"Oh my fucking God, Lo!" A voice that must have belonged to Tori screamed from the computer. "I saw the pictures from Disneyland—that was *so* cute—and Kyle is *so* hot! I can't believe he's your *stepbrother*. That sucks *so* hard! I swear, you two look like you were *made* for each other! Holy freaking—"

"Enough," Lo shrieked. "Kyle's right here!"

Hmm. Maybe this was why she'd kept us apart.

"Oh geez, I'm sorry!" Tori wailed, and I tried not to laugh as Lo adjusted her dress and tried not to die of embarrassment. "Is he still right there?"

"Yesss," Lo said through gritted teeth.

"Oops." Tori promptly stopped talking.

"Can you check my outfit before I go out for the night?" Lo asked, sounding defeated.

"Your dress looks wicked hot," Tori said, regaining her enthusiasm. "I was there when you picked that out, remember? We went shopping for slutty clothes so you could finally get over your dry spell? Well, this is it! That dress screams sex!"

Lo glared at the computer screen, her shoulders rising and falling as she tried to maintain her composure.

"He's still right there, isn't he," Tori squeaked, not bothering to make it a question. "I'm so sorry. I'm just excited!"

"Oh, I can tell you're excited. Everyone can."

"You *do* look wicked hot," I called from across the room.

"Is that him?" Tori squealed. "Is he always that nice? It sounds like he really likes you!"

Lo looked absolutely livid. "Tori, I'm assuming from everything you've said that you approve of my dress. As my stylist, do I have your permission to go out like this?"

"As your stylist, I absolutely approve of that dress. Go forth and have fun." It sounded as if Tori was trying to be serious.

"As my best friend, do you understand that I'm totally pissed at you and I'm going to hang up now?" Lo asked.

"As your best friend, I thoroughly understand your position."

"One more thing—Kyle and I are heading to Boston tomorrow. He has a meeting. Can you deal with the travel arrangements for me?"

"Ooooh, an east coast getaway!"

Lo glared at the computer screen, and Tori stopped.

She cleared her throat. "Of course," Tori said primly, pretending to be all business. "I can take care of that." She cleared her throat again. "But do you acknowledge that you have to call me tomorrow morning and tell me *everything*?"

Lo smiled indulgently. "Of course I'll call you tomorrow. You're still my BFF." She closed the computer and looked at me. "Sorry about that. Tori gets a little... excited for me sometimes."

"Someone who's rooting for you is my kind of gal. I haven't had the pleasure of meeting her, but I'm looking forward to it." I grinned at her. Her face was still flushed, but she looked as though she was trying to pull herself together. "Are you ready for our fabulous evening out, princess?"

"Only if you stop calling me princess."

"Okay, boss," I said and reached for her hand.

She took a deep breath. "Oh, I don't want to do this. I really hate clubs."

"I got you." I squeezed her hand and tried to calm her. "Let's just do this tonight, and we can leave tomorrow for Boston. We'll hide out there."

"But you know what we're going to there is probably just as bad as what we're leaving."

I nodded. "Actually, my dad is definitely worse than these guys." I jerked my thumb toward the window.

Lowell grimaced and nodded. "Oh, I remember." She looked miserable. "Can't we just put on our sweats and watch a movie tonight?"

I smiled and rubbed her hand gently, trying to calm her down. "I would love to do that, but we need to strike while the iron is hot. Think about Lucas. Think about Ellie, with her little headset. She's rooting for you."

She nodded, resigned and clearly gathering her courage. "Okay. Okay."

Of course, the press went nuts when they got a look at her. "Lowell! You look gorgeous!"

"Is that dress a statement about looking great at any

size?" asked Katie from *XYZ*, who was headed directly to the top of my "To Punch" list.

I stopped dead in my tracks. "Are you kidding me? Did you actually just *say* that?"

Katie managed to look a little abashed but not enough for my liking. "I thought that after what she said the other day about being a healthy role model, this dress was some sort of statement."

She looked at us expectantly. She knew full well that Lowell still couldn't afford to say no comment or, worse, have an outburst.

Lowell gave Katie a brave smile. "This dress is totally a statement piece. Guess what this statement is?"

A million flashes went off.

"I'm guessing the *real* statement is geared at Katie and that it's unprintable," I whispered into Lowell's ear.

"You got that right," she whispered back. "Someday, I'll tell her what I really think. Just not today." She sounded resigned.

"What's the statement, Lowell?" everyone asked.

"That being healthy and happy is being beautiful," she said.

"You are beautiful," one of the male reporters said. "And I bet you're going to get some great endorsement offers because of your awesome attitude. You go, girl!"

The other reporters looked at him as if he had three heads.

"If it's still okay to say that," he called sheepishly.

"I appreciate all your support," Lowell said. "See you at El Campo!"

"Thank you, Lowell!"

"Thank you so much!"

"I wish everyone kept us posted about their whereabouts like you two do. It makes things so much easier!"

Lowell smiled at them like a queen, then she strutted to the car with her head held high. I watched Katie, another sour look on her face, watching Lowell.

Lowell sighed, and her face relaxed into a scowl once we were safely inside the confines of the tinted windows. "This is exhausting."

"Good thing you're good at it," I offered.

"You're the one who's good at it. Thanks for sticking up for me back there."

"That Katie…"

"Oh, that Katie…" Lowell agreed.

"She'll get hers someday," I said confidently. "I'll make sure of it."

I MADE Lowell eat her dinner, and I made her drink her wine.

"Relax," I said. "You want to project a healthy body image? Eat, for Christ's sake. Then get up and go back to the gym with me tomorrow. You burned, like, five thousand calories today."

Lo sighed and pushed the food around on her plate. "I don't want Lucas to freak out." She took a sip of wine, looking guilty.

"Fuck Lucas. He can't fire you unless you break the contract terms, right?"

She nodded warily.

"So what do the contract terms actually state?" I asked.

"That I have to be 'fit enough to undertake the action sequences in the film,'" she recited.

"What sort of action is it?"

"Running on a beach. I also have to jump into the back of a moving Jeep." She chewed and looked thoughtful. "I think I have to sprint down a bridge too. Maybe climb some rock walls. They were talking about adding in some stuff like that."

"So every day at the gym from now on, we sprint. We run, jump, and climb. You'll show Lucas exactly how dedicated you are."

"Awesome," she said, finally breaking down and eating her food. "Just awesome."

"ANYTHING BUT THE CLUB," Lowell whined, dragging her heels. "I don't even know what to do in a club. I don't dance, I shouldn't be drinking hard liquor, and you and I don't know anybody."

"Even better," I said, pulling her toward the velvet rope. "C'mon. They're watching us, you know." I looked up at the handful of photographers who'd followed us. "We're taking one for the team."

"The team freaking owes me by this point." Lowell sounded weary, but she had her game face on, beaming at all the other club-goers and the photographers.

The club was packed, but the hostess magically produced a table for us anyway.

"I can only do this for fifteen minutes," Lo said, looking at all the undulating bodies on the dance floor and the beautiful people dancing on tables. "This is silly."

"Do you think the photographers can get in here?" I asked, looking around.

She wrinkled her nose. "No. Gigi said the shots of us coming and going were the most important. Since they already have one of us coming, do you think we can get that 'going' picture now?"

"We don't have to stay long. But any one of these people could take our picture." I motioned with my chin to the crowd around us. "So... do you wanna dance? Just once?" I already knew the answer.

"Absolutely not. I already told you that."

I put my hand on her wrist and pulled her up. "Just once."

She looked at me miserably. "I can't dance to this type of music."

I dragged her onto the crowded dance floor and carved out a small space for us. "You don't have to do anything. Just follow my lead."

I wrapped my arms around her, swayed in time to the throbbing hip-hop beat, and moved her with me. She moved easily and elegantly.

"See?" I asked, leaning down. "You don't give yourself enough credit."

She frowned and shook her head, looking embarrassed.

I wrapped my body around hers, protecting her and moving her more urgently to the music. Heat radiated through me as I felt her body against mine. I pulled her tighter against me, where I'd been aching to have her. My body notched against hers, and she pressed back against me. Lowell's body was saying one thing, but when she looked up at me, her face looked guilty. I knew her head was saying something else entirely.

I ran my thumb across her bottom lip, stroking it. Her eyes met mine, and I leaned down and kissed her slowly.

She pulled back almost immediately. "Kyle, stop."

A yearning grew so fierce inside me that it was almost scary. But I took a deep breath and pushed the heavy feeling away. "Okay, boss." Trying to make light of it, I smiled and pulled her back to me. "But at least dance with me for the rest of the song."

She frowned, then she rested her head on my chest. I ran my hands over her, guiding her to the music and wishing desperately that she wanted me as much as I wanted her.

It was honestly the first time in my life I'd ever felt this way—unsure.

WE SMILED for the cameras and didn't say a word on our way home.

Later, back on her couch, I looked at the latest pictures of us together and tried to forget what it had felt like to have her body pressed against mine.

"We look so good together," I said, slurring from all the champagne I'd drank at the club after she rebuffed me.

Lowell leaned over me and looked at the pictures. "I know. It's ironic, isn't it?"

"Why's that?" I asked, facing her.

"Because we're pretending. And because we couldn't ever actually be together." She sounded as though she was forcing her voice to sound neutral and matter-of-fact. But her eyes were searching mine, as if she wondered if I agreed.

"Why not?" I asked, sitting up. I was suddenly alert, the slurring erased from my speech.

"Because we're *related*. That's why we shouldn't have been dancing like that. It's not okay."

"We aren't related," I said hotly, watching her face. "We weren't ever related."

"Close enough." She shrugged.

"If we actually wanted to be together, we could, you know." I felt a knot forming in my stomach as I waited to hear what she'd say.

She shook her head. "Not really. We lived together when we were kids—that makes it icky. Besides, your father hates me. And my mother hates you."

"So what? *Icky* is subjective. I don't think it's icky. And I don't care what either of our parents have to say."

Again, I waited on edge to see what she'd say. I felt like a lovesick teenager, and I'd never even been a lovesick teenager.

You've got all the cards, Lo. Show me one. Not having the upper hand sucked balls.

She just looked at me, as if she wanted to ask me a question but wouldn't.

"What?" I asked.

She shook her head. "Nothing. All that's bad enough —about our families. Then there's the fact that you're a male escort. Not that there's anything wrong with that, but can you imagine what the press would do if they found out?"

"No," I lied. "I can't."

I knew exactly what would happen. Her reputation would be ruined, my father would reach the emotional state beyond livid, and I would never escape the reality of the bad choices I'd made. My story would be available forever, courtesy of a little technological advance called the internet.

I stood and noticed I was clenching my fists. Frustration and sour disappointment coursed through me. "I'm really tired. I'm going to bed." I walked out of the room before she could see my face.

"Are you okay?" she asked.

"Just tired," I called and slammed my door. *Of everything I'm not.*

I clicked open my phone and stared at the picture of the two of us, wishing it wasn't a lie. If I'd been looking for an answer from her, I'd just gotten it.

It just wasn't the one I wanted.

THE FOLLOWING MORNING, I got up before Lo and called Elena at AccommoDating.

"How's it going, all-star?" she asked, picking up after the first ring and sounding slightly out of breath.

I looked at the clock, incredulous. *Five thirty in the morning.* "Do you ever sleep, Elena?"

"I just finished my Kundalini workout. Why're you calling me if you thought I'd be asleep?" She was quiet for a second. "Oh no, Kyle. Do not fuck with me. Not now."

"What?" I asked innocently. "I didn't even say anything!"

"Why're you calling me at five thirty in the morning, Kyle? After you were out dancing with my client until midnight?"

I made a fist and watched my knuckles turn white.

"I don't have time for this. My girls are going to get up in twenty minutes for school. Speak," she commanded. I could just picture her short hair spiked with sweat, a pristine white workout towel draped around her neck.

"I can't do this anymore."

She sighed. "But you're doing a great job. The press *loves* you. I haven't received communication from the client, but she wired in another payment on top of the retainer. She must be pleased, or I would have heard something."

"I think she's happy with my services," I mumbled, watching my fist.

"You two look *ah*-mazing together, and everyone loves your story," she said encouragingly.

"I can't be an escort anymore. I have real-life issues."

Elena snorted. "Honey, you don't have to tell me that —everybody who works for me has real-life issues! It's almost a professional requirement."

"I mean, I have real-life issues at the moment. I have things going on. It's no longer possible for me to fulfill the requirements of my job."

"Kyle." She was silent as, I assumed, she got her anger in check. "You can't quit on me. If you walk out on that girl right now, it'll ruin everything. For her and for my company."

"You can keep all the money Lowell's given you. I

don't want it. Then we'll be even, right? If you don't have to pay me, it'll be as if you got paid in full. Even if I quit right now."

"Why are you going to do that to this poor girl?"

"I'm not doing it to her. I'm doing it for her."

Elena sighed. "I'm not giving you a dime of this money."

"Good," I said. "Then maybe it'll be like this never happened."

LOWELL

THE TRAFFIC to LAX was insane, as usual. Wishing I'd brought coffee with me, I watched the throng of vehicles from the back of our hired Town Car.

"Do you think we're going to miss our flight?" Kyle asked.

I checked the GPS; even with the traffic we'd make it to the airport in an hour. "We should be okay. I'm worried that there'll be a ton of reporters we have to get through, though." Our regulars knew where we were heading, and there was usually a group that camped out at LAX, waiting to snap pictures of disheveled or perfectly composed celebrities departing and landing.

I was probably looking more on the disheveled end of the spectrum, although I'd dressed carefully. My nerves were frayed, and I was running on nervous adrenaline; the dance I'd shared with Kyle last night, followed by the conversation we had, had unnerved me. *If we actually wanted to be together, we could, you know.* His words rang in my ears, leaving me a jangling mess.

Maybe it was a good thing I'd left my coffee at home.

On top of that, we were headed to Boston for Kyle's mandatory meeting with Pierce. I was happy to go and support Kyle, as he'd been supporting me, but I was petrified of his dad. The last time I'd seen Pierce Richards, he'd been white with anger, shaking at the sight of my mother exiting the courtroom with buckets of his money. *Ugh.*

I pulled out my compact and looked at my traitorous reflection. I looked as though I hadn't skipped a meal in weeks. Because I hadn't. Lucas was going to kill me. "Ugh."

"Don't say *ugh* when you look at yourself—that's sacrilege." Kyle squeezed my hand. "And don't worry about the photographers. We'll get through them, and this time, we won't tell them where we're going."

He squeezed my hand again, making my stomach lurch with excitement.

I pulled away from him. "You don't have to do that right now."

He sat back and grimaced. "You don't always have to pull away from me. Maybe you could, like, relax. For once in your life." He stared at me, forcing me to confront those green eyes and that square, luscious jaw.

Luscious? WTF's up with the word choice, Lo? Like you don't have enough problems already?

Kyle narrowed his eyes at me. "I enjoy being with you, Lo. I've had *fun* with you. I can't remember the last time I had fun that didn't involve getting so drunk I couldn't see straight."

"Disneyland was great. It *was* fun," I agreed quickly. I wanted to keep my distance from him for a variety of reasons, but I didn't want to hurt his feelings. "You're doing a great job. Thank you for everything. Really. You've turned a bad situation into a redeeming success, and you even managed to keep me from looking like a total klutz on the dance floor. You're like a miracle worker."

His face relaxed into a smile. "Yes. Yes, I am."

He threw his arm around me. I looked at him pleadingly, not wanting to hurt his feelings, as I scooted out from under it.

"I'm not used to people touching me," I explained lamely. "Can we just save that for the cameras? Is that okay? It's just...easier for me that way."

Easier for me to keep from hopping onto your lap and straddling you when your arms aren't around me.

I grimaced, digging my nails into my palms,

desperate to get a grip. *Mental slap, Lo. Mental. Fucking. Slap.*

"Of course it's okay," he said too easily. He turned away and looked out the window. "Lo...I know you said it's because you work all the time...but really. Why no boyfriend?"

I blew out a deep breath and stared out the window at the traffic. "You want the truth?"

He looked at me expectantly.

"I have a hard time trusting people. If a guy's interested, I never know if it's for me or for the publicity. I've just heard too many nightmare stories—girls who thought their boyfriend was all about them, then suddenly they're trying out for commercials, calling the paparazzi to follow them so they can be in the magazines, all sorts of horrible things. And after seeing my mother go through guy after guy, I guess...I guess I'd just rather be alone. Build my own empire. If I meet somebody at some point, okay. But if not, it's not the end of the world. There are other things in life."

"That sounds awfully lonely."

I turned back to him, my eyebrow raised. "How about you? When was *your* last serious relationship?"

"Never. But it's not like I've been lonely, if you know what I mean."

I shook my head. "Sometimes I think being around people you don't really care about is a lot lonelier."

Kyle's eyes went dark, and he turned back toward the window. "You're smart. Must've been all the books you read growing up."

THE LAX TERMINAL was teeming with yelling paparazzi.

"Lo! Where are you guys headed?"

"Kyle, are you taking her away to propose to her?"

"Are you in trouble with your director?"

"Are you pregnant?"

"Are you two really a couple? Or is this a publicity stunt?" a female voice called.

I saw that damned Katie from *XYZ*, watching us with her brow furrowed.

I furrowed my brow back at her and inwardly cursed. "I'm not sure why you're asking that, but it's real." I turned to Kyle. "I'm going to kiss you, okay?" I whispered a little breathlessly.

He didn't even hesitate. He swept me into his arms and kissed me tenderly, running his hands down my back and sending shockwaves through my body.

He pulled away and grinned at the press. "Did you

guys get that? Or do you need me to do it again?" He looked at Katie, challenging her. "For more evidence?"

There were whoops and hollers from the majority of our onlookers, but Katie just watched us skeptically. Kyle put his arm around me protectively, and now I welcomed it. He smiled at the press and squeezed my shoulder.

"We're taking a quick *romantic* getaway." Kyle pulled his sunglasses up on top of his thick hair and grinned at them. It seemed as if a thousand flashes went off. "Emphasis on the romance, for you non-believers. We won't tell you where we're going—that'd just spoil the fun—but we'll see you when we get back. Behave while we're gone."

"Lowell, what about that exclusive?" one of the reporters called.

"Call my agent, Shirley Reeder," I called. "She'd love to book it."

"Who's going to get it?"

Kyle beamed at them again. "Whoever asks nicest." His eyes found Katie's. "We've narrowed the list down quite a bit."

He grabbed my hand and pulled me into the security line, waving good-bye to all the photographers and grinning madly. I shook my head and laughed at him.

"What?" he asked, sounding extremely pleased with himself.

"You've got a gift." He was still holding my hand, and that made me feel warm and protected; I pulled my hand away.

He pulled his sunglasses back down and gave me a little frown. "Don't look now—they're right behind us." He took my hand back possessively.

I didn't turn and look. I just stood with him in line, my fingers twined through his, and tried to ignore all the feelings rushing through me. There was heat, yes, but it was something more than that—something even more terrifying.

I was having fun. I *liked* him. And I didn't want to stop being next to him.

It was our turn at security, and I took the opportunity to disengage myself from Kyle to get my identification. I felt Kyle look at me briefly, but I didn't look back.

It was clear to me, now: I knew what I wanted. It was what I could never have.

Now I just had to get my shit together and accept it.

FIRST CLASS WAS ALMOST FULL, but we still managed to find a little corner all to ourselves.

"Why was Katie asking us that?" I asked, playing the scene over and over in my mind.

Kyle shook his head. "I don't know where that came from. I *do* know it can't be good."

"Maybe we're not doing a good enough job pretending?" I asked in low tones.

"Who's pretending?" Kyle asked innocently. He laced his fingers through mine, then he just sat there, stubbornly holding my hand.

"We're clear. No one followed us," I whispered, pulling away from him. "You don't have to do that."

He wouldn't let go of my hand. "I want to do *that*." He jerked his chin toward our hands.

"Why?" I asked, my heart pounding.

"My hand feels lonely without your hand," He grinned at me. "So deal with it. If you don't want to hold my hand, then don't."

I just sat there, looking at our entwined hands as if they belonged to aliens. "But what...but why..." I was flustered, unable to decide which question to ask.

"Talk to the hand, Lo," Kyle said, leaning back in his seat and closing his eyes. "You want to get into semantics? Talk to it. Tell me if you get the response you're looking for." He didn't let go of me for an instant.

I bent down toward his hand. "You are being very stubborn," I whispered at it.

With his eyes closed, Kyle smiled briefly. But he didn't budge. Sighing in defeat, neither did I.

Because I didn't want to.

Shortly thereafter, the plane took off, and Kyle fell asleep. I watched his handsome face, turned toward me, completely oblivious and innocent. In my past dealings with Kyle, he'd never been innocent. But really, he seemed as though he'd changed.

Hitting rock bottom can do that to you. I looked at our entwined hands. I ought to know.

I looked out the window, grateful that he was next to me. I listened to his even, regular breathing and clung to him in a way I never would have had he been awake.

I was dangerously close to having real feelings for Kyle. I'd always wanted him to like me when we were kids, but this was different. And much worse. Because now we were adults. I was in a precarious situation to start with—publicly shamed and about to be fired from my movie. Kyle had saved me, at least for now. But if the press found out the truth about our circumstances, they'd crucify me, and I'd never work in Hollywood again. I was still too new to be inoculated from the fall-out. If they found out I'd hired an escort, I'd be done for. If they also found out that he was my ex-stepbrother, my walk of shame would last all the way back to Texas.

But it wasn't just that. It was his father and my

mother. If my mother were Stateside right now, she'd probably have to be involuntarily held at a yoga retreat so she wouldn't attack him. She'd never forgiven him about those drapes. Knowing my mother, she never would.

I looked at Kyle. His face was relaxed in sleep, belying none of the stress I knew he felt about seeing his father again. I was glad that he was here with me, but it was a sharp feeling. I was so glad it hurt.

I went back to looking out the window, not letting go of his hand.

I woke up a few hours later when I felt water dripping down my chin. I sat up straight and wiped it...only to realize I'd been drooling. I shot a surreptitious look at Kyle, who was unfortunately wide awake and reading the sports section of the *Los Angeles Times.*

"Hey there," he said, smirking, as he handed me a napkin. "It looks like you were dreaming about me."

"Ha-ha." I furiously wiped my reddening face.

"We're almost there," he said.

I noticed he was no longer holding my hand.

"Missing something?" he asked, wriggling his fingers and flashing me a mischievous grin.

"No," I said, scoffing and still wiping my face. "You wish."

He put his head on my shoulder. I tried not to notice how good he smelled. I didn't even know what it was—some sort of mixture of shampoo and sleep and… virility. I shivered as my mouth filled with saliva again. I was literally drooling over him.

For fuck's sake, get a grip.

"Do you know where we're staying?" He sat up and stretched, yawning.

"No, Tori booked everything. She's supposed to send me an itinerary text when we land."

"Great." Kyle folded up the sports section and linked his hand back through mine. "I love romantic getaways."

I glared at him, a mixture of excitement and annoyance coursing through me. "You know that this isn't—"

He held up our linked hands again, his eyes glimmering with mischief. "You know what I'm going to say."

I wished I had a human sexuality textbook handy. I felt as if I might need it, for a variety of reasons.

KYLE

There was a man holding a sign: *JORDAN.*

"Here we are," I told Lowell. I nodded toward the driver.

She looked at me quizzically. "Why does it say your fake last name?"

"We're trying to be incognito, right? Plus, I need to alpha this"—I pointed from me to her—"up a little bit. I gotta take the lead." I grabbed her hand and pulled her toward the driver.

"I'm Evan," the driver said, flashing us a smile and shaking our hands. He was six-foot-three and had the neck of an NFL linebacker. "Tori arranged for me to drive you while you're here. I'll bring you out to the car and have your luggage brought out."

We settled into the back of an enormous Range Rover. Lowell was studying my face.

"If Tori made the reservations, how did he have your last name?" she asked.

I smiled and patted her head. "Because Tori and I finally met last night over Skype. I told her that we needed this trip to look like I was pursuing you—hard. I want it to be big. Romantic. Grand gestures, Lo. Grand gestures."

"You talked to Tori?" She looked mystified.

"Yup. I Skyped with her on your laptop while you were packing."

Lo furrowed her brow, looking more suspicious than mystified now, and her phone buzzed. She glared at it. "Tori," she answered angrily. "We just landed. You didn't tell me you talked to *Kyle*. On *Skype*."

She was quiet for a minute, and I heard Tori's muffled voice talking in what sounded like her normal, excited tones.

"Well, what if that's not okay with me?" Lo huffed.

Now Tori's tone sounded pleading.

Lo rolled her eyes, but her expression softened, just as it always did when she spoke to her friend. "No, I know...I know, Tor. I'm not mad." She looked at me and frowned. "At you."

They talked for a few more minutes while Evan

arranged our luggage and pulled out into the airport traffic.

"I understand I'm taking you to the Stratum," he said after Lowell had hung up. "Have you stayed there before?"

"No," Lowell and I said in unison.

He smiled at us in the rearview mirror. "You're in for a treat. It's impressive."

I turned to Lo and smiled. "See? Impressive. I'm all about the impressing."

"You and Tori better watch it," she said through gritted teeth. "Or you're both going to get voted off the island."

"You'd miss me," I said, making sure my dimples were on full display. "Admit it."

"I admit nothing," she said under her breath.

I watched her face as she examined the unfamiliar skyline of Boston. We drove through what appeared to be the financial district, and a few minutes later, Evan maneuvered the SUV down Newbury Street and pulled up in front of a massive, opulent building. I looked at the Stratum, impressed, and let out a low whistle.

Just then my phone vibrated. I pulled it out, a pit of dread in my stomach.

You just landed, correct?

Please come see me at my office. Immediately.

The address for an office building located within MIT followed shortly thereafter.

Evan looked back at us expectantly, but Lowell must have seen the pure dread on my face.

"I think there's been a change in plans," she said. "What is it?" she asked me quietly.

"My father wants to see me. Now." I turned to her. "I'm going to have Evan take you upstairs. I'll be back soon."

Lowell shook her head. "I'm coming with you. If Pierce doesn't want to see me, I can wait for you outside or in the car. But you're in trouble because of *me*. I'll be there even if it's just for moral support." She squeezed my hand, and the despair I felt was somewhat eclipsed by her warmth and the fact that she was standing by me.

I nodded. "Okay. But you might want to stay out of sight, at least for now." I gave Evan the address in Cambridge then leaned back, preparing for what would surely be an ugly family reunion.

UNFORTUNATELY, MIT was right across the Massachusetts Avenue bridge, close to Newbury Street. I was sitting outside his office sooner than expected and certainly sooner than I was ready for.

In spite of her objections, I'd deposited Lowell at a coffee shop nearby, filled with students getting their caffeine fix and solving math theorems.

"I need to do this alone," I'd said as I grabbed her hand. "At least I know you're here."

She'd nodded, but her eyes told me she felt guilty and worried.

"It's going be okay," I'd said, sounding much more confident than I felt.

I was pretty sure that the MIT campus was lovely, but I couldn't concentrate on my surroundings. All I could feel was the throb of my nerves. It'd been almost a year since I'd seen my father. A year since he'd cut me off from our family fortune. Months since I'd started hooking. I hung my head, waves of nausea rolling through me.

The fact that I was about to see my father made my job seem more real and more horrible.

He poked his head out of his office door.

"Hey, Dad."

"Come in." His voice was all business. He closed the door behind me.

Pierce looked different. His hair was sparser, and he looked more rumpled. In California, he'd always taken time to hit the gym and hike in the canyon. The Boston version of Pierce looked haggard and a little thin, his usual tan faded, as if he'd been working non-stop.

I forgot about my dread enough to worry about him for a second. "Are you doing okay, Dad?"

He looked at me and scoffed. "You don't have to pretend you care. There's no one else here."

I felt my blood pressure spike, so I took a deep breath. Pierce had a way of getting under my skin. "Of course I care. You're my father."

"Did you care so much about me when you started dating your stepsister? Or should I say when you started being your stepsister's *hooker*? Were you wondering about my feelings when you decided to do that?" His voice was dangerous, the even tone masking the fury behind his words.

I took another deep breath. I looked my father in the eyes. "I didn't think about you then. All I was thinking about was how to support myself. It was survival mode, I guess."

"So you chose to become a prostitute?" He ran his hands through what remained of his hair, making it stick up in crazy directions. "Was that really the best you could come up with?"

Shame flooded through me, but I held his gaze. "I tried waiting tables. I got fired. I tried giving surfing lessons, but it wasn't enough money for an apartment and food. As you might remember, I have no skill set. The only things I studied were the bottom of a bottle, my surfboard, and the occasional hot model—okay, the more than occasional hot model."

He didn't say anything.

"I'm sorry I've disappointed you, but it's not like that's anything new, is it?" To my horror, I felt my eyes fill with tears. I took another deep breath and willed them back. I wasn't some stupid fourteen-year-old boy being chastised for another failing grade.

He watched my crumpling face, but I saw no softening on his. "I cut you off from your trust fund because you almost killed yourself, remember? When you stole my car and drove completely drunk? You're lucky to be alive. You're lucky you didn't kill someone. What kind of father would I be if I hadn't taken action? What would your poor mother have said if she'd lived to see that?" He sat back in his chair. "If I hadn't done it then, son, I wouldn't ever have done it, and I was worried the next phone call I got from the police would be telling me that you were dead."

I scrubbed my hands over my face. "I know I've made some bad decisions—a lot of bad decisions—and I understand why you did what you did. I was out of control."

Pierce nodded. "It's a first to hear you say that. But

that doesn't make it okay that you're…hooking. Or whatever you call it. And whatever it is you're doing with Lowell—that's just beyond my comprehension." He pinched the bridge of his nose as he always did when he was really frustrated, as though he was trying to open his airways to get more oxygen to his brain.

As if that was going to help his son not be a hooker.

"The escort job just sort of fell into my lap. It wasn't like I had a lot of other options at the time. And I've only done it for a few months," I said quickly. I wished that I didn't feel as though I owed him an explanation, but now that we were sitting across from each other, the words just poured out. "But this thing with Lowell is different. She called the service I work for because she needed to hire someone for PR. She was in a bind. I've been helping her—strictly business. And I've already left the escort service. I'm doing this just to help her now."

Pierce's eyes softened but only for a moment. "I studied up on her. She was in trouble because she was drunk in public, right?"

"That's right. It was a PR disaster."

Pierce snorted. "Obviously. But did she really think hiring a prostitute would save the day?"

"She's smart, Dad. She understands how the industry works. It's like if you flash something shiny in front of them, they get confused and can't remember what they were doing."

"And you're the shiny thing." He pinched the bridge of his nose again. "But this is all for show? The relationship part that the press is having a field day with?"

I nodded.

"What does her mother have to say about it?"

"She doesn't know. She's out of the country right now."

"Lucky her."

I waited until he removed his hand from the bridge of his nose. "Dad?"

He sat up straight and looked at me. "You need to stop working for her and never go back to that…lifestyle…again. We can make some sort of arrangement. I realize that I might have been too harsh. Cutting you off like that wasn't the right thing to do. I didn't give you any options. I should have made you get a job and go to school."

"You'd already given me options. You tried, remember? I was stubborn. I wasn't ready to grow up. But I've changed—this experience changed me."

"Please." He winced and held up his hand to stop me. "I don't want to know."

We were both quiet for a minute, but I realized that

the pit in my stomach had dissipated. Telling my father the truth felt good.

"I'm thinking of where I can use you right now. I could actually use some help in the publicity department for my new app launch." He pointed at the office around him, which was bare and academic, holding just a messy bookcase and a scarred desk. "People I'm working with are great, but they're not public-image savvy. I'm hiring an agency…maybe you could be my liaison with them. Help me get the exact branding I'm looking for."

I was stunned. Not only was my father offering me a job, he was offering me a job that I actually understood. "Dad. Wow."

He actually smiled at me. "Does that sound like something you'd be interested in?"

"It does."

"Maybe I'm not such a crap father after all." He sat back, satisfied. "You start tomorrow, Kyle. Be here at eight. I'll give you a synopsis of the app, and we can talk about branding. Then you can make arrangements to meet with the agency."

"Tomorrow? I can't. I can't come to work for you until I finish this thing with Lowell. I told you, I'm not an escort right now—I'm being a friend. She needs me. At least until she starts shooting again. Her premiere's coming up. Maybe I can still go to that with her…"

Pierce shook his head. "No, son. This stops today. I'm making you this offer based on the assumption that you're leaving your current situation behind. No more Lowell Barton. I told you before: I can't have you dating your stepsister, especially when it started out as you *hooking*. I have a feature in *Forbes* coming up. I'm launching this app in a month. You can't do this to me. Especially not with that girl." He scrubbed his hand across his face. "We're lucky the press hasn't found out about you already."

"I can't just walk away from her." I heard the stubbornness in my own voice.

"It sounds like you have feelings for her." I didn't say a word as he leaned across the desk and held my gaze. "You grew up with her. I was married to her *mother*. You are—were—her *escort*. If the press gets a hold of this, it'll be the end of her career. Don't you get that what you're doing is wrong?"

"Don't you mean the end of *your* career?" My eyes held his, but he didn't flinch. "Don't pretend to care about hers."

"I'm not pretending. I don't care about hers, but I'm trying to reason with you. For all the good that's ever done me."

I scrubbed my hands over my face; I suddenly felt as tired and worn-out as my father looked. "What I'm doing with her isn't wrong. And with all the bad things I've done, I should be a pretty good judge of that." I stood.

"Wait." My father stood too. "I just want you to stop seeing her. Yes, I have that profile coming up, but it's not only about that. You're my son. I don't want you…struggling. Come work for me. If you show up every morning and show me that you're responsible now, not only will I give you a competitive salary, I'll reinstate your trust."

Whoa. Of all the outcomes I'd expected from this meeting, my trust being dangled in front of me wasn't one of them. What he was offering me was enormous. *A real job. My money back, my security back. I could afford to take Lowell to Hawaii, just like we'd talked about.*

But I couldn't just leave her.

"I won't do that to her. I made a commitment. For once, I'd like to know what it feels like to not disappoint someone." I headed to the door. "We're here for a couple of days. If you want to have dinner or something, just text me."

Pierce snorted again. "That'd be real fun. One big happy family."

"Yeah, that'd be a first, huh?" I started to walk out.

"If you don't do what I ask, I'll make sure you regret it."

I turned toward him. "Really, Dad? You're going to be like *that*?" He was like a child who wasn't getting what he wanted and was about to throw a massive, potentially dangerous temper tantrum. "I'm not saying *no*. I'm just saying I can't do it right now."

"If you continue on this course, you're not leaving me much choice."

I shook my head and stormed out of the office, anger coursing through me. *I'm the one who doesn't have a choice, Dad. I can't leave her like that.* But I could never explain why to him.

I could barely admit it to myself.

LOWELL

"How did that go?" I asked once we were safely back in the car.

"It...went." He looked out the window. It seemed as though a black mood had descended on him.

"Do you want to talk about it?"

He shrugged. "In some ways, it was better than I expected. He actually apologized for cutting me off."

"Wow! That's great, right?"

"Sort of."

I didn't want to pry, but I was overcome with curiosity. "Did he say he was going to the press about us?"

"No. He...can't. He doesn't want it getting out about me. What I've been doing for work." He hesitated. "He offered me a job, Lo. He said if I came to work for him and stay out of trouble, all would be forgiven. He wants me to work with the agency launching the new brand for his app."

"That's great!" Relief washed through me. Pierce Richards had never been my favorite person, but back when I'd known him, he'd at least been a caring father. He'd been preoccupied with my mother and let Kyle push him away, but Kyle had been tough back then. Still, I'd always felt that Pierce loved his son. Disinheriting him had just been the tough side of that love.

Kyle shook his head. "It's not great. He wants me to start tomorrow."

My heart sank a little. *He's not coming back to LA with me.* But I didn't let myself think about that. I quashed my disappointment and smiled. "That's okay. This is a great opportunity for you."

He looked at me then turned away. "I'm not ready to walk away just yet."

Hope and guilt mingled inside me. I wanted to hear what he was saying, but I knew he shouldn't say it. "Does Pierce want to you come work for him right now because he wants you away from me?"

He shrugged. "It doesn't matter. It's not going to happen."

"Kyle—"

"Enough," he snapped. "I don't remember saying that I wanted committee approval."

I shut my mouth, hurt by his tone. If Pierce wanted Kyle to quit right now—and I was pretty sure that was exactly what he wanted—then Kyle had to do it. I had a feeling Pierce didn't offer second chances with much frequency; thirds were probably out of the question.

I had to convince Kyle to take the offer, and I only had a few hours to do it. Even if it meant a public relations disaster for me.

I could handle a public relations disaster.

Ruining Kyle's life? That was another matter altogether.

EVAN BROUGHT us back to the hotel. I grabbed Kyle's hand when we got out of the car, and he looked at me, surprised.

"Just in case," I whispered in his ear. All of a sudden, I felt as if my time with him was running out.

"I like just in case." He smiled at me, and it seemed as if the black cloud went away, my sunny, good-natured Kyle returning.

I grinned back even though my heart was twisting. I looked up at the Stratum. "This is nice. I might not be that mad at you and Tori after all."

We entered the imposing lobby, which boasted

marble floors, marble columns, and teak woodwork accents in unexpected places. It was beautiful and pristine. Our footsteps echoed across the lobby.

"You see a front desk anywhere?" I asked.

Kyle shook his head. "The new hotel lobbies don't have front desks. They think Millennials don't like them and want everything to be decentralized."

"Huh?" I asked. I was pretty sure I was a Millennial, and I had no idea what he was talking about.

"It's just the new thing—don't worry about it. I've spent a lot of time in hotels recently." His face went dark at the thought.

I squeezed his hand. "It's okay, Kyle."

He looked at me, his face bleak. "It's not okay."

"I think I see someone who works here," I said, trying to distract him for the moment. We headed toward a stunning young blonde, wearing a headset, in a simple black dress.

"Welcome," she said warmly. "You must be Mr. Jordan and Ms. Barton. We're honored to have you staying with us at the Stratum. I'm a huge fan of your work, Ms. Barton."

She smiled and motioned for us to follow her. "I'm Britta. I'll have your luggage brought up. You'll be staying on the fiftieth floor, in the penthouse suite. I hope that you enjoy your stay, and please let me know if you need anything while you're here."

We reached the fiftieth floor, and Britta gave us one final smile as Kyle and I got off the elevator. "You have the floor to yourselves." Her eyes glittered with good-hearted mischief. "Just call downstairs if you need anything."

Kyle let out a low whistle as we entered the room. It wasn't just the penthouse suite—it was clearly the *honeymoon* suite, built for romantic and most likely naked behavior. Unlike the minimalist space in the lobby, our suite had plenty of romantic flourishes: roses in crystal vases, champagne in a bucket, a view of the Commons, intimate seating throughout the room and a fire roaring in the fireplace.

It was August. *Who the hell needs a fire in August?*

Lusty, love-struck couples on a sexy vacation. That's who.

I stared around, taking everything in. "Maybe I *am* mad at Tori."

"Don't be." He pulled me against him and looked at me hungrily. "She did a good job—and I'm pretty sure I won't have to call Britta—because I have every single thing that I need."

"Kyle!" I said in protest, extricating myself before I accidentally-on-purpose jumped him. I was happy he'd briefly escaped the dark cloud again, but that didn't mean I could throw myself at him.

I, for one, didn't need the roaring fire. I already had a very inconvenient one between my legs at the thought of being trapped here with Kyle for a whole weekend. We could skip talking about Pierce and his offer. I could turn off my phone and pretend Lucas and his list of athletic and calorie-restrictive demands were figments of my imagination. We could order room service and defile every available surface of this suite with our sweating, naked bodies. We could…

Mental slap. Mental-fucking-slap, Lo. You have to break up with him—fire him, I mean. So that he can have a normal life again.

Furious for more reasons than I cared to entertain, I stomped into the bedroom. It was luxurious and decadent, with a crystal chandelier hanging over an enormous four-poster bed. Red draperies hung on the wall; I felt as if I were in an ultra-expensive brothel. I peered into the bathroom, and it was exactly as I'd feared: clear glass shower, enormous tub built for sharing, bubble bath, everything that a couple having a sexy weekend would want. I tore through the rest of the suite—but that only confirmed my worst fears. There was only one bedroom and only one bed.

I stood next to the floor-to-ceiling windows, my fists clenched, my breathing rapid.

"What's the matter, Lo?" Kyle asked, and I heard that shit-eating grin in his voice again. At least he was in a better mood.

My mood, however, had taken a turn for the worst. "There's only one bed."

He was stretched out on the couch, and he put his enormous arms behind his head. I tried in vain to look away from those bulging biceps.

"I can sleep on the couch," he said, grinning. "If that's what you want."

I gritted my teeth, stalked over to the champagne, and opened it. Anything to avoid staring at his biceps. When in Rome, the least you could do was drink the available alcohol.

"Okay. Sleep on the couch." Two could play this game. "If that's what *you* want."

He sat up a little and watched me. "It's not what I want."

Oh, holy hell. Now he was being completely direct.

I rolled my eyes as if he were being ridiculous. "Stop. You just met with your father. We have enough problems right now." I swigged some champagne.

His eyes didn't leave my face as he shrugged. "Okay, boss."

"Don't call me boss."

"Okay, princess."

"Stop. It." I sighed. "At least you're in a better mood. I do hate it when you call me names, though."

"Does it remind you of the good old days when I called you bookworm? Or pencil-neck?" Kyle grinned at me.

I grunted. "It's not like I still call you scrotumhead."

Kyle raised eyebrows. "You called me scrotumhead?"

I shrugged, feeling my face reddening. "I only called you that... in my head...when we were growing up and you were being mean to me. Which was pretty much all the time."

Kyle nodded thoughtfully, as if considering his nickname. "Scrotumhead had a certain something to it, I guess. At least you were thinking about my scrotum." He continued to grin at me, and I felt my face go from pink to crimson.

I stalked around the room, clutching my champagne and no longer wanting to discuss scrotums. I had enough to worry about: my upcoming premiere, the fact that Kyle might very well quit this weekend, and that I hadn't lost a pound. Not one.

"You can come sit next to me, you know. It's not like I'm going to bite. Although a bite from a scrotumhead might be... interesting." Kyle laughed, and it was great to hear. I'd hated it when he came out of his father's office, pale and fuming.

In spite of all the trouble mounting around me, I laughed too. Shoulders shaking, I sat at the foot of the couch.

Kyle made himself comfortable and put his feet on my lap. "That's more like it, Lowell. Just give in to it."

I shook my head. "I don't even know what to say anymore."

"Then don't say anything. Just relax, for once."

I smiled weakly. I was going to put "relax for once" on my ever-growing list of things that were never going to happen.

IN AN UNFORTUNATE TURN OF EVENTS, Kyle's father called him that afternoon at the same time my mother called me. We looked at our respective phones and exchanged wary looks. Kyle retreated to the bedroom; I headed for the far end of the living room.

"Hey, Mom," I said through the crackling line. "Can you call me from a different phone? I can barely hear you."

"What about now?" she asked, and suddenly her voice was perfectly clear. "I moved into the sanctuary.

I'm forbidden from being on the phone in here, but you're my only child, so whatever."

I could just picture her stalking around the temple in capri yoga pants and a gauzy organic tank, her face smooth and unnaturally plump with filler. Her hair, frosted only with the most expensive chlorine-free bleach, was probably hanging past her shoulders in age-inappropriate waves.

"I can hear you now." I swallowed and realized I had a lump in my throat. I was hiding so many things from her, and that wasn't like me. "How are you, Mom?"

"I'm great, darling. I tried to tell you last time we talked, but then we got cut off. This has been the best trip ever. It's not even a trip—it's a *journey*. I'm so mentally clear right now, you could probably see right through my head." She chuckled. "How are *you*? I've been worrying about you non-stop."

"I'm...fine." I tried to sound like I meant it.

"Did you wrap *Renegade Hearts* yet? Did you get everything straightened out with Lucas? Did you tighten up your derriere, darling?"

I groaned. I couldn't say anything about my ass, lest she offer to fly home immediately or sic her personal chef on me. "We're not finished filming yet. We're on break right now. They had some... things they needed to work out."

The issue is still my ass, Mom. And yes, it's still too big for Lucas's taste.

No, I haven't lost a pound.

Even though I've been going to the gym. Every. Single. Friggin. Day.

"I'm actually in Boston right now for a long weekend."

"Huh? What was that, sweetie? I thought you said you were in *Boston*," she said.

"I am."

"Are you on a *vacation?*" She sounded thoroughly confused. I hadn't taken a vacation…ever.

"We're sort of on vacation," I mumbled. Then I groaned, realizing my mistake.

"I'm sorry," my mother shrieked, probably breaking every rule ever made about the sanctuary she was in, "but did you just say *we*? As in you and an actual someone else?"

I swallowed, hard, over that lump. "I'm, um…here with someone." *Please dear God, don't let her have had an internet connection on her spiritual expedition.*

"Is it a *man?*" she asked.

"Um… yep?" I let my answer trail up in a question. Because I was afraid.

"Lowell, darling, I need details. *Now.* Who is it? What does he do? Is it serious?" *Is he rich? Does he have any single friends you can set me up with?* Those questions were coming. It was only a matter of time.

I took a deep breath. "His name is Kyle...Jordan. He's in consulting. He likes to surf...he's nice. You'd like him." *You'd hate him. Actually, you* do *hate him.* "But you probably won't meet him. I'm pretty sure it's not going to work out."

"He's *nice?*" she screeched, ignoring every other important detail. "You never say guys are nice!"

"That's because they're usually not," I said. "Especially not yours."

"Well, I guess I have a bad habit of picking the wrong men... maybe someday I'll meet 'the one'..." Even though my mother was stunned by my news, she was incapable of talking about anyone other than herself for longer than a minute. She prattled on about the nonexistent state of her love life while my mind raced a mile a minute.

Knowing she could go on forever, I interrupted her with the million-dollar question. "When're you coming home?"

"Sooner than expected, honey." The line crackled again. It sounded as though I was about to lose her. "I'll come find you—"

The line went dead, cutting her off mid-sentence.

That was just perfect. My mom was coming back

sooner than expected, she knew I was in Boston, and she knew I was dating someone. Why had I opened my mouth? I could have just let her blather on about her yoga poses. I'd just made everything worse. Again.

Kyle walked in, his normal tan replaced by a slightly ashen color. His father seemed to have that effect on him.

"Pierce wants to see us. Together."

I gulped. "When?"

"He has meetings over the next few days, so first thing in the morning on Sunday."

"Awesome," I said, a pit of dread forming in my stomach. "Just awesome."

KYLE

My stomach growled, and I looked at my phone. It was only five, too early to just get room service and go to bed. "Can we just go get a quick dinner then call it a night? This has been the longest day ever. I'm beat." I scrubbed my hands over my face.

"Of course," Lowell said.

We didn't ask each other about our simultaneous parental phone calls. I guessed hers had probably gone as poorly as mine—she looked as tired as I felt.

Evan picked us up and took us to the North End, the Italian section of Boston. It was a relief to be there, out and largely anonymous on the East Coast, without worrying about fifty photographers waiting to ambush us.

The North End was perfectly charming with narrow

streets, cobblestoned sidewalks, and cafes with their windows open wide. After several failed attempts to pull away, Lowell held my hand without objection. We wandered around the neighborhood, enjoying the delicious smells and reading the different menus. My fatigue eventually evaporated, and I relaxed, relishing the time with Lowell.

We finally decided on a tiny restaurant on the corner. They served us red wine in small plastic cups. The day melted away as we shared stuffed clams and fresh, hot bread.

After our entrees arrived, Lowell twirled her black pasta and moaned with pleasure when she had a bite. "Why do carbs have to be so good?" She eyed her plate, which was filled with homemade pasta and smothered in puttanesca sauce.

"Because God wants you to eat," I said right before I stuffed a large chunk of lobster meat into my mouth. God was on my mind at the moment. I'd ordered the Lobster *Fra Diavolo*, and it was so good, I was pretty sure that I'd died and gone to heaven.

Lowell stole a piece of lobster from my plate. I shot her a look, and she raised her eyebrow, daring me to object.

"You *said* God wants me to eat. I'm just following orders."

"Don't be fresh," I warned. "I might have to spank you when we get home."

Lo spluttered and coughed while I laughed. She took a sip of wine and collected herself. She cleared her throat and tried to look all-business. "So... what did your dad want this time? What on Earth does he want to talk to both of us about?"

I didn't want to tell her everything that Pierce had said. If she knew, she'd pack me up and deliver me to my father in a suit, ready to go to work first thing in the morning. Not because she wanted to get rid of me—at least I hoped she didn't. She'd do it because she was a good person and would put my needs before hers.

I wasn't going back to my father's company. Not yet. But I did have to find a way to protect Lowell from whatever my father had planned. Or find a way for him to understand that hurting her was completely off-limits.

"He probably wants to make us an offer. Or deliver a threat."

Lowell shrugged. "He can't make my situation much worse."

I watched her for a beat. "Of course he can. He can out me as an escort who is tangentially related to you."

She held my gaze. "He won't do that. You already said he won't do that to you."

I snorted. "You mean he won't do that to himself."

"Kyle." She put her hand on top of mine. "Your dad loves you. I remember how difficult he can be—I watched what he did to my mom. And I know he cut you off. But I think he did it because he was trying to protect you."

I pulled my hand away. "You don't have to make me feel any worse about it. I know what a fuckup I was. Am."

"You're not a fuckup. Look at me."

I raised my eyes back to hers.

"And give me back your hand, dammit," she commanded.

I did as I was told, happy and angry at the same time. She was about to deliver a lethal blow. I knew it.

"You made mistakes. You're paying for them." She cracked a smile. "Your father wants something better for you. That's what I want too."

"I'm not going to leave you and get you fired. Lucas would have a fit if we parted ways right now, and so would Shirley and Gigi. You know that's true." I watched her face. "It'd be the end of everything we've been trying to do. I don't want it to end that way—do you?"

She shook her head. "No, of course not. But I don't really see what other options we have. I want what's best for you."

"You can't make me leave you," I said.

She smiled, but it was a sad smile that made my insides ache. "No. I guess I can't, huh?"

AFTER WE WERE BACK at the hotel, I clicked on ESPN and watched from the couch. Lowell paced, probably worrying about my father or the sleeping arrangements. Or both.

"Lowell, stop pacing."

"Huh?" She looked at me and wrung her hands.

I patted the couch next to me. "Come here and tell me what's the matter."

She sat stiffly next to me. "I don't want you to say no to your father. And I don't want to get in any more trouble with Lucas and Shirley. And there's only one bed here." She miserably jutted her chin toward the over-the-top bedroom.

Oh, what I would do to you in that four-poster bed. My cock twitched. *Stop it,* I ordered. She was upset. I didn't want to scare her away—or worse, take advantage of her vulnerability.

"You can have the bed. I'll take the couch," I said.

She still looked miserable.

"About the rest of it—we'll just have to get my dad to

understand that what we're doing has an expiration date." I swallowed hard at the thought. "Once he understands that I *will* eventually come to work for him, that should reduce his drama."

"But is he going to let you stay with me for that long? Until the *Hearts Wide Open* premiere? Because I think that's the thing Shirley's the most concerned with."

I shrugged. "If he wants to get what he wants, he'll have to agree." I said it with confidence, but I knew my father—when he wanted something, he wanted it *now*. Not a few weeks from now. "Whatever happens, we'll deal with it."

She nodded, but she looked troubled. "Let's talk about it more in the morning. I'm going to go to bed." She gently kissed my cheek, making desire tear through me. She stood. "Good night, Kyle."

"Good night, Lowell."

If she was feeling what I was—the unmistakable, almost painful longing—I couldn't believe she would walk away. But she did.

She looked at me one last time at the bedroom door, a mixture of desire and regret on her face. "You can have the bedroom tomorrow night, okay?"

"Okay." I nodded. *But only if you're in it.*

LOWELL

I LAY AWAKE THAT NIGHT. I could feel him on the other side of the door. My body, heavy with lust, was practically screaming for him.

Shut up, I warned it. *We're in enough trouble as it is.*

I hadn't told Kyle that my mother might be coming home soon; I didn't want to put him any more on edge than he already was. Besides, this was my mother we were talking about. She could end up staying in Japan for another month, going to a random *reiki* retreat or finding some Japanese businessman to fawn over.

When I slept, I slept fitfully, dreaming of Kyle naked and on top of me, his big biceps holding me down. *Oh yes, yes, yes—*

"Yes!" I yelled, waking myself.

I sat straight up in bed, my breath heaving, early morning light coming through the window. I looked around, flustered and wishing that either the dream had been real or I could somehow manage to stop craving Kyle's hands on me.

"Are you okay in there?" Kyle called.

He heard me. Just perfect.

"I'm good," I croaked, embarrassed beyond belief. I looked at the clock—six o'clock. "I'm going to go for a run." *And burn off some of this sexual energy before I burst into flames.*

Kyle knocked on the door and poked his head through. "I'll come with you. I can't sleep for shit."

I nodded warily, wondering what he'd been dreaming about and hoping he couldn't read the guilty look on my face.

We ran in the Boston Commons, past the quiet swan boats, past the empty benches still covered in dew.

"Do you wanna go for a long run today?" Kyle asked.

"Uh-huh. I think that would be good. I seem to have some extra nervous energy."

He snorted. "If that's what you wanna call it."

I didn't ask him what he meant. Strategically.

We ran for about six miles, looping back to Newbury Street. I stopped on the corner near a coffee shop.

My breathing was ragged. "Well, that hurt." At least I had something to focus on other than my yearning and frustration.

Kyle put his hands on his hips and bent over. "I know." Sweat made his shirt cling to his back, and I could see every muscle. He stood back up and caught me looking at him.

"What," he said, not bothering to make it a question.

I just opened and closed my mouth, like a guppy at a loss for words.

He gave me that shit-eating grin and came toward me. "You enjoying the view, boss?" He put his hands on my hips and pulled me to him.

I tried to pull back. "I'm all sweaty. And don't call me boss."

He held me firmly in place, and it became more than just the run that created heat between us. I struggled to catch my breath.

"One of these days, Lowell Barton," he said and grazed his lips against mine. "One of these days you aren't going to pull away from me."

I just gulped.

He released me and looked at me darkly. "Let's get some coffee."

I nodded and followed him obediently. For once.

I CALLED Tori a little while later, while Kyle was in the shower.

"What were you thinking?" I hissed as I stalked around the too-sexy hotel room. "This suite is a sex trap!"

"Oh, lighten up," Tori said, and I could just picture her twirling her hair. "It's not a sex trap. It's just the honeymoon suite."

"This. Is no. Honeymoon," I said through gritted teeth.

"Aren't you having at least a little fun?" Tori asked. "The pictures from this morning looked a little intense though…"

"What pictures?"

"The ones on *XYZ*. Didn't you see them?"

"Hold on." I ran for my tablet and fired it up, clicking quickly to the gossip website. We were on the front page. It was a shot from earlier this morning, with Kyle's hands on my hips. He was leaning over me, and his intense expression gave me the shivers all over again. "Huh."

"Huh?" Tori sounded confused. "You didn't know the photographer was there?"

"No." I tried to remember the people around us on

the street. Things had been so intense between us at that moment, and I'd been so beat from our run, I hadn't even noticed anyone else.

"You didn't think there were any photographers around and you were looking at each other like that? You're *so* totally sleeping together!" Tori sounded triumphant.

"I'm *not* sleeping with him!" I fumed.

"It didn't just…slip in there? Even once?" She sounded crushed. "You can tell, me! I won't breathe a word!"

"No." My teeth were clamped together so hard, I was worried I would get lockjaw. "It didn't just *slip in*. I gotta go."

I clicked off my phone and stomped to the bathroom, still clutching my tablet. I knocked on the bathroom door while Kyle was in the shower.

"Come on in," he called.

He peered at me through the shower door, and I tried not to look at his full frontal. But I might have peeked a little…

The news was good. Very, very good. Or very, very bad, depending on how I looked at it.

I kept looking at it.

"I knew you'd come around," Kyle said seductively.

"I have not *come* around. I haven't come anywhere." I mentally slapped myself for using the word *come*.

Kyle laughed as I got redder, clutching the tablet until it almost shattered.

Oh yeah—the tablet.

"There is a reason for my visit," I said, keeping my eyes off of him and trying to sound dignified. I hit the screen, and the picture of us came up. The headline read: *Trouble in Paradise?*

"Someone followed us here." I held up the screen toward him, in front of my face. For better or for worse, part of him was dangling *below* the screen, so I could still get a pretty good look...

"Lowell?" He paused for a second. "Lowell, stop looking at my dick."

I moved the screen down so I couldn't see it anymore. "I wasn't," I lied. "And it's not like it's so big I can see it from here, anyway."

"Oh, but it *is*." There was a smirk in his voice.

I continued to hold the screen in front of my face and talk through it, ignoring his taunt and trying not to investigate his naked body further. "My point is that someone from *XYZ* followed us here. We need to be more careful. I don't want anyone tracing us back to your father."

I heard him turn off the water. A second later, his

dripping hand pushed the tablet screen down from my face.

"Okay." He proceeded to towel-dry his hair as the rest of the water dripped off his glorious body onto the tiled floor.

I peered down. "Um…"

"You want something else?" he asked, grinning.

"No," I said, backing out of the room. "No, I do not."

I closed the door and flopped down on the bed, exhausted. I'd never lied so much as I had just then.

"SINCE WE'RE BEING FOLLOWED, we should take advantage of it." Kyle was dressed in camouflage shorts and a *Hawaii* T-shirt.

For some reason, I found that combination mouthwatering. I followed him with my eyes as he paced restlessly. "Okay."

He looked at me with mild surprise.

If we were going to go out and put on a show, that meant I got to feel his hands on me for the rest of the day. That meant kissing all over town. That meant all the things I wanted—well, most of the things I wanted—without having to feel conflicted and guilty about it. It would also give me the opportunity to work on him about going to work for Pierce. I hadn't had the heart to broach the topic yet this morning, but I needed to.

"I mean, we absolutely should." I stood eagerly. "We don't see your father again until tomorrow. There's no way they can trace us to him today."

He held out his hand to me, and I took it, excitement coursing through me. *Mine for the day.* I was surprised by the thread of sadness that laced the thought.

This was just for now, but I wanted more.

I wanted more, and I could never have it.

EITHER BOSTON WAS A ROMANTIC CITY, or it was just us. As the day progressed, I couldn't tell anymore, and it seemed to matter less and less.

First we went to breakfast at an outdoor cafe on Newbury Street. We had fresh orange juice, tomato-and-spinach eggs Benedict, and cheese-covered grits.

"I hope nobody gets a shot of this food," I said through a delicious mouthful. "Lucas'll have a fit."

"You ran six miles today." Kyle leaned over and kissed me quickly. Heat shot through me, and his eyes searched mine. "Remember?"

I nodded and leaned back over to kiss him again. I was

taking this further than I should, but I couldn't help myself. He was only mine for right now. I pulled back and he was still looking at me the same way, his eyes searching mine.

"You going for an Oscar today?"

I shrugged. "Something like that. Maybe a Golden Globe."

After breakfast, we wandered the city streets with his arm draped over me. Going for a walk for him like this was an event. Every part of my body tingled because I was next to him, his body pressed against mine. I'd never felt this before—this alive, aware of every second —and I didn't want it to end. I clung to him all day, knowing that when he wasn't next to me anymore, it would hurt.

We went to Faneuil Hall and watched the street performers, then we headed into the park and watched the children ride the carousel. Unlike LA, Boston didn't house many celebrities. No one seemed to recognize me, and I welcomed the anonymity. At one point we stopped at a tiny restaurant for raw oysters, clam chowder, and Bloody Marys.

Kyle threw his arm around me again as we sauntered back to the hotel that afternoon.

"This has been the perfect day. I don't want it to end," I said and leaned against him.

"Then let's not let it end, yet." His lips twitched into a smile. "Did you bring a dress?"

I nodded.

"Good. Then let's go take showers and get ready to go out. I'm taking my beautiful fake-girlfriend on a proper date."

KYLE

Elena had bought me a suit. I put it on, along with a lavender tie, feeling guilty that I'd kept it. I would send it back to her when we returned to LA, after I'd had it properly dry-cleaned.

I was starting to sound like an adult. It both scared and thrilled me.

Lowell stepped out of the bedroom a second later, her blond hair in waves over one shoulder. She was wearing an ice-blue dress that brought out her eyes and hugged every curve.

I sucked in a breath when I saw her. "You look gorgeous."

She blushed but smiled, clearly pleased. "And you look dashing. I've never seen you in a suit before." She came over and straightened my tie. "I like it. It's very Kyle 2.0."

I beamed and held out my arm. "Shall we?"

She giggled and took it, following me out to the elevator. "Where are we going?"

"To the most romantic restaurant in the city."

"Says who?" she asked.

"Says *Boston Hub*, and about fifteen other websites I checked." I grinned. "There's going to be lobster. And steak. And dancing."

"Dancing?" she asked, obviously horrified.

I grabbed her hand and twirled her in a circle in the elevator. "Trust me. You can handle it."

She tripped a little, and we both laughed.

When we got to the lobby floor, she looked at me. "You can't let me trip like that. It's embarrassing."

I put my arm around her and pulled her against me. "I've got you. Don't you worry."

Britta, the blond concierge, caught sight of us and waved. "I have a message for you guys!"

I raised my hand to her as I hustled Lo out the door. "When we get back!"

I didn't want anything to interfere with my night with Lowell. I didn't want a single interruption.

Evan drove us to the Financial District. We watched

through the windows as the city lit up around us, the darkening sky a purplish-blue.

Lowell turned to me. "It's beautiful, isn't it?"

I stared at her gorgeous face. "You have no idea."

Her eyes widened for a second, then she shook her head and playfully punched my shoulder. "Once a player, always a player."

"What are you going to do when you finally figure out I'm not playing?"

She studied my face for a minute. I thought I saw a mixture of longing and hope on hers, but I could have been hoping for it, not seeing it.

"I don't know," she said finally.

I put my hand over hers. "You might want to figure it out."

THE RESTAURANT WAS LOCATED on the top floor of the highest building in Boston. We could see the whole city spread out below us. Lowell looked out the windows in delight, clutching my hand as she had at Disneyland, the same wonder on her face.

"This is so pretty," she gushed, taking in the view, then the restaurant itself.

The restaurant was set up with tables circling a dance floor. Couples glided over it as a big band played.

"It's fun, isn't it?"

We drank champagne, danced, and shared a lobster dinner. Lowell didn't trip once, so around midnight, we agreed to one last dance. Lowell had announced she was about to turn into a pumpkin if she didn't get to bed soon.

We swayed to the music, our bodies melded together on the dance floor. We'd been like this all day—pressed up against every inch of each other—and I wasn't sure how we would ever get back to normal. Whatever that was.

I tilted her chin up and leaned down to kiss her.

"Is there a photographer near us or something?" she asked, looking at me warily.

"Yes," I whispered. "Right behind you."

I leaned down and claimed her mouth, wrapping my arms around her and pulling her against me. My body told me how much I wanted her. Still, I didn't want to scare her away, and I wanted to do the right thing. So I pulled back.

"Why'd you do that?" she asked breathlessly.

"Because I thought I saw a photographer," I lied.

She shook her head. "No. Why'd you stop?" She

leaned up and kissed me, making my heart race and my temples throb.

We stopped for a second, halted in the middle of the dance floor.

"You don't want me to stop?" I asked.

She shook her head, her eyes wide and urgent. "No. I don't."

We practically ran back to the hotel.

LOWELL

I TOLD MYSELF, over and over, that I wasn't going to do it. But when he kissed me like that, and when he stopped—my body took over.

My body—the shameless sex-goddess.

This wasn't a good idea, but I no longer cared. With his mouth on me like that, I couldn't think straight. He pulled me against him in the car, and I clung to him, blocking out all rational thought.

Britta was waiting in the lobby when Kyle hustled me toward the elevator. We ignored her even when she raised her hand at us.

"I still have a message for you," she called.

"Text it to me," Kyle snapped.

He seemed completely single-minded as he rushed me to the elevator. No one else joined us, so he took the liberty of pinning me against the wall. He looked down at me intently.

"Do you want to do this?" His eyes were hooded. "Are you sure?"

I nodded bravely. "Yes."

That seemed to be all the encouragement he needed. "Good." He claimed my mouth hungrily, his tongue searching for mine as he ran his hands down my torso.

I shivered against him then threw all my self-control out the window. *Good riddance.* I put my hands on his fine ass and crushed him against me. Finally feeling him, all of him, pressed against me felt so good.

He hoisted my legs up around his waist and carried me out of the elevator. Somehow he managed to swipe our room key, and we burst through the door of the suite, our lips still crushed together. Then he stopped, placing me gently on the floor and closing the door.

He stalked toward me, his eyes fiery. "You have to mean this. You have to want this as much as me. I can't do it otherwise."

I nodded, shaky and unable to say anything. I just knew that I wanted him—I wanted him so much that nothing else made sense.

I wanted to show him how I felt. I kissed him deeply, our tongues connecting again. Electricity shot through me, and I ran my hand down his back, feeling all of the muscles on his glorious body. He lifted me again and carried me into the bedroom. He laid me gently, reverently, on the bed. My whole body was throbbing in anticipation.

"You have no idea how much I want you," he said, his voice hoarse.

"Yes, I do. I know exactly how much."

He ran his thumb across my cheek and leaned down to kiss me deeply. I grabbed his hand and placed it over my heart.

"I know this is wrong, but it doesn't feel wrong," I whispered breathlessly. I almost tore his coat as I ripped it off him. "It feels right."

"That's because it *is* right." He unbuttoned his shirt, revealing his gloriously enormous chest.

"It's still not a good idea," I whispered as my body was screamed at me to just shut the hell up.

"Doing the right thing is *always* a good idea, babe. Now stop talking." He started to kiss me again then pulled back, hesitating. "Lowell, if you don't want to do this—"

I interrupted him by kissing him hard, letting my body tell him what I was too afraid to say. *I want you. I want you more than I've ever wanted anything.*

"I'll shut up if you shut up," I offered breathlessly.

"Deal," he said, grinning wickedly. He unzipped his pants. "At least until you scream my name."

His cock sprang out, enormous and thick and ready for me. Looking at it close up, I was pretty sure I would soon be screaming *something.*

I sat up and tentatively wrapped my fingers around him, stroking him slowly as he stepped out of his pants. He moaned and moved against my palm. I got bolder, gripping him more firmly. Then I knelt down and took the tip of him into my mouth, moaning when I tasted him.

"Holy fuck, Lowell," he said hotly as I swirled my tongue around his tip and continued to work my hands up and down his length.

He flexed his hips, and I could see that he'd closed his eyes, his head thrown back. I took all of him, to the base of his shaft, into my mouth. He moaned, and I moved my mouth up his cock, back to the tip, until he moaned again.

"Stop," he growled. "You're going to make me come like that."

He lifted me and slowly unzipped my dress, stopping to kiss me. His tongue, probing and urgent, found mine. My dress fell to the floor, and he pulled back enough to look at me, stroking my lacy bra reverently.

"You're so beautiful," he whispered.

I just stared at him, every part of my body on fire, and didn't even chastise him for talking. His hands trailed down to my lace underwear. He twisted the bikini strap in his fingers and put his cock between my legs, rubbing against the lace. I heard myself moan in pleasure, but I no longer felt self-conscious. *Holy fuck.* I rubbed against him artlessly, amazed at how good he felt. How thick and hard.

Every wild dream I'd been having about him was coming true. I ran my hands down his chest to the divots near his hips before I kissed his chest, running my tongue along the lines of his pectoral muscles. If this was wrong, if I was going to pay for this—all those thoughts hurtled out the window. I officially no longer gave a fuck.

He undid my bra and cupped my breasts as I took off my underwear. I was wet, ready for him. He used my slickness against me, rubbing his cock against my slit until I was panting. His fingers found my clit and swirled it, lazily, playfully, then pinched it.

I didn't feel lazy or playful. I felt as though if he didn't put his cock in me right now, I was going to burst into flames.

Kyle must have sensed my need. He pushed me back onto the bed gently, his naked body looming gloriously over me. He brushed the hair off my face and just watched me for a moment. Then he went to his bag, grabbed a condom, and rolled it on.

My breath caught in my throat as he straddled me, his cock enormous and thick against me. I grabbed his muscled ass and pulled him to me, running the head of his cock over my sex, getting it even more slick.

"Are you ready for me?" he asked, and I nodded. He eased himself inside me, just the tip, making me moan and writhe.

He put his forehead against mine. "Are you sure?"

In answer, I put my hands on his ass and pushed him into me.

We both cried out. He paused as we caught our breath, then he buried himself in me, my body stretching to accommodate his. He was gentle, but I was impatient, wanting to feel him deeper inside me. His body listened to mine, and his long, deep strokes brought me wave after wave of pleasure.

He continued to thrust, and I greedily drank in the sight of his taut, muscled body over mine. I kept my hands on his hips and his ass, relishing the feel of having him all the way inside me. I hadn't realized how much my body had truly been craving his. Now that he was inside me, I felt complete.

He leaned up on his forearms, pumping into me

more urgently. Waves of pleasure tore through me, taking me to the edge.

"Kyle," I moaned, "Kyle…"

"I'm right there with you, babe."

His strokes got deeper, even more urgent, and I shattered, my body clenching around him as he found his release. Our orgasms shook the bed.

"Kyle!" He'd been right. Of course I screamed his name.

LATER, he leaned over and ran his thumb along my jawline. "So beautiful…"

I smiled. "Thank you." I meant it for a lot more than just the compliment.

He sighed and threw himself back on the bed. "So what happens now?" There was an edge to his voice.

"Well," I said, flopping onto his chest, "I could be on top again, or we could try it from behind…"

"Naughty girl." He grinned, then his face turned serious. "But I mean it. What happens now?"

I took a deep breath and rolled onto my back, looking at the ceiling. "I don't know. What do you want to happen?" The endless myriad of obstacles we faced whirled in my mind, but I ignored them, holding my breath. *What on earth does Kyle Richards actually want from me?*

"I sort of just want you to be my girlfriend." The edge in his voice was jagged now, as if it took a lot for him to say that.

"I am your girlfriend," I said.

"No. I mean, for *real.*"

"So do I." I laced my fingers through his, and we continued to lie next to each other. I was still flushed and tingling from Kyle's exploration of my body. "I think this is about as real as it gets."

I was being honest. It was the truth.

But what I'd left out was the more important, more ugly truth: the fact that it was real just made everything that much worse.

KYLE

I ROLLED over and looked at Lowell the next morning. She was still asleep. I ran my hand down her hair and just stared, hoping I didn't wake her.

She was so beautiful that looking at her hurt.

Last night had been the best night of my life. Lowell didn't know that…and she didn't know that being with her was the first time I'd actually been able to have an orgasm in months.

That wasn't why it was the best night, though. It was because I'd been with her.

We had to go see my father this morning. The fact that he wanted to speak with Lowell was ominous. I knew he'd made me an excellent offer; I also knew I couldn't accept it—not right now. But Lowell wanted me to. My father was smart; if he suspected that Lowell cared for me, he'd want her to hear him out.

But I couldn't leave Lowell. She had her premiere coming up. She still had to deal with Lucas and the fallout from her puking incident. She still needed me.

But I was fooling myself. She didn't need me. I needed her.

I watched her chest rise and fall peacefully. The truth was, I didn't want to be away from her. I didn't want to send her back to big, bad Los Angeles alone, even though she was more than capable of handling herself. It wasn't just that I didn't want to let her down—I didn't want to be away from her.

Not now. Not ever.

Last night had confirmed my feelings for her. But I had to make some real changes in my life. If I was ever going to have something to offer her, I needed a career. I couldn't be her boyfriend if I was just an ex-escort or a less-than-minimum-wage surfing instructor.

I also knew my father's offer was the only one I would get. I had no resume, no education, no experience. So I had to find a way for him to understand that I would accept the position, but I needed a little more time. After Lowell's premiere, I would go to work for him and become legitimate and build my own life.

Then I would finally be the man Lowell deserved.

∼

WE WAITED outside Pierce's office. A cold sweat trickled down my back, but I tried to appear calm. Lowell smiled at me, but I saw the stress in her eyes. It had been over ten years since she'd seen my father, and they hadn't parted under friendly circumstances.

After what seemed like forever, his MIT assistant poked her head out. "Pierce will see you now."

I looked at Lowell. "Are you sure you want to do this? You don't have to come in there with me if you don't want to."

She put her hand in mine and squeezed. "I'm coming to support you. We're in this together, remember? Plus, we don't need to make him any more upset than he already is."

I tried to draw strength from her as we went inside. Now I felt as if I were the one walking the plank. We rounded the corner of the cool, concrete room, and there he was, scowling out the window.

He turned toward us, his eyes running over me briefly before turning to Lowell. Shock registered on his face. "Lowell? Is that… really you? I can't even believe you're the same girl."

"Hello, Pierce."

He just continued to stare at her as though he was in shock.

"You've seen her movies, Dad. And the pictures. You knew she looked different."

My father looked at her as if she had three heads. "*That* is not just different. No offense, young lady, but you were never a looker like your mother."

"Watch it," I said, my tone warning.

Lowell was being strong for me. She seemed to shrug off his brash rudeness. "Coming from you, Pierce, I'll take that as a compliment."

My father looked chastised. He ran his hands through his hair—what was left of it. "I didn't say that to be mean. Sorry. I think I used up all of my mean where your mother was concerned. How is she, anyway?"

Lowell's face went from surprised, to confused, to wary in an instant. "She's okay. She's in Asia right now on a spiritual retreat. I just spoke with her."

"I heard she got divorced again," Pierce said.

"She didn't like Number Four that much," Lowell admitted.

"Poor bastard," my father said. "Well, when you speak to her again, please give her my regards."

Lowell raised her eyebrows. "You're kidding, right?"

Pierce sighed heavily. "No, young lady, I'm not."

She watched his face. "Well… excuse me for being

surprised, but the last time I saw you two together, it was really ugly."

"I remember. I've had a lot of time on my hands lately. I've been thinking about her and about him." He jerked his head at me. "How I screwed things up."

Lowell's face softened. "My mother is a piece of work. I'll be the first one to admit that."

"I shouldn't have pushed so hard in court. What's more money anyway? Then maybe she wouldn't have had to get married again. She's never had a job. It's not like she could support herself."

My jaw was practically on the floor as I listened to my father. *He has sympathy for Caroline Barton? Since when?*

"Well… that's very chivalrous of you. My mother would probably pass out if she heard you say it." Lowell looked baffled.

Pierce nodded. "Maybe I should tell her when she gets back."

Lowell's eyes were huge in her face. "Right. Huh."

"As for you two"—he pointed at us—"I called you in here for a reason. This ends today. Right now. Kyle, you come to work for me. I'll give you a competitive salary. After six months, if you prove yourself, I'll reinstate your trust. I want you to be successful. I've always wanted that. This is the first time in years that you've actually seemed capable of being responsible. But I can't have you being a paid 'date,' or whatever you are. And you two can't be together. It's wrong on so many levels, it literally makes my head hurt."

Lowell responded first. "If I could just say one thing, Mr. Richards? Kyle has been nothing short of wonderful to me. I made some really big mistakes, and he's helped me turn everything around. I called the service as a last-ditch effort to save my career. He didn't know it was me who was…hiring him until he showed up at my house."

"He told me the same story."

Lowell looked at Pierce, her eyes pleading. "It's true. This has all been a show for the press. Kyle's actually really gifted at public relations. He'll be great working for your company in that capacity. Everybody loves him."

"That's part of my son's problem," Pierce said. "Everybody *does* love him. He's had it too easy—he's never worked a day in his life."

"He's been working for me," she said, "and he's amazing at winning the press over. It's not a bad thing that everyone loves him, sir. It's a gift."

Her words left me with a weird mix of emotions. Her kindness never ceased to amaze me. She saw me in a way nobody else did.

I faced my father, who was looking at me with raised eyebrows. "What?"

He crossed his arms. "You have a *gift*?"

I smiled, feeling exposed. "I guess Lowell sees the best in me."

"But you two aren't a real couple." He sounded extremely skeptical, and also as if he were waiting for an answer.

I didn't have one for him. "I'm ready to come to work for you, Dad. I just need more time. I made a promise to Lowell, and part of me acting like an adult is not going back on my promises."

Pierce inspected my face. "What's the difference with you? Is it her?" He motioned to Lowell, who was sitting perfectly still, silent and pale. "Because really, you two *can't* be together. If the press finds out that she's your stepsister, her career's over. She isn't going to choose you over her career."

Lowell opened her mouth and then shut it again.

"You shouldn't choose her over your career either," my father said. Satisfied that he'd won the argument, he sat back in his chair.

"I don't want her to give up her career for me, and I don't want this to get out." I looked at him. "I told you—I'll come to work for you, but I have to wrap things up in Los Angeles first."

My father leaned over his desk. "Eric showed me the pictures of you two from yesterday. You've been followed here. Your every move is being documented. Hell, somebody could be waiting outside my door right now." He pinched the bridge of his nose. "Giving you a chance is a risk for me, Kyle. I can't have it come out that you've been a male escort and that you've been escorting your *stepsister*. That'd completely ruin me." He jerked his thumb at Lowell. "Her too. And I can tell you don't want that." He took a deep breath. "I'm truly sorry. Lowell, I'd be happy to reimburse you for what you paid Kyle. I'll give you enough to start another PR blitz. Or hire another young man."

Lowell shook her head. "You don't have to do that, Mr. Richards. I don't need your money. I'm fine."

I turned to her. "You're fine because I'm not leaving you. We're going to that premiere."

"Not if you want your trust back, you're not." My father looked at me. I must've looked stricken, because his face changed from stern to apologetic. "I'm sorry, son, but I can't risk this right now. I have too much at stake."

"Actually, I'm the one who's got—"

"It's okay, Kyle," Lowell said. "Your father's right. If he's got a big press blitz coming up, it's too risky for all of us. I don't want the public to find out how we…came together. And I don't want them finding out about our parents." She looked at me. "I'll be fine. You've done wonders for me. I'm going to be okay."

I clenched my hands into fists. "Let's talk about this outside." I turned to my father and nodded at him tightly. "Dad."

"You need to come back here tomorrow morning. You start work then," he said. "Lowell, it was a pleasure seeing you. You've grown into a mature, thoughtful young woman. Thank you for cooperating. Give Caroline my regards. Tell her I've been...thinking about her."

Lowell nodded, clearly shocked by his lack of animosity toward her mother. It was weird, but I ignored it, grabbing her elbow and dragging her out of the office. I had bigger things to deal with right now.

"You have to listen to him," she said as I stalked down the hall beside her.

"I'm an adult." I heard the anger in my own voice. "He can't tell me what to do."

She shook her head. "You need to listen to *me* then. This is your one shot. He's going to give you a position that you'll be brilliant at, *and* you'll get your trust back. That's millions of dollars we're talking about. You can't give that up for me."

I stopped, and turning, I pressed her back against the wall. Anger and sadness ripped through me as I looked at her beautiful face. "I'm not leaving you. Period. He's my father. He'll wait."

She shook her head, and although I saw sadness in her eyes, stubbornness rolled off of her in waves. "He's not going to give you another chance, Kyle. He has his launch coming up—if you cross him now, it's all over."

I leaned over her, wanting to crush my lips against hers and stop this stupid conversation. "Your premiere's next week." Unable to stop myself, I ran my lips along her jawline. "It's just a week. He'll be fine."

Her breathing deepened, and she looked at me, lips parted, responding to my touch. Our eyes locked but only for a second; she shook her head as if to shake off the heat between us.

"No," she said, her tone final, "he won't. And I can't let you lose this opportunity. Not for me."

"It's not your choice. It's mine."

She drew herself up to her full height and pulled away from me stiffly. "You should always make the right choice. Staying with me is the wrong one, and I can't accept that."

"What are you saying?" I felt stupidly, ridiculously close to tears.

She must have sensed my impending breakdown, because she seemed to calm down. She smiled weakly and patted my arm. "Let's not talk about it anymore right now. We're both upset. We'll figure it out."

"Together," I said stubbornly. For some reason, even though my arms were still around her, I felt as though I was losing her.

"Together."

I wrapped my arms tighter around her as we headed to the car, but I felt as if she was already gone.

LOWELL

WE WERE quiet on the drive back to the hotel. At least on the outside. On the inside, my mind was racing a thousand miles a minute.

How am I going to do this? How am I going to do any of this?

I was forming a plan that I hated. But I felt as though I had to see it through, because it was the best thing for Kyle, and that was the most important thing to me. I had to at least be honest with myself about that. I looked at his profile. His handsome face was turned toward the window, dark circles under his eyes. I squeezed his hand.

"What?" he asked flatly.

I love you. "Nothing," I said.

Even though I was lost in my thoughts, as we walked

hand-in-hand through the hotel lobby, I felt eyes on me. I turned around, the hair on my neck standing up.

And I locked eyes with the one and only Caroline Barton.

I saw the concierge, Britta, waving wildly at me. She pointed at my mother then shrugged helplessly. "I told you there was a message," she said.

I turned back to my mother, steeling myself for what would surely be another fucked-up family reunion.

"Darling!" My mom sprang up out of her chair when she spotted us.

A nanosecond too late, I dropped Kyle's hand and jumped away from him. My mother eyed me curiously then turned her gaze to Kyle, her carefully-mascaraed eyes taking in every sexy, hulking inch of him.

"How did you know I was here?" I stammered.

She looked at me as if I had three heads. "I called your agent, darling." She gave me a perfunctory hug and practically pushed me out of the way, extending her hand to Kyle. "Hello there, I'm Caroline Barton, Lowell's mother. And you are…?"

I watched as she studied his face, a look of suspicion and stupefied recognition dawning.

"It's me. Kyle." He offered his hand to her, clearly steeling himself for her impending reaction.

She dropped his hand like a dead fish. "Kyle as in Kyle *Richards?*" Her face was a pale mask.

I almost felt sorry for her, but I was too busy feeling annoyed by her presence and sorry for myself.

"The one and only." He smiled at her, putting his dimples on full display.

But the dimples had never done much for my mother. She turned to me. "You've got to be fucking kidding me, young lady."

"Uh…" I shrugged helplessly. "If only I had such a great sense of humor. Or irony. Or whatever you want to call it."

Caroline raised herself to her full height and tossed her frosted hair over her shoulder. "I call it *spite*. I cannot believe you're doing this to me. I cannot believe that I'm coming home to *this*." She pointed at Kyle as though he were Exhibit A of my presumed guilt.

I shrugged again and rolled my eyes. "For once, Mom, you need to realize that not everything is about you. Now come upstairs, and we'll explain. You're making a scene." I looked around the lobby nervously, hoping that no one from *XYZ* was hiding behind a potted plant or teak column.

She looked taken aback—probably mystified by my tone. I normally sugar-coated everything for my mother. For once, I didn't have the energy. For once, my own problems seemed a lot more pressing.

My mother kept her mouth shut for exactly one minute. The peace ended when the elevator doors closed behind us.

She whirled toward me, eyes flashing and frosted hair flying. "When you said you were in Boston with a man, you never once mentioned it was *this* man." She turned to him. "Does your father know about this?"

He nodded.

"I'm surprised he hasn't had you two physically separated," she fumed.

"He's trying." Kyle looked as if he wanted to say something more, but I put my hand on his—a move that was not lost on my mother.

"You have a lot of explaining to do, young lady."

Kyle opened his mouth then shut it, a move that only made me love him more.

"You don't really have a lot of room to take the moral high road." I took in her expensive-looking cotton tunic and perfectly highlighted hair. "It's not like *your* typical behavior is beyond reproach."

"Don't you use your fancy words on me," she practically spat.

Although I was surprised she was so upset, I shouldn't have been. Pierce and Caroline hated each other. Even though it seemed he'd softened toward her during the years since their divorce, she hadn't budged an inch. She believed he owed her more than she'd gotten in the settlement, and she was still bitter.

My mother wasn't one to blame herself for too much. Or for anything really.

The elevator opened, and I tried to remember if we'd left any incriminating evidence around. Were my underwear somewhere on the floor? Were the champagne glasses still sitting on the counter? I hustled in first and picked up the glasses and kicked my damning underwear under the chaise lounge. I turned around and saw my mother frowning, her eyes trained on the spot where I'd just kicked my lace thong.

She looked at me. "What is going on with you? I read a magazine article on the plane that said you'd gotten drunk in public. And now this?" She jerked her thumb toward Kyle. "Have you gone completely crazy? He's your *stepbrother*. Isn't that illegal?" She turned and looked him up and down, his muscled shoulders clearly evident underneath his tight-fitted T-shirt. She turned back to me. "It's totally illegal. I'm sure of it."

"It's not illegal. We aren't related. We never were, and you and Pierce got divorced a decade ago. There's no scandal here."

Except for all the... scandal.

She snorted. "That's a ridiculous statement—there is *only* scandal here. Do you know what the press will do if they find out that you two lived under the same roof as kids? They're going to have a field day!"

Kyle shuffled his feet, and I twirled my hair.

My mother looked back and forth between us. "What," she said, not bothering to make it a question. "Why do you both look guilty *now?*"

I shrugged and washed the glasses. Kyle picked imaginary lint from his shirt.

"Answer me. One of you. Now." My mother folded her arms across her chest.

"Um..." I said.

"Uh..." Kyle said.

"Maybe you should sit down, Mom. And have a drink."

"A strong one." Kyle smiled at me. "I'll have one too, babe. Lowell. I meant Lowell." He looked sheepishly at my mother then immediately at the floor, as if he wished it would swallow him up.

"Make mine a double," my mother snapped. "Then please tell me what the hell is going on. I have a feeling I'm going to have to call Dr. Klein this afternoon and order a new Valium prescription."

You'd better make that a double too. I dutifully poured the drinks.

"So," I said, a while later, "not knowing what else to do, I called an escort service. AccommoDating. Everything was confidential, they had insurance… it seemed like the right thing to do. Actually, it seemed like the *only* thing I could do. I hired an escort to come live at my house, pretend to be my boyfriend, and go to events with me. I needed to make the press more interested in my love life than the fact that I'd just spilled my guts, literally and figuratively, all over the internet."

My mother swallowed some of her drink. "And they sent Kyle?"

I nodded. Kyle was nursing his own drink and staring out the window, listening to me.

"He showed up, and I freaked out when I recognized him. But I had an event that night, so I took a chance. Best thing I ever did." I looked at him longingly, hating that we had to be apart from each other right now.

"Why is that?" my mother asked sharply.

I lifted my chin. "Because the press love him, Mother. He's brilliant at keeping me on message and in the public eye. And because he's important to me. He's in my corner. I trust him… and I can't say that about too many people."

She snorted. "You trust *him*? An *escort*? Son of the

man who ruined us?"

Now it was my turn to snort. "Pierce hardly ruined us. You just wanted more money from him. Like a tip for being such a pain in the ass to live with."

It looked as if she tried to raise her eyebrow at me but failed. Probably too much Botox. "You're being really mean, Lowell."

Kyle shot me a look, and I leaned back on the couch, exhausted by dealing with both of our parents. "I'm not trying to be mean. This has been a rough day, and I wasn't expecting you. What are you doing back so early? And where are you staying?"

"I came home because I thought my daughter needed me. And also, really, I needed a change of scenery. I meditated and meditated, and after a while, it just got boring." She finished her drink. "I needed more action."

I groaned inwardly. Of course she did.

"I've got a suite at the Plaza."

Of course she did.

I said nothing, even though I was sure it was costing me a small fortune. Sometimes being rich and famous seemed in direct opposition to my overall financial health.

"Pierce asked about you," I said. "He told me to tell you hello."

"He never got over me." She tossed her hair over her

shoulder. "Typical."

"He was trying to be nice, I think."

She shivered. "Ugh. Just talking about him makes all sorts of unpleasant memories come back."

Kyle took that as a cue and stood. "I'm going to give you two a minute alone. It was nice to see you, Caroline. Take care." He nodded at her.

"Thank you. I'll see you…again?"

He smiled tightly. "I hope so." With that, he disappeared into the bedroom.

Caroline watched him retreat and turned back to me. "This is crazy. This is totally out of character for you."

"I don't think that's true. I've always been very solution-oriented. I needed a distraction, so I created one."

She jerked her thumb toward the closed bedroom door. "That's certainly a distraction. He turned out… nicely. Those are quite the biceps."

"There's nothing going on with us," I lied. "It's a business arrangement."

"I don't believe you. And I can't believe my own daughter is lying to my face. You're not *that* good of an actress, dear."

I counted backward from ten, not wanting to argue with her or, worse, blurt out the truth. *I love him, and I'm going to cut you off this year. I swear it.*

"Pierce was asking lots of questions about you," I said, trying to distract her.

She looked slightly mollified. "I'm sure he was. Like I said, he never got over me."

"He's up here working on some new app in conjunction with MIT. Some sort of social media innovator or aggregator or something. He has a launch coming up. He said this is his biggest deal yet." I watched her as she picked imaginary lint off of her yoga pants. "He seems lonely."

"There's a good reason for that, darling. He's a wildebeest." She searched for more lint. "Is he seeing anyone?"

I knew she'd come around. "Actually, no. He seems lonely…"

I EVENTUALLY PACKED my mother up and sent her back to the Plaza. Even though the thought gave me a wicked headache, I promised to call her later.

Kyle hadn't come out of the room. I knocked tentatively on the door.

"Come in," he said flatly. It sounded as if that black cloud was back.

I went in and sat on the edge of the bed. "She's gone… for now."

"Why is she here? Why now?" He propped himself up on the pillows and clicked off the television, studying my face.

"She was just... worried. Or bored. Or something." I looked at him. "At least she's gone now. Ugh, our parents really give me a headache."

"You're speaking my language, babe." He patted the bed next to him. "C'mere."

I scooted toward him, and he pulled me close and kissed the top of my head.

"She's furious about you. That I kept you a secret from her. She was furious at me anyway—for putting my career in jeopardy by drinking. She'll probably try to stick me in Betty Ford to get me away from you and make it look like I've officially cleaned up."

"Do you trust her?" he asked.

I looked at him sharply. "She's my mother, Kyle. I don't trust her *judgment*, per se, but I don't think she'd ever do anything to intentionally hurt me. Why do you ask?"

He shook his head. "It's... nothing. I just remember what she was like when she was divorcing my father. It was like there was no limit to what she would ask for. And the stuff you've told me about how she takes advantage of you? She just seems... predatory. I'm sorry to say that."

I sat up and pulled away from him. "Maybe that's because you shouldn't have said it."

He sighed and gave me a long look. "Is it wrong that I want to protect you?"

I bristled, even though part of me was collapsing all over myself at his words. "I don't need to be protected."

"I know." He brushed my hair back from my forehead. "But even though I know that, I still feel that way. And it's probably not going to change."

"But you *have* to trust my judgment. You have to trust that I can take care of myself—and my mother, for that matter."

"I know. I do." He pulled me against him again, and I didn't resist; our time was running out. I could feel it. "But can you accept that I'm still going to watch your back? And worry about you, even if you don't need me to?"

"Why?" I leaned my head against his chest and luxuriated in the feel of his muscles all around me, protecting me even when I said it was the last thing I needed.

"Because." He kissed the top of my head. "You can get used to that, can't you?"

"Of course I can." And that was exactly what I was worried about.

KYLE

A LITTLE WHILE LATER, after Lowell had let me make love to her again, I slipped out of the room while she slept. My phone had been buzzing for the past hour.

Balls deep in the woman I loved, I'd chosen to ignore it. But I had a sinking feeling that it was something that needed my attention.

Call me immediately, read a text from my father.

He picked up after one ring.

"Hey," I said.

"Hey yourself." Anger rolled off of him through the phone, and I braced myself. "I had a rather unexpected phone call from Caroline Barton after you left. You saw her?"

"Unfortunately, yes."

"Well, apparently I'm not the only one who has

objections to your…circumstances with Lowell. Her mother's very upset."

"I can't imagine that you really care. Not after what she did to you."

He sighed. "She was practically hysterical."

Drama queen. Actress. Grifter. "That's too bad. She seemed okay when she was here. Not that I trust her."

"Well, I don't trust her either. She said some other things too, son. I'm not sure what I'm going to do with her."

"What do you mean? What'd she say?"

"Well, first, she asked to see me. When I said no, that I was too busy with meetings, she went on and on about how she doesn't have any financial security right now. And she said she's worried about Lowell, that she seems off-balance."

"I think she's on a treasure hunt. Stay away from her."

"She probably is. She usually is." He snorted, as if dismissing the topic of Caroline Barton. "Am I going to see you tomorrow?"

I looked toward the bedroom door. Lowell had suddenly appeared there, her brow furrowed, staring at me.

"I don't know," I said, because I didn't.

"WHAT THE HELL WAS THAT?" Lowell asked. Her face had gone pale. "Who were you just talking to?"

"My father."

"Were you talking about my mother?"

I nodded tightly. "She called him. He said she was going on and on about how she doesn't have any financial security right now and how she's worried about you."

"I told her he seemed lonely, but I didn't think she was going to call him today." Lowell sank onto a nearby couch. "Ugh."

I sat gingerly across from her. "I'm sorry."

"Are you sorry that she called him? Or that I caught you telling your dad my mother is a gold-digger on a treasure hunt?" Her eyes flashed at me.

"Both. I'm sorry about both." I started to get defensive, but I reeled myself in.

I believed Lowell knew who her mother was. But as much as I wanted to protect her from her mother and from everyone else, I needed to tread lightly. Caroline was her mother. You only got one, and most people preferred it if people didn't insult theirs.

She looked at me warily. "This is just going from bad

to worse. Just when I thought it couldn't get more complicated..."

"It was always going to be an awkward family reunion, Lo. Both of our parents are difficult. They both have their agendas. We just need to separate them from ours."

She shook her head, and my heart sank. "I can't do that. I can't forget where I came from. Or where you did. And you need to go back, Kyle. Back to your Dad."

"It doesn't matter." To me, it didn't. "Nothing else matters to me except you."

She stood suddenly. "I have to go."

She headed into the bedroom, and I scrambled after her.

"Go where?" I watched as she fumbled for her suitcase and randomly stuffed clothes into it.

"Home. Back to Los Angeles. Away from our crazy parents. I can't do this to you. I can't unleash the crazy of my mom on you. You're so close to making everything okay with your dad."

"Okay," I said as nonchalantly as I could manage. I grabbed my suitcase from the closet and put it on the bed.

"What're you doing?"

"Packing to go back to LA with you."

She shook her head, and although I didn't think it

was possible, my heart sank even lower. "No. You're staying. You have a deal with your father."

I stared at her. "I had a deal with you first."

"That deal's off." She wouldn't look at me.

"You have a commitment to Lucas. And Shirley. The premiere's coming up. Just let me come out for that." I hated the wheedling tone in my voice, but I felt panic descending on me.

"No." She stalked into the bathroom and almost violently threw her shower kit into her bag. "This stops now. I've already told more lies than I thought I was capable of. We've already hurt our parents. I don't want to keep going until we hurt each other." She grabbed her bag, threw on her flip-flops, and headed toward the door.

"You are *not* walking out on me right now. This is fucking ridiculous. You're acting like a child."

"I am not." She still wouldn't look at me as she headed out the door.

"Dammit! Stop!"

But she didn't. I ran out after her, shoeless and wearing no shirt.

The elevator doors were about to close, but I wedged myself in and grabbed her wrist. "You said you didn't want to hurt me. You're hurting me now."

"I can't do this. I can't ruin your life," she said. Her

eyes were filled with tears, but she had that stubborn set to her jaw.

"You haven't! You've made it a thousand times better! I'm a better man because I've been with you!"

The elevator doors opened to the lobby, and she rushed out.

"Just come back upstairs," I pleaded.

"No." Lowell stormed through the lobby doors. The skies were darkening as if it was about to rain. She turned to me. "Kyle"—she sounded as if she was trying to keep her voice on an even keel—"go back upstairs. Go to work tomorrow. I'll call you from home."

"Don't do this to me, Lo." My voice was shaking, and my hands were clenched into fists.

"I'll send the full fee to Elena. Don't worry about that." She sounded as though she was trying to be all business, intentionally cold.

"I'm not worried!" I practically spit. "I already quit! I don't care about the stupid money! Yours or my father's!"

Her face faltered a little, but fine actress that she was, she recovered almost immediately.

I stared at her until she looked at me. "If you want to leave me, think it through. And please don't do it because you think you're protecting me."

Her eyes flashed, and I couldn't tell if it was in anger or because I'd hit a nerve.

"What do you want from me?" she asked.

I reached for her, but she stepped back. "You know what I want."

"What'd you think was going to happen between us? Really?"

"Not this," I said. "Not you leaving me."

"Being around our parents is the reality check I needed. I don't want this either, but I have to get out before… before things go too far. Which is already." She raised her hand at a passing cab, and it pulled over. "I just don't want to make it worse."

I stood there, watching her, as the sky opened up. "I said I was sorry about what I said about your mom. I'm sorry." I sounded like a sniveling shadow of a man, and I didn't care.

"It's okay. I've probably said just as bad about your father." She shook her head. "But look at what we're doing to each other. There's too much history. Thank you for everything you've done for me." She looked as though she was going to lean over and kiss me good-bye, but she hesitated, and the moment passed. "Go back inside. You're getting soaked."

Then she got into the car and disappeared. I just stood there, with no shirt and no shoes, as the rain crashed miserably over my head. Once her car had disappeared in the traffic, I shuffled back into the hotel, trekking water across the marble floors.

"Mr. Jordan—" Britta started breathlessly.

My glare cut her off cold. "Please have a bottle of Grey Goose sent up to my room." I sloshed past her. "And if anyone calls for me, tell them to fuck off."

LOWELL

I don't want to keep going until we hurt each other. My words rang in my ears. But I was already hurting. I felt as if I'd ripped out my own heart.

I shut my eyes tight against the image of Kyle looking at me like that—betrayed, shirtless, standing in the rain. But of course shutting my eyes couldn't stop the images from playing in my head.

I'd never hated myself as much as I did in that moment.

"Please take me to the Plaza," I told the driver.

I was going to go to my mother's suite, get cleaned up, and take the first flight out of Boston. The idea of dealing with Lucas, Shirley, Gigi, my producers, and everyone else when I got back was sickening, so I shut my mind against it. I would be fine, no matter what.

Because Kyle was better off without me.

"You look like shit." My mother stood aside and let me in.

"Gee, thanks, Mom." I stood in front of her bathroom mirror and wiped mascara from underneath my eyes.

"What happened?" she asked.

"I'm going back to LA." I shrugged and hustled past her to the suite's kitchen, which she would surely never touch. I grabbed a paper towel and tried to squeeze-dry my hair. "I'm going to take the redeye."

"What about Kyle?"

I shrugged again, as if I had no answer for her.

"I spoke with Pierce."

All I wanted to do was get away from her and go home. "I heard."

"He didn't seem as interested in me as you said."

I rolled my eyes. "I said he *asked* about you. I didn't say he wanted to marry you again."

Sighing, she sat on the couch. "You know dear, I'm not as young as I used to be. My options are...more limited."

"Mom, get over it. You're still hot."

"Well, I appreciate that, but I *am* getting older,

darling." She spoke if she was trying to sound dignified. "That's why I need to think about making sure I'm okay in the future. That I'm taken care of. That's why it's so important that you're successful. I need you to be able to take care of us. I was hoping Pierce might be interested so I didn't have to lean on you so hard…"

I looked at her, incredulous. "Are you asking me for more money? After that crazy-expensive trip I just paid for?"

She shifted in apparent discomfort. "You don't have to put it that baldly."

"I'm not being bald. I'm being direct—which is more than I can say for you. How much do you need?"

She shrugged nonchalantly. "Enough for my condo association fees for the rest of the year. And some refreshing." She pointed at her eyes. "My crow's-feet have decided this is a good time for a comeback. I also need to update my wardrobe. I'm starting a new barre class—"

I shook my head, trying to ward off the headache I felt looming. "Now's really not a good time. I just gave you all that money for your trip, and the condo, and I'm probably going to get fired when I get back."

Caroline sprang up and paced, wringing her hands. "My daughter, the famous actress, can't afford to help her own mother?"

"I can *help* you, but I can't foot the bill while you live like a billionaire socialite." My mother didn't understand, or didn't care, that this suite at the Plaza alone would cost me over ten thousand dollars by the time she checked out. She'd gotten so used to extreme wealth, it was as if she wasn't even aware of the value of a dollar.

"Well, that's all I'm asking for—help."

"Fine. I can help you get what you need. Maybe not what you *want*, but definitely what you need. So how much is that?"

"Seven hundred thousand should do it." She didn't even blink.

"Are you out of your mind?" I snapped.

She just looked at me blankly.

I shook my head. "I can't give you that much. I don't have it."

My mother snorted. "You're a famous actress. You have a premiere coming up for a movie that everyone's saying will be a hit. I feel certain that you can help your mother out."

Rage bubbled inside me. I was still too emotionally raw from leaving Kyle to handle this right now. I clenched my hands into fists. "I don't *have* it. I told you."

"Are you telling me you're going to leave me in the lurch? Let your own mother live on the streets?"

"You don't have to live on the street. You just can't

buy a new ballet-inspired wardrobe for a hundred thousand dollars and have your tenth elective plastic surgery. I don't think I'm being unfair."

"I don't think I'm being unfair either." She tried to look serene; I wondered if that was a trick she'd picked up in Japan. "If you cannot or will not help me, I'll be forced to take other action. I have to protect myself, darling. I'm not getting any younger. I have to make sure I'm taken care of."

I stood, my hands shaking, and I grabbed my bag. "Exactly what constitutes 'other action' in your frail mind, Mother?"

Again, she didn't flinch. *Fucking yoga. Must've given her all sorts of steely resolve, even though it's wildly misguided.*

"Pierce doesn't want this story about you and Kyle to get out. Perhaps I'll let him know that if he wants to be as generous as he should have been during our divorce, it won't?"

I opened my mouth then closed it again, surprised by this new low. "Seriously? You're going to blackmail Pierce? I thought you wanted to date him again."

"I told you, he didn't really seem interested. He owes me, Lowell. This would be one way of finally collecting on that."

"That's disgusting."

She shrugged. "Not as disgusting as going directly to the press to sell my story. The story of my daughter, the famous actress, hiring a male escort, who happens to be her estranged stepbrother."

I stopped dead in my tracks. "You would do that?"

"You would cut off your own mother?"

"I'm not cutting you off!" I yelled. "I'm saying you can't afford to live like Paris Hilton!"

"You're not leaving me with too many choices, dear."

I dropped my suitcase and stalked over to her, my finger jutted out at her bony chest. "You've got some nerve." I poked her, but she didn't wince. "This is exactly what you were like with husbands one through four. Your greed had no floor and no ceiling. No wonder they divorced your ungrateful ass."

"I can't believe my own daughter would speak to me like this." Caroline actually managed a sniffle.

"You"—I poked her chest again—"are being an ass. I've done everything for you, and this is how you treat me?" I stood back, really looking at her. "You do what you want. Blackmail Pierce, go to the press. I don't care anymore."

I made it to the door before she spoke again. "I guess that means you don't care about protecting poor Kyle either. I don't think Pierce will take it too well, whatever scenario I choose. If this gets out, Pierce will probably push Kyle away again. For good."

My chest heaved, but I refused, I absolutely refused, to cry in front of her. "You leave him out of it."

"You're the one leaving him out of it, darling. You're only thinking of yourself."

I actually laughed, leaning back against the door so I didn't just collapse. "*I'm* the one thinking only of myself? That's a good one, Mom."

"Your actions have consequences. Just think about what would happen to your career if this comes out. What will happen to Kyle's relationship with his father? And it'll ruin Pierce. His launch will go so far south, it'll be in the South Pole."

"That's the North Pole, Mother."

She shrugged. "Whatever."

"So now you're blackmailing me, too?"

At least she had the decency to examine her nails instead of staring blatantly at my face. "A girl's gotta do what a girl's gotta do."

"You aren't a *girl*." I laughed again, but this time I was closer to tears. "It's official: your lifestyle, your clothes, your pocketbooks, and your face are more important to you than your daughter."

She looked back at me. "That's not true. But I can't go back to living like a Texan hick. I can't live in an apartment building somewhere and go… *grocery shopping*. And wear clothes from Target. And watch cable for fun. I'd die like that—wither away."

"I think I'd like to test that theory."

She looked as if I'd just slapped her. "What is the difference with you? You've always supported me—financially and emotionally. Why're you turning on me like this? Is it this boy?"

"He's not a boy. He's a man."

"From what I remember, he was always trouble." She crossed her arms and stood there, waiting for more of an explanation, which was more than she deserved.

"He's changed. He's not like that anymore." I sighed; Kyle seemed like a more mature adult than most people in my life by the nanosecond. "But it's not just him. It's everything that's happened this year: the stuff with Lucas about my weight, that video… and yeah, Kyle. I'm starting to wonder what it would be like to have a normal life." I shook my head, furious with myself. "Ugh, why am I even talking to you? You threatened to blackmail me two seconds ago!"

She smiled a little. "Sorry about that, but you're talking to me because I'm your mother." She came over and touched my hair, fixing it and making me wince. "It's always just been you and me against the world. You can't turn your back on me. I'm your blood. You and I would never do that to each other. Not after your father walked away from us."

I swallowed hard. For all of her faults, I loved my mother. "I'd never turn my back on you, but that doesn't mean I'm giving you seven hundred thousand dollars for pocket money either."

She dropped my hair and stepped back.

"I don't have it, Mom. I'm not saying that to be mean."

"You're not leaving me with a lot of choices, Lowell."

My mother had burned through four husbands and tons of my money with that very tactic: the threat of a temper tantrum and a bitch-slap to the person saying no. But I was no longer negotiating with her. "Do what you gotta do, Mom." I just wanted to get on the plane, go to sleep, and block out this entire miserable day.

In spite of all the Botox, she still managed to look surprised. That did nothing to sway me. For the first time in my good-girl life, I walked out and slammed the door on my mother.

I WAS SITTING in the waiting area at Logan, extra-large sunglasses plastered onto my face, when my phone buzzed. I looked at it warily. I hoped it was Kyle, then

I really hoped it wasn't, because I would probably crack.

It was Pierce. *Oh, fuck.*

"Hello?"

"Lowell, it's Pierce. Your mother just called me. Again."

"Ugh." That was all I could come up with.

"Did Kyle tell you she called me earlier?"

"Yes… but I'm not with Kyle now, sir. I'm at the airport."

He was quiet for a moment. "You're flying out? Alone?"

"Mm-hmm." I figured the less I spoke, the less of a chance there was I'd cry.

"Well, when she called me just now, she said you were cutting her off and that she's in a tight spot. She said she was going to have to sell your story to the press in order to have enough cash to survive."

Wow, my mother wasted no time. If I weren't so sickened, I'd be impressed. "Are you accusing me or empathizing with me?" I asked.

"Uh… both. I just wanted you to know I took care of it."

I sat there, stunned. "What do you mean?"

"I'm giving Caroline the money she needs in exchange for keeping Kyle's situation… private."

"You know she's just going to keep soaking you for that, right?"

"I'm well aware of your mother's tactics." Pierce sounded as if he were amused. "I didn't mention it to her just now, but I have some leverage of my own. Just in case she gets out of hand, which we know she will."

I perked up a little at that. "What's that?"

"Just some old personal photos of your mother. From when she lived in Texas. She had big hair. Very big. And do you remember what her teeth looked like before she had them done?" He laughed, and I realized that even though he was talking about revenge-black-mailing my mother, he was speaking of her in doting tones, as if she were a spoiled, naughty, favorite child.

"I thought she burned all those pictures."

"She thought she did too." I could imagine him smiling in his office.

"Well, it's good you have them. You'll probably have to threaten to sell them to *XYZ*." I hesitated, wanting to ask about his son but also afraid to. "Did you talk to Kyle just now?"

"Yes. He didn't... he was his typical monosyllabic self, but he didn't mention anything about you leaving. But as I said before, I can tell that you've turned into a mature young woman. You're doing the right thing by going back, you know. Kyle needs to get his life together."

"I know." I felt my heart break a little bit more because Pierce was right.

"He starts work tomorrow morning."

"He's going to be great. Your launch will be amazing because of him."

"It'll be interesting to see."

"Are you going to see my mother again?" I asked out of morbid curiosity. He'd been kind about her when I'd seen him, but I still remember their red-faced yelling in those days leading up to their separation. "I'm surprised you're giving her the money and being so... relaxed about it. You were anything but relaxed about the divorce."

"I remember. I hated her with the fire of a thousand suns. I felt like every dollar she took was a slap in my face." Then he...*chuckled*. "Funny thing. She was such a pain in the ass back then... but it's just sort of boring without her around. You know what I mean?"

I ached without Kyle being next to me, and I still felt the sting of my fight with my mother. Even though I felt as if I'd been alone my whole life, I'd never felt as lonely as I did in that moment. Still, I was doing what I thought was right. For both of them.

"Yeah, I do, Pierce. I know exactly what you mean."

Tori met me at LAX. She spotted me before the photographers did and got to me quickly. "You look like shit. Keep your sunglasses on and put your hood up. There's a ton of press here."

"Awesome," I said. "Just awesome."

The photographers started calling my name as soon as we got outside. A thousand flashes went off as Tori pulled me toward the Town Car.

"What happened with Kyle? Did you two break up?"

"Are the rumors true? Did he cheat on you?"

"Are you two taking a break?"

"Knock it off!" Tori hollered. "Just let us get to our car!"

She managed to push me through the throng and to the car. We both collapsed inside, exhausted.

"Please get us out of here," she asked the driver.

We sped off into the early morning light. I kept my sunglasses on and my hood up so Tori couldn't inspect me.

"How are you *dealing* with that?" she asked, motioning back toward LAX.

I shook my head. "I have no idea. Kyle made it a lot better." Saying his name made me choke up, so I was relieved that I had my sunglasses on.

But of course, this was Tori I was dealing with. She put the divider up and turned back to me. "Lo?" She patted my knee. "Talk to me. Where's Kyle? When I got your text to pick you up, I assumed you meant both of you. What happened?"

"I broke up with him," I said, and tears spilled traitorously down my cheeks.

"But I thought you guys weren't even really together," she said, trying to be comforting.

"We weren't." I sniffled.

She handed me a tissue, and I honked my nose into it.

"But?"

"But I still broke up with him." I blew my nose again. "His dad offered him a position with his company—*if* he agreed not to see me anymore."

"Did Kyle take it?"

I shook my head. "He said... he said he wanted to stay with me." My words came out in puffy little sobs.

Tori patted my knee again. "Aww, that's sweet, Lo. That's really nice."

"I know. He even said he'd quit being my escort before we left—but he hadn't told me that before."

"So he was just with you because he wanted to be with you?"

"Yes."

"I think I like this Kyle," Tori said.

"But that's exactly why I had to let him go. I can't ruin his life, Tor. I can't make him miss out on a great opportunity because… because… I'm selfish." I collapsed into tears.

Tori pulled me into her arms and shushed me. "It's okay, Lo. It's okay."

I pulled back and continued to ugly-cry. "N-n-no, it's not. His father forbid him from being with me. And it made sense. Because it *makes* sense. Then my mother showed up, and she freaked out when she saw him. She asked me for more money—"

"Ugh! I knew she was going to do that!" Tori fumed.

"And when I said no, she freaked out even worse. She threatened to blackmail me." I tore off my sunglasses and wiped my face. "It's such a mess. I was trying to do the right thing. That's all I was ever trying to do, I swear."

"I know," she said soothingly. "I know."

We were quiet for a minute while I collected myself.

"So…what happens now?" my friend asked.

"Kyle goes to work for his dad. That's the important thing. He'll get the chance he deserves."

"What about *you*?"

I shrugged. "I go deal with Lucas and Shirley and everybody else who's going to be disappointed in me.

And just pick up the pieces. Maybe… quit the business."

"So that's it? You're just going to give up? On your career and on Kyle?"

"I'll figure work out." I blew my nose again. "It's not as if I really have a choice about Kyle."

Tori snorted. "Of course you have a choice. You're either going to give him a chance, or you're not going to give him a chance."

"Did you not hear a word that I just said?" I asked incredulously. "His father will do anything to keep us apart. So will my mother. On top of that, there are some minor details you might remember: He is my step-brother. He is my escort."

Tori held my gaze. "He *was* your stepbrother. He *was* your escort."

"Still sounds pretty insurmountable to me."

"I think he's nice. I think you should give him a chance."

"I *can't*." I shook my head, feeling desolate. "It's not a good time."

My best friend, who knew me too well, patted my knee again. "When's it ever going to be a good time?"

KYLE

I DRANK HALF the bottle of vodka, but it did nothing to dull the pain. I sat on the bed, running my hands down the sheets, just thinking about Lowell.

My heart hurt. I didn't know that was actually a thing, aside from in movies and books, but it was happening. To me. It actually hurt pretty badly.

Then my father called, going on about Caroline Barton. Some nonsense about her threatening to go to the press and him giving her money to stop her. I only half-listened through the haze of vodka, but it sounded as if Caroline would be able to afford her next series of cosmetic procedures, along with another Louis Vuitton bucket bag, courtesy of my father.

As if I gave a fuck.

We hung up, and I sat there, fuming. I wanted to tell

him I wasn't coming in tomorrow. I wanted to tell him I had more pressing matters to attend to, but I didn't. I wasn't sure if Lowell would want me if I walked away from him. She might think I was never going to grow up, never going to be the man she needed.

Old Kyle would have just finished the bottle, passed out, and slept in late. *Fuck you* to my dad, *fuck you* to my questionable future, *fuck you* to the woman who left me.

But Kyle 2.0 couldn't do that.

For once, I felt as though I had something at stake that mattered. And I wanted it more than I'd ever wanted anything.

I put down the bottle and called my father back.

SOME PHOTOGRAPHER—ONE I would be punching later, when I could get my hands on him or her—had taken pictures of Lo and me in front of the Stratum. We were clearly fighting. In the picture, her face was angry and mine was despondent. My abs had made it into the shot; at least they looked good.

The headline on *XYZ* read: *Lovebirds Done Already?*

Then there was another shot of Lowell, looking exhausted with puffy eyes, getting out of a cab at the Boston airport: *Lowell Packs on Pounds Amidst Breakup.*

I cracked my knuckles, just thinking of what I was going to do to Katie from *XYZ*.

～

I PULLED up in front of Lo's house the next afternoon. I'd only made one stop between LAX and her house. I hoped she would understand what I was about to do.

I also hoped she would be happy to see me, but I kind of doubted it.

There was a full-on campground of reporters splayed out on the sidewalk, drinking coffee, chatting, and waiting for Lowell to come out of the house.

I triple-parked and got out, waving to my favorites. "Hey, Jimmy. Jose. Hey, Lila." I stopped when I saw Katie. "Your click-bait headlines had it all wrong. Again."

"Really?" she asked, not missing a beat. She snapped about a thousand pictures of me as I forced myself to smile pleasantly at her. "Tell me how I got it wrong. That wasn't a fight? It sure looked like one. Is she expecting you today, or is this a surprise visit?"

I flashed my dimples. These pictures would be a far cry from the ones last night, dammit. "I don't think I owe you a detailed explanation," I said, flashing my teeth at her, "but I *will* say that I'm thrilled to be here."

She snapped some more pictures as I moved on, then

she trained her zoom lens on the door and waited like a cheetah stalking its prey.

I ignored her. I would deal with her later.

I smiled and nodded at the other reporters as I headed toward the door; I would allow nothing in my face to give away the jagged nerves in my stomach. It was as if I'd swallowed a bunch of teeth and they were rattling around in there, chattering. I took a deep breath. I rang the doorbell and took the box out of my pocket.

My back was to the reporters—hopefully they couldn't tell I was scared shitless.

Lo came to the door and peered through the side pane of glass, her brow furrowed. She probably thought one of the paparazzi had had the audacity to ring her doorbell. When she saw me, shock registered clearly on her face. I nodded at her, praying that she'd regain her composure quickly. We had a job to do. By the time she opened the door, her face was serene.

I'd always said she was a fabulous actress.

"Come in," she said, motioning me through the door.

"Not yet," I called, loud enough so the closest reporters could hear me. "I wanted to say something first."

Her brow furrowed again. I noted, stupidly, that she was wearing jean shorts and a tank top with flowers on it. She looked innocent and adorable, her face scrubbed clean of makeup.

I had a feeling I would always remember this moment. For better or for worse.

She crossed her arms and watched me. "What?"

"I just wanted to say I'm sorry," I said, again loud enough to be heard. "I'm so sorry about how I'm doing this," I mouthed to her.

I watched one of her eyebrows go up as I went down on one knee. I opened the small box to reveal a square-cut diamond engagement ring, fit for a princess and paid for by the credit card I'd begged my father to lend me.

Now both of her eyebrows were up.

I looked at her pleadingly. "I'm sorry about last night, Lowell. I said things I should never have said. But after you left, it got me thinking…" I was still speaking loudly enough for the press to hear, but I was getting choked up because I meant every word. "I don't ever want to be away from you again."

She still wore a skeptical expression, her arms crossed firmly. "What is it y'all is asking me?" The Texas that had leaked into her question was the only giveaway that she was freaking out.

She's going to kill me once she lets me into her house. That was surely the truth, but it was too late to stop now.

"Are we back to *y'all* status?" I asked.

She continued to look at me skeptically. "Some of us are. Let me see that." She edged closer, and her face softened when she saw the ring. "That's...pretty. You have pretty good taste."

"I actually have excellent taste."

She looked at me and blushed, knowing full well I wasn't talking about the ring. I took a deep breath, praying for several things all at once. First, that she would forgive me for this someday. Second, that she'd say yes. Third, that the reporters would get a good shot.

I was still looking at her pleadingly, inwardly begging her forgiveness. "Lowell Barton, would you do me the undeniable honor of becoming my wife? Will you marry me, Lo?"

Our eyes locked for a second, and a thousand different emotions shone in hers.

Then she flashed me her megawatt smile—the one she saved for the press. "Why, Kyle Jordan, I thought you'd never ask."

She threw herself at me, and I put the ring on her finger, petrified of what her private reaction would be—but thrilled nonetheless to have her back in my arms. I pulled her tight against me.

"I love you," I whispered against her hair.

"I freaking hope so, because everyone thinks we're engaged," she whispered back.

We turned around and posed for the cameras, the ring front and center, my arms wrapped around her like a vise.

LOWELL

"You have a lot of explaining to do, Kyle Richards." I stomped toward my couch and collapsed on it, spent from the performance on my front porch.

"Don't you mean *y'all* have a lot of explaining to do?" He threw himself into the chair across from me and grinned.

"Ha ha." I looked at the ring on my finger, temporarily distracted.

"Pretty, isn't it? Just like you."

I looked up and found him watching my face. "That was some stunt."

"It wasn't a stunt."

I raised my eyebrows, and he looked sheepish.

"Okay, it was sort of a stunt."

I winced as if he'd kicked me in the stomach and automatically wished that I hadn't.

He sat up straighter, watching my face. "Lowell, I meant it. What I said."

Which thing you said? I wanted to ask, but I couldn't, because I was holding my breath.

He came over to me and kneeled in front of me. My eyes filled with hot, traitorous tears, and I blinked them back. He pulled my left hand to him and ran his fingertips gently over the ring, looking so deep into my eyes I felt it in my stomach.

"I love you."

I still wasn't breathing. He looked at me, waiting for an answer. I finally gave up, blew out a deep breath, and roughly wiped the tears from my face.

"I love you too," I admitted.

He smiled. "You don't sound too happy about it."

I pulled my hand back and defensively put my other hand over it, as if to protect the ring. "That's because I'm not. What're you doing here? You're supposed to be at work. In Boston."

He looked a little wounded and went back to sitting across from me. "I called my dad last night. I told him that I love you and that I need to be with you for your premiere. Then I told him that I really, *really* want to come back to work for him and that I'm going to follow through as soon as I feel okay about coming back east."

"You know he's going to cut you off for good, right?"

I sounded accusatory, and I was—but not for the reasons he might think. *I* didn't care if Kyle had a lucrative career or a massive trust. I would take him shoeless and shirtless, just as he was last night. But I didn't want him to miss out on a great opportunity, and I didn't want him to lose the chance to mend his relationship with his father. Not because of me.

"I don't want you to give all that up. Not for me. I'm not worth it." My voice wobbled, and I inwardly cursed as I wiped more tears away.

"Lowell, knock it off." Kyle looked exasperated. "Of course you're worth it. But I don't have to choose—Pierce agreed to let me start after the premiere. He was surprised I had the balls to call him and tell him the truth. It was definitely a first for me."

"What about his app launch?"

Kyle shrugged. "We just have to keep the truth about our past a secret. We've done it so far…"

"Did he tell you about Caroline? That she called him again?" I didn't want to give Kyle any more of a reason to hate my mother, but he deserved to know what we were up against.

"Yes. She threatened him, and for some reason, he

agreed to give her exactly what she wants. He seemed...happy about it." He looked baffled. "Your mother seems to have a knack for keeping my dad's attention. I think they might go on a date, or something."

I shook my head. I was just as confused by our parents' love-hate relationship. "That is completely messed up."

I didn't even want to think about the ramifications, for us, if our parents dated again. *Ew.*

"I went to see my mother after I left the Stratum last night. We had a terrible fight." I looked at him. "She said she was going after Pierce for hush money, and if that didn't work, she would sell her story—*our* story—to the press. So we're only safe for as long as your dad keeps her satisfied, which is a tall freaking order, let me tell you."

He shrugged. "My dad seems happy to give her money, at least for now."

"Until she gets too greedy, like last time."

"Hopefully she's learned her lesson. Maybe they both have." He paused as if he was thinking it through. "But for the short term, we should be safe. I think my dad said he has pictures of her she wouldn't like going public. They'll keep each other busy by blackmailing each other for now. They really might deserve each other. But your mother won't go to the press, and my father won't cut me off. Done and done."

"So we *could* be okay," I mused.

"As long as nobody else finds out about our past." Kyle chuckled. "This really is sort of crazy, huh?"

"That's a massive understatement." I took a deep breath and held up my left hand. "What about *this*?" I wriggled my fingers, secretly loving the weight of the engagement ring. "What're we going to do about this?"

"What do you want to do about it?" His voice was dead serious.

A pit formed in my stomach. "Everyone's going to think we're getting married."

"Okay." He shrugged a loaded shrug.

"Okay?" I wailed, my voice reaching a near-hysterical pitch.

"That's what I said." He didn't falter.

I put my hand back in my lap and fiddled with the gorgeous ring. "You really are a PR artist, you know."

"I know." He gave me a lopsided grin that made my heart speed up.

"So what're we going to tell the press?"

"The truth." He kept grinning. "That we're getting married. Whenever you're ready."

I stared at him. I had the sense, for once, to just keep my mouth shut. But that was where the sensibility ended. I threw myself into his lap and kissed him with wild abandon, letting my body say what I was too chicken to.

After our kissing became more frantic, he carried me to the bedroom.

"I missed you," he said quietly.

His mouth claimed mine, his tongue probing my mouth until I was dizzy with lust. I arched my back beneath him, trying to get as close to him as possible.

"I need you," I said urgently. I felt as if I was going to cry if I didn't have him inside me right now.

I whipped off my tank top and my shorts. The self-consciousness I'd felt before was long gone. It was just me and Kyle, his glorious chest pressed against me, his strong arms wrapped around me.

I unzipped his shorts, somehow struggling to get him out of them, while he fisted my hair. His enormous cock, hard and glorious, sprang out to meet me. I leaned down to stroke him, feeling him get even thicker. I greedily took him into my mouth and heard him suck in a sharp breath. I took him all the way to the base of his shaft, wanting to taste every inch of him. He moaned and threw his head back as I sucked on him hard, wanting to get him ready to be inside me.

"Oh, *fuck* yeah."

Lost in the moment, he thrust into my mouth, and I

felt myself getting even more turned on. I loved how he responded to me, like he loved me being in control. I was throbbing though. I needed him. Being apart from him, thinking I was going to lose him—even for a little while—had been too much, and now my body physically craved his.

He gently stopped and pulled me up to him. He ran his hands through my hair and looked at me, his eyes urgent.

"I love you," he said.

"I love you, too." I leaned over and kissed him, my need for him overpowering.

He grabbed a condom from his pocket of his discarded shorts and handed it to me. I ripped the foil packet open, pinched the tip, and rolled it down his length. He pushed me back onto the bed with a deep, probing kiss that made me moan. He trailed his fingers down to my sex as he kissed my nipples. His fingers circled me, making me arch against his hand. Finally his fingers touched my clit and he rolled it back and forth. Pressure built up inside me. I arched up to him again, greedy for more.

"You looking for something?" he whispered in my ear. I heard the grin in his voice.

All I could do was nod and hope like hell he knew what I needed. *Now.*

He slid his tip into me, and I groaned. Then he hitched himself in farther, with small thrusts, and my body stretched to accommodate him. His thrusts became harder and deeper, bringing me to the edge already. He put his hand against my hip bone and pulled me against him for every thrust, making my vision go blurry, a scream building up in my throat.

"Come for me, baby."

As soon as he said it, an orgasm ripped through me. I was shaking, screaming his name as I shattered around him.

He fucked me ruthlessly through my orgasm. Then he took my hands and held them over my head. He licked and sucked my nipples between thrusts, making me moan. Every roll of his hips sent shockwaves through me. It was as if my body had been built for his— he filled every inch inside me. Every thrust brought me closer to the edge again.

"Tell me you're mine now. Tell me you mean it." He slid into me, making it difficult to breathe.

"I'm yours. I mean it."

He thrust all the way into me again, making my heart speed up and my world go woozy, as if my impending orgasm was going to knock me out.

"Tell me you love me, Lo. That you're mine."

I felt my body clench. "I love you, Kyle." I was crying

and laughing, moans escaping my lips without my consent. "I'm fucking yours."

Now his thrusts were deliberate, deep, and bracing. I could tell he was about to come, and he was holding on until the very last second. I adjusted my hips and forced his cock all the way into me. I moaned deeply as he fucked me until I found another release.

I shattered beneath him, screaming his name again. He slid even deeper inside me, lacing his fingers through mine, his thrusts ragged.

I heard myself still screaming, but I also heard Kyle.

"Mine. You're mine," he said as he came inside me, holding onto me for dear life.

"ARE YOU ALWAYS THAT LOUD?" he asked later with a self-satisfied grin.

I smacked him. "Apparently I am with you."

He managed to look even more self-satisfied.

Both of our phones were blowing up, but we were in bed and ignoring them.

"Our parents are going to freak out when they see the headlines," I said.

"What else is new?"

I considered that. "With the two of them? Not too much."

"Tori's *really* going to freak out." Kyle laughed.

"Yeah, she is. And my agent. And Lucas. They're all going to go nuts." I snuggled into him. "And Katie, that bitch from *XYZ*. I think she's carrying a torch for you. She's probably crying right now Because you're off the market."

"And because everybody loves you. No matter how hard she tries." He kissed me.

I beamed at him. "Can we just stay in bed for the rest of the day?"

"Hell, yeah," he answered, beaming back. "Until we go out to dinner to celebrate. And show off that bling. Gotta feed the machine, babe."

We grinned at each other.

"Let's feed some other machines," I said.

He laughed. "That doesn't make any sense, but somehow I know exactly what you mean." He pulled me on top of him. "Now, shh. No more talking."

"Until I scream your name," I reminded him.

"Until you scream my name. Again. I could get used to this, babe."

"Well, you better," I reminded him.

"I MISSED YOU SO MUCH," he said after we'd had sex for about the zillionth time. He trailed lazy kisses over my shoulder.

I laughed. "We were only apart for a day." I flopped over and put my head on his chest, snuggling into him and relishing the feel of his naked body against mine.

"It was a long day."

I smiled into his chest. "I agree."

He took my hand and ran his fingers over the diamond again, as he'd done repeatedly since we landed back in bed. "This is just a placeholder. Once I start working and I can save some money, I'm going to get you something killer."

I sat up and looked at him. "You're going to replace my fake engagement ring?"

He looked appalled. "It's not a *fake*. It's real, not CZ."

"That's not what I meant, and you know it." I wanted to shut myself up, but I couldn't.

He scrubbed his hands across his face. "I said it was a placeholder ring because I eventually want to get you something else. Something spectacular. After I've earned the money to do it. That would really mean something to me. In fact, I'd like that to be my first act as a responsible, salaried adult."

His thumb stroked the ring again, and I pulled my

hand away. I held it up and looked at it in the light. "This one's pretty. I like it."

Kyle stared at me. "I'm getting you another one." He hesitated for a second. "If you want it, that is."

I sighed and rolled onto my stomach. I couldn't look at him. A million emotions were running through me. Kyle was smart. He rolled on top of me so I could feel his long, perfectly muscled body pressed against mine.

"Do you want it?" he asked and kissed the back of my neck.

I felt him, erect and extraordinarily hard again, pressing against the small of my back. I groaned. "Of course I want it! What are you, crazy?"

"Which it?" He poked me with one of the *it*s I wanted, and I automatically spread my legs a little.

But then I remembered what we were talking about. I tried to muster my last dregs of self-discipline and swatted him away. "I want *it*"—I jerked my thumb at his lovely, erect, large piece of man fun—"and *it*." I waggled my ring finger. I turned to look at him. "But we can't be engaged, Kyle."

He sat up and ran his hands through his hair. "You're really doing this? After all *that*?" He jerked his thumb at the bed.

I sat up too. Even in my glowing post-sex haze, I felt as though I needed to be responsible. To be serious about this. "It hasn't been long enough, first of all. We've only been together for a little over a month. Second of all, our parents were married, and they might be... dating again. I don't even know if we *can* ever get... you know."

"*You know?* You sound like a middle-schooler." He cocked an eyebrow at me, and I desperately wished I'd thought of a different word than *cocked.* "You can't even say it?"

"I can say it. *Married.* I'm worried we can't ever really get... married. And I'm not even sure that's what this is." I held up the ring again, as if it were evidence of some plot to cruelly confuse and embarrass me.

"Let me try this again. Because apparently I didn't do a very good job." He traced my jawline with his thumb, making me shiver. "I asked you to marry me because I love you. I did it in that obnoxious manner because we needed a headline to trump our fight. Your premiere's coming up fast. You don't need any more trouble. You need to be on top." At that, he laid back and pulled me on top of him.

I relished the feel of him beneath me, his strong, muscled body fulfilling every wild dream I'd had about him. But this was serious, so I slid off him. "I'd love to be on top. Hell, I'd love to stay on top forever, but we need to figure this out."

He sat up again, undeterred. "You said yes, right?"

I nodded.

"Did you mean it?" he asked.

"What exactly did I say yes to?" I noticed that my heart was hammering.

"You said yes, in front of the press, to marrying me, which means they think we're engaged. You said yes when I asked you to marry me... which means *I* think we're engaged." He was quiet for a heavy beat. "And that means, to me, that we're committed to each other. Exclusively. Forever."

I held my breath and felt my eyes well up with stupid, inconvenient tears.

"And for me, forever starts right now," he continued. "But we can wait to get married for as long as you want. Because I agree, six weeks is soon. Not too soon, but soon. I want to do this right. I want to give our marriage every chance to be successful. I'm only ready when you're ready." He stroked my back. "And I want to buy you a different ring. I've been thinking about this for a while, Lo. Like I'm a *girl* or something. I totally have a picture in my mind of what I want to get you." He looked stupefied by his own thoughts.

That was so adorable, I almost died. "That's really nice."

"I know, right? But listen—I know what I want. I

know what *this*"—he pointed at the ring—"means to *me*. And if we went to Vegas tomorrow to elope, I wouldn't even hesitate." He watched my face. "But that's me. What about you? What did *you* say yes to?"

A tear slid down my cheek. I couldn't help it. I couldn't believe that he loved me like I loved him.

"So?" His jaw clenched at my silence and crying. "Are we engaged or aren't we?"

I wiped my face and looked at him. Tension rolled off him as his eyes searched my face.

"Of course we are, you big lug." I threw myself into his chest again. He wrapped his powerful arms around me, and I let myself cry against him. "Like I could ever be away from you again. Y'all is family."

"I'm not a plural, babe. Even though I totally understand you wishing I was." I heard the grin and dimples in his voice.

"I'll teach you one of these days—y'all can absolutely be used in the singular."

He kissed me, our lips coming together delicately at first, then changing into something deeper, more urgent. Kyle pulled back. "I'm going to teach *you* a few things, young lady. Now that you've agreed to be mine, I can afford to take my time."

He ran his hands down me, and I giggled a little

breathlessly. "That sounds exciting and bad all at the same time."

"It's both, babe—and it's bad in a very, very good way," he said, his massive form looming over me. "You better get used to it."

He kissed my neck, and I took a deep breath. *I could get used to this. Very, very used to this.*

"Are you sure this is what you want?" I didn't want him to stop, but I couldn't stop asking questions.

He sighed and leaned up. "We're still talking, aren't we?" He sounded humorously resigned.

"I can't help myself." I smiled at him, feeling guilty for stopping him again. But I had to know that this was real, and I needed to feel all the corners of the situation out. "How's this going to work? You're going to go back to Boston, and I'm going to stay here, or go on location, and we'll see each other…when, exactly?"

Kyle sighed and rolled off me. "You're really trying to keep me outta there, aren't you?" I must've looked stressed because he smiled indulgently and patted my hand. "We'll make it work, babe. I can fly out here on weekends, or we can take turns. When you go on location, I'll take vacation days to see you. We can Skype." He tucked my hair behind my ear. "People do it all the time. We can do it too."

"And what about… our parents? For real? They're

going to freak. You know that, right? We were joking about it before, but it's not funny."

Kyle shook his head. "We're just going to tell them the truth. And they're just going to have to live with it."

"But people are going to find out about us eventually." I swallowed hard. "At some point, the press will discover your real name. They'll figure out who your father is and that our parents were married. It's going to happen. It's just a matter of time." I looked over at our phones, which hadn't stopped beeping with texts and media alerts. "What happens then?"

He pulled me against him. "I don't know. I only know that what we have is the most important thing to me. Everything else will just have to work itself out."

I looked at him, knowing in my heart that he was right. "I love you, Kyle." Saying it felt so good. "That's what matters to me now."

He grinned. "I love you too, babe. Everything else will be okay. Trust me."

KYLE

TRUST ME. Of all the bright ideas I'd had, maybe that had been the worst one yet.

I read the latest text message on my phone and groaned inwardly, then I looked over at Lowell. I loved watching her sleep. I loved it as much as I loved watching the 49ers, and that was saying something.

I turned back to the message. Lowell was going to freak, and it was all my fault.

I shouldn't have come out here. It was selfish. But I shoved that idea from my head. It was probably true, but it was also true that Lowell and I loved each other. We'd agreed that our relationship was more important than everything else.

I really hoped she still felt that way once she'd had a chance to think about it some more. And once I told her what was coming. I sighed and gently nudged her awake.

She opened one eye and squinted at me adorably, a huge smile spreading over her face. "Well, hello, *fiancé*."

My heart leapt. Then I remembered the text, and my stomach dropped.

"Hello fiancée, yourself." I swallowed hard. "There've been some…uh, developments while you slept."

She sat up and opened both eyes. "What?"

I held up my phone. "Katie from *XYZ* texted me. She said she had some new information and wanted to verify it before she went to press."

"Since when does she ever verify anything?" Lowell asked skeptically.

"Exactly. Never. So this has gotta be a big deal."

"It can't be good."

"Nope, it definitely can't be good." I rolled out of bed and threw on some clothes.

Just then, Lowell's phone rang. She looked at it suspiciously before picking up. "Hello, Tor." She held the phone away from her ear as Tori screamed a few things. When she'd subsided, a grinning Lowell brought the phone back to her face. "I know, right? He totally surprised me! And yes, it's a real engagement. To be followed by a real wedding. When we're ready." She listened to Tori babble.

"No, you can't start planning. *No*, we're not ready to book a venue. We just got engaged two hours ago!" Her brow wrinkled as she listened to her friend. "Listen, if you want to live to be my maid of honor, you'd better relax."

I heard more squealing through the phone, and I decided it was a good time to grab a snack. I was searching through the refrigerator for the organic peanut butter, when I heard a knock at the door. *Uh oh.* Lowell was still in the bedroom, so I went to the door and looked through the side glass panel. It was Katie from *XYZ*, looking smugger than usual, and who I assumed was her assistant.

I cracked the door open and peered through. "I got your text about two seconds ago. Do you mind giving my fiancée and me a minute to talk it through?"

She looked at her watch. "You have about one minute." She was antsy, tapping her foot and fidgeting. "I need to publish this before anyone else does."

"Stay right there," I said, not trusting her enough to leave her alone for more than a second.

I ran back to Lo and stuck my head through the bedroom door. Lowell was on her back, chatting and smiling like a normal newly engaged person. Which she was not.

"Hey," I said, interrupting her, "Barracuda Lady's at

the front door. She doesn't seem like she has a lot of patience."

Lowell rolled her eyes and hung up with Tori, promising to call her later for more dissection of the happy news. "She didn't give us much time."

"She's antsy, tapping her foot on your front step."

"Great," Lo said, getting up. She looked down at herself in a rumpled T-shirt. Then she peered in the mirror at her hair, which was mussed and wild. "I totally look like I've been having sex all afternoon."

"That's because you have." I grinned, ridiculously proud.

She sighed and grabbed some clothes. "Let her in while I take a quick shower. But don't let her past the living room! I don't trust her!"

"What do you want me to tell her?" I asked.

"Nothing. Not yet."

"YOU CAN COME IN," I told Katie the Barracuda. "But give your cell phone and any other electronic devices to your assistant. Nothing's coming in here."

"Picky, picky." She tsked, but she did as I asked.

"I have to be," I said, letting her in. "You can't trust anybody nowadays."

"You can say that again." She looked greedily around Lowell's house, her eyes drinking in every square inch. "This is lovely and perfect. Much like Lowell Barton herself."

"I agree," I said, although I didn't care for Katie's snide tone. *She's just jealous.* I was sure that was true, but it didn't make her any less dangerous. "Have a seat. I'd offer you something to drink, but I'm not leaving you unattended."

She raised an eyebrow at me. "You were a lot friendlier when you first showed up."

"I had to learn the hard way."

We looked at each other for a beat, with fake smiles, until she broke the silence. "I have information about you, Kyle. I wanted to give you the courtesy of telling you first."

"That's so thoughtful of you," Lowell said, sailing in from the kitchen, wearing clean clothes, her hair pulled back in a ponytail. She carried three lemonades on a tray.

"Lemonade." Katie rolled her eyes at the tray. "You really are something, you know that?"

Lowell handed her a drink and sat across from her. "Yes, I know that." Lowell flashed her a megawatt smile. "Now, what can we do for you? I'm assuming you're not here just to offer your congratulations—thank you anyway. I did, however, overhear you telling Kyle that you have information about him. How fascinating. I just can't imagine what that might be." Lowell linked her hands through mine and squeezed, the only indication that she was on edge.

Katie set down her drink without taking a sip. "I'm pretty sure that you know, but I appreciate the little flourishes of your performance. Tell me, how's it going to be to kiss all of that good-bye? Because I happen to know for a fact that Lucas Dresden won't appreciate the story that's going to break about you two later this afternoon." She motioned toward the ring on Lowell's finger. "That was a nice try, though."

Lowell held up the ring. "It's not a try, Katie. It's an engagement ring. Because we're engaged."

The reporter raised her eyebrows. "I don't believe you."

"Why's that?" I asked, but the pit in my stomach told me I already knew.

"I knew there was something off between you two. It was too cute and too convenient. So I did a little digging," she said, licking her lips. "And I found out that you're related. So that's why I don't believe you're engaged—the last time I checked, in the state of California at least, siblings can't get married."

"We're not siblings." I waited to see what she'd say next.

"According to my source, your parents were married. You lived in the same house during your adolescence, raised as siblings."

"That's bullshit." I'd been able to tolerate her thus far, but she was making my blood boil. So this was going to turn into a shit show, after all. I started to say something more, but Lowell clutched my hand.

"What you're saying isn't true," Lo said. "I would say that if you care about your credentials as a journalist, you won't go forward with that story. But since I know you couldn't give a flying fuck about journalistic integrity, I'll just save my breath." Lowell stood. "You can go now. Do what you like."

Lowell marched her to the door. Katie looked a little flustered, as if this wasn't what she was expecting.

"We can cut a deal," she offered Lowell at the threshold. "I'm the only one who knows. For now."

Lowell leaned toward Katie's ear. "Go fuck yourself. Deal?" Lowell slammed the door behind her then pressed herself against it, her chest heaving. She was quiet for a minute. Then she said, "We're so fucked."

I nodded, feeling guilty as hell. She seemed to pull herself together a little. She stood, a faraway look on her face as if she was lost in her thoughts.

"What's the name of your favorite reporter out there?" she asked.

"Jose."

Lowell opened the door. "Go get him. And tell him he's going to need a camera crew."

LOWELL

Kyle was taking care of the arrangements for our interview, which would take place first thing in the morning. In the interim, I had to make the call I'd been dreading since Kyle came back into my life.

My mother. Always my mother.

I decided to call Pierce first. Kyle and I had already talked about it and decided on what to say to each of them. Dealing with his father's anger would be like baby-stepping toward dealing with my mother's.

"Lowell," he answered before it even rang. "You've got to be fucking kidding me. When Kyle asked for a credit card, I assumed it was for a plane ticket, not an engagement ring."

I swallowed hard. "That's not exactly the reaction I was hoping for, Pierce."

He sighed. "You know that it's not personal. But the timing for all this couldn't be worse for me. Now that it's an engagement, your story's going to turn into even more of a media circus."

"I know," I said quickly. "But Kyle did it to protect me."

"I know. And I see how much he cares for you. But his being in the public eye like this, one week before my launch, is too risky for me. I've already told you both that."

"I know, but... he puts me first. Even when I tell him not to." I lovingly fingered my placeholder engagement ring. Now that I knew what it felt like to have someone fight for me, I understood it wasn't something I would give up easily. Still, I felt bad for Pierce. "I didn't want him to come out here honestly. I wanted him to stay in Cambridge. And stay away from me."

"So why'd you say yes?" That was Pierce for you. Always cutting to the chase.

But I felt that even though I'd made a mess out of Kyle's new life—the life he might not have now, if the launch went sour—I'd done the right thing. "Because I love him. And I want to marry him. I want that more than I want your app to be successful. More than I want my mom to be happy. And more than I want my acting career, I guess."

"What do you mean? I thought this would be your crowning moment in social media."

I shook my head. "No, sir." Taking a deep breath, I prepared for the worst. "A reporter told us about an hour ago that she's found out about our past." I steeled myself for his reaction, but all I heard was silence. "Pierce? Are you still there?"

"I'm here," he said. "I was just inwardly cursing."

"Well, Kyle and I are going to handle it. I promise."

"How the fuck do you plan on 'handling' it? It's a disaster is what it is. Put on a hazmat suit. That's about as much as you can do before a shit storm." He hung up on me.

I didn't really feel any better after those baby steps. I still had to call my mother though. I looked at myself in the mirror. *Big girl panties, Lowell. Come on.* I groaned and hit her number.

"Well, well, well," she said before the phone even had a chance to ring. "I knew you would ruin everything. You have a lot of explaining to do, young lady." She took a deep breath, winding up. "You're *engaged?* To your *step-brother?* Who's been *disinherited?* Would it really be so difficult for you to just date a hot actor with a house in the Hills? Like a *normal* person?"

"You can't help who you fall in love with, Mom."

"Oh, cut the crap. Of course you can. Do you think

it was *fate* I fell in love with four millionaires after your father left me penniless and with a baby? Do you think my *heart* told me to do that? No, young lady. Those were decisions based on rational thought. I needed someone to take care of us, so I found someone to take care of us. Several someones. And my heart didn't have any say in the matter. Have you met Pierce Richards? The man is ugly. He's a hairy *beast*. The man has more hair on his chest than he ever had on his head. He even has hair on his *ass*, Lowell. Like fur. But I married him anyway. Because it was the right thing to do for our future. Do you understand what I'm saying to you?"

"Not really," I answered weakly. "Which is pretty normal."

Caroline sighed. "It's time to grow up, young lady. Part of what you find out when you're an adult is that fairytales don't happen to those of us who live in the real world. You don't love Kyle. You just want him to put his dick inside you because he's a bad boy and because it's taboo. I know you. This is a *phase.* You'll grow out of it as soon as you two stop having sex all the time, then you'll realize what this is—lust. And maybe a late-stage temper tantrum."

"Please don't ever talk about Kyle's dick again." My voice was flat. "This is not about sex, Mother. I know you can't understand what being in love means. You don't love anybody except for yourself."

"That's not true," she said, and I almost felt her seething through the phone. "I love *you*. I loved your father—before he knocked me up and took off. I just don't let my emotions rule me. That's called being *practical*. That's called being a *grown-up*."

I paused for a second. "I'm sorry you're disappointed. I'm sorry I'm disappointing you."

"Then don't disappoint me, dear," she snapped. "You're the only one who never has. Don't start now."

I shook my head, tears welling up. "I don't want to be like you." The tears ran down my face. "I don't want to end up like you."

"Like what?" She snorted. "Thin, rich, and fashionable? There are far worse things, let me tell you."

"I don't want to be bitter. A bitter *cougar*. Aren't you lonely, Mom? Aren't you tired? Don't you want to be with someone who cares about you?"

She groaned. "Before you went and messed things up, I thought that Pierce was interested in me again."

But you don't love him. You just want to go shopping again. And plan dinners at all the right places. That's all you want. You don't care about anybody.

Not even me.

Not even me.

"Good luck with that, Mother." I willed my tears away. "And you might want to pour yourself a drink before you watch the Entertainment channel this week. Make it a stiff one."

"What on earth does that mean?" she shrieked. "I'm coming out there to put a stop to this. You're the one who needs something stiff! A stiff dose of reality! You've lost it."

But I knew, I just knew, I'd only just found it. "Speaking of stiff, Kyle *does* have a nice dick. And I *do* enjoy it. And he *is* a bad boy." I heard her inhale sharply, and I almost relished making her upset. "But do you know the best thing about him? Do you?" I realized I was yelling at her and my whole body was shaking. "It's that he *loves* me, Mom. And I can trust him."

"I can't believe my own daughter is so naive that she's—"

"I feel sorry for you," I interrupted. "Because you will never, ever know what love like that feels like. But I hope your new barre class is great. And your new ten-thousand-dollar bucket bag. Good luck with keeping your face up. It's turning into a regular full-time job, whether you want one or not."

"I cannot believe this is you, Lowell. You're going to pay for this. I am going to make you *pay*," she screeched.

But it was as if someone had dropped a house on her

and she'd lost all her power over me. Suddenly, I didn't care if she went on screeching till her next facelift. I just shook my head. "I've already paid, Mother. So I guess this is good-bye."

I hung up, looking in my own eyes in the mirror for signs of despair. None came.

As if it were a new wrinkle, I took that as a visible sign of growing up.

THE INTERVIEW WAS BOOKED for first thing in the morning. I had no idea what Katie would do between now and then, but I figured it couldn't be good. It was time to come clean. I invited Tori, Shirley, and Gigi over, and I made them pack their bags to stay the night. We needed to close ranks. After they arrived, they all fussed and cooed over Kyle, as if he were the conquering hero of my Hollywood image empire, which I suppose he was.

With a pit fully formed in my stomach, I called Lucas. "I've got good news, and I've got bad news."

"I always like to hear my good news first," he said. "Go."

"I'm engaged. Yay."

"I already saw that. That's fine news. Much better than the fight you two had up in Boston. Nicely done."

He waited for a minute while I paced. "Is that it for the good news?"

"Um… it depends on how you define *good*, I guess."

I could almost hear him looking at his watch. "You know I don't have time for guessing games. Go."

"Kyle and I are doing an exclusive interview with the Entertainment network first thing in the morning."

"Did you clear that with your agent? I'm sending our PR person over. She needs to be on set—I already told you that. She'll have to vet the interview."

"Great," I said tightly. "That's great."

"So what's the bad news? Go," he commanded.

"I haven't lost a pound. But I've been working out, and I think I look pretty good."

"She looks great," Kyle called from the other side of the room. He, Tori, and Gigi were researching wedding venues and honeymoon destinations, in spite of my protests. "If you give her a hard time, I'm coming down to the set tomorrow to break your face."

I made a shushing motion at Kyle, but I was secretly thrilled by his threat. It was just so *mas macho*.

Lucas just ignored him. "Per our contract, you have to be in shape enough for our shoot."

"Per our contract, I'm in shape enough. I'm in *better* shape. I'm just not skinny."

Shirley came over. "Give me that phone."

I handed it to her and watched her stalk around my kitchen.

"Real body types are in, Lucas. Your movie sucks, but Lowell's body just might save it. You might get numbers if people think she's representing a new Hollywood standard in beauty." She listened to him and rolled her eyes. "No, I don't think your movie should be a clinical trial. That's not what I'm saying."

He must have yelled at her because she closed her eyes and braced herself against the phone.

"Say what you want. I've been in this business a long time, and I know what I'm talking about. You can thank me when it does well." She hung up and handed the phone back to me. "That guy's a real asshole."

"I told you," I complained.

"He's a successful asshole, though. You still need this part." She wagged a red, gel-manicured fingertip at me.

"I know. I don't know if I'm going to be able to keep it, though." I looked nervously at Kyle. Now that I'd sort of dealt with Lucas, it was time to deal with my inner circle. We hadn't told anyone about us yet. Tori was the only person outside of our parents and Katie who knew about our past.

Shirley rarely, if ever, missed a trick. "What does that mean?"

I swallowed nervously. "It just means that Kyle and I

are going to answer every question at the interview tomorrow."

"I would expect that. So what's the problem?" Shirley looked at my face, which was clearly guilty, and raised her eyebrows. Then she looked at Tori, who was looking down, picking imaginary lint off her blouse. She turned to Kyle, who was inspecting his nails. Gigi just shrugged at her, mystified, so Shirley turned back to me. "Out with it. Right now, please. I'm not getting any younger."

"Kyle and I… have known each other for longer than you think." I shot him a quick look and saw the smile spreading on his face. "We… knew each other when we were younger."

"Go on." Shirley crossed her arms. "Because I know that's not the whole story."

"We grew up together. For part of the time, anyway."

"My father was married to her mother," Kyle said. He put some crushed ice into a tumbler and poured vodka in it, squeezed in a lime, and handed it to Shirley.

Shirley frowned and took a large swig of her drink.

"They were married for four years. Lowell and I were stepsiblings from the time she was ten until she was fourteen and I was seventeen, when they got divorced. That was the last time I saw her. Before this."

"So…" Shirley looked as if her mind was racing a mile a minute. She didn't look upset anymore, more like she was plotting and scheming—her normal look. "Did you two have feelings for each other back then? Did you ever do anything?"

"No," we said in unison, horrified.

"He was really mean back then," I offered.

"She was sort of a dork," he explained.

"Okay, okay. We can work with this," Gigi piped up, her blond ponytail swinging excitedly. "You two didn't like each other back then, but you met years later and felt an instant spark." She sounded as if she was giving a movie pitch to an executive.

"Umm...no," Kyle said, shaking his head. "I mean, I obviously thought she was hot when I saw her again, but we didn't exactly... get along." He looked at me and smiled. "She totally wanted me though. I could tell."

I snorted. "As *if.*"

Shirley looked confused. She elbowed Tori, who was still busy picking imaginary lint off her shirt. "I thought you said you set them up and they hit it off instantly."

Tori pressed her lips together, pretending to think. "Is that what I said? I really don't remember." Shirley towered over her, and Tori winced. "Okay, okay...I might have made some stuff up."

"Which stuff?" Shirley asked.

"All the stuff?" Tori asked, even though it wasn't a question.

"Tori didn't set us up," I interjected. "I'm the one who called Kyle. Actually, I called Kyle's... pimp."

"Pimp?" Shirley asked, aghast. She drained the rest of her drink and shoved the tumbler back into Kyle's chest. "Does that mean you're a—"

"Escort," Kyle said smoothly. He poured her another vodka. "I'm an escort. Well, I was anyway, until I accepted a new position with my father's company."

"You're a hooker." Shirley couldn't hide her shock.

"I'm retired now." He gently handed her the drink. "You should probably sit down. You look a little pasty."

Shirley sat down obediently and drank some more. Gigi watched us all with avid interest. Tori twirled her hair, trying to look innocent. I just paced, knowing that I was anything but.

"You hired a hooker," Shirley said to me, and I nodded. "And he showed up." She jerked her thumb in Kyle's direction. "And you recognized him... because he was your stepbrother."

I smiled at her in sympathy. "It gets a little convoluted, I know."

"And did the reporter from *XYZ* find out all of this?" Shirley asked.

I shook my head. "She knows that our parents were married. I don't think she knows about the... other part." I looked at Kyle. "I guess we'll find out when she posts something."

"What about the proposal?" Shirley asked. "Was that just for show?"

"Yes," I said at the same time Kyle said, "No."

"We're getting married. For real. That's the important thing," I said soothingly. "I know. It gets a little convoluted."

IT WAS a long night of refreshing: refreshing the *XYZ* website and refreshing our drinks. Shirley, Gigi, and Tori were sleeping over in order to be there for the interview early the next morning. Pierce hadn't called again, and neither had my mother. I would be relieved about that, but somehow it didn't seem right.

Finally a picture of us from earlier in the day was posted to *XYZ* with the headline: *Stepbrother Fiancé?*

We clicked on the article—if you could call it that—and my heart sank. It named Kyle as Kyle Richards and speculated that "Kyle Jordan" was a name fabricated to fool the press. It told all about our time living together in northern California and how our parents had been bitterly divorced. To my horror, there was even a school picture of me in glasses and braces, smiling pleadingly at the camera.

I wondered who had sold them this information. It was mostly banal, with few details, so I wondered if it could have been someone who had worked at the house and recognized both Kyle and me.

There was no mention about AccommoDating. Not yet.

But I knew it was only a matter of time.

KYLE

Lowell and I went to bed a little after that. I felt thoroughly dejected.

"It's just a matter of time," I said. "They're going to find out that I was working for Elena and that you hired me. It's all going to come out."

Lowell wrapped her arms around me and pulled me close.

"I'm so sorry," I said.

"For what?" She put her head against my chest.

"For being your stepbrother. And your escort. And all this drama." I gently kissed the top of her head.

"I'm not sorry anymore." She looked at me. "I love you, and we're getting married. End of drama."

"Lucas is going to fire you. And then your

premiere… the producers of *Hearts Wide Open* aren't exactly going to be happy either. There's plenty of drama."

"What if I told you I don't care anymore?" she asked softly.

"I'd say I don't believe it." I watched her face, which was defiant. "Or that it was a damn shame, because you're a talented actress."

"There are some things that're more important than that. Like you." She blew out a deep breath. "I'm worried about your father."

"What about your mother?"

She shrugged. "My mother… is a pain in the ass."

"I know that. But she's going to freak."

"She already did. She screamed at me and threatened to come out here."

I scrubbed my hands over my face. The idea of seeing Caroline Barton again exhausted me. "Great."

"I know, right?" Lowell groaned.

We just snuggled against each other, each of us lost in our thoughts.

"What do you want to do tomorrow, Lo? During the interview?"

She looked at me again, her eyes searching my face. Then she smiled. "We're going to do the right thing, babe. Together. From here on out."

WE HAD SCHEDULED the interview for the ass crack of dawn. I groaned when the alarm beeped. I slammed it off then reached for Lowell's nipple and rubbed it slowly with my thumb. I kissed her shoulder, feeling heat shoot through me.

"Mmmm," she said, then she sat bolt upright. "Kyle. Stop." She swatted me off of her. "We've got work to do."

I groaned again. "Do you think you're always going to be so Type-A?"

She shot me a filthy look. "You can play with my boobs later. Now shush. You're going to wake up the others."

She bustled around the room, and I took small comfort in her promise about her boobs and later.

Lowell made me wear a suit, claiming that I would look dashing and respectable. I knew what she really meant was that I wouldn't look remotely like a hooker, but that was fine with me. She chose a simple white dress that showed off her curves, which she was apparently through with hiding.

The network showed up, and they did our hair and makeup.

"There," the artist told me, putting a final puff of powder on my nose. "You're gorgeous."

I flashed him a smile. "I kind of get that a lot." I needed to feel some bravado right now to counteract the nervous boulder of dread sitting like deadweight in the center of my stomach.

"I bet you do, honey. I bet you do," he said as he hustled off.

I turned around to find Lowell watching me with raised eyebrows.

"Are you flirting?" she asked.

I shrugged. "Maybe a little."

"Aww, you're nervous." She took my hand. "Don't be. We're going to be all right."

I laced my fingers through hers. "If you say so."

She leaned against me. "I do."

LUCAS SENT over his PR person, Jenny, a grim, razor-thin woman with black nail polish and a cool haircut. Gigi tried to make small talk with her but finally gave up. Jenny smiled at no one and constantly tapped things into her phone. She was sitting in the room with some of the network's crew, and I had a feeling she would get a nasty surprise today.

Or two.

Gigi was staying out in the room with us too, doing nothing to earn her commission except flicking her hair and smiling. Tori and Shirley sat in the kitchen, drinking coffee and vigilantly checking every website known to man for signs of trouble. They were also researching Caribbean resorts for our honeymoon, but fearing reprisal, they'd made me promise not to tell Lo.

Finally the lighting was arranged, the sound check was done, and it was time.

"So," Jose said, smiling and sitting on the couch across from us. He was a reporter for the Entertainment network, and he'd always seemed like a nice guy, always polite and smiling, no nasty questions. "I landed the exclusive interview of the year. Thank you. I thought that bitch from *XYZ* was going to get it."

"She wasn't an option," Lowell said, smiling at him. "We wanted to save the good stuff for someone we liked. By the way, love the jacket."

Jose beamed at her, and she beamed back. The girl had been studying me. And she was pretty good.

"We're ready when you are, Jose." I twined my fingers through Lowell's and took a deep breath.

"Three, two, one," the camera man said.

"I'm here with Lowell Barton and her fiancé, Kyle Richards. Kyle, up until yesterday, I thought your last name was Jordan. Can you catch me up with what's been going on?" Jose asked.

I put on my best smile, making sure my dimples were on full display. I was going to need them. "Well, Jose, it all started eight years ago…"

LOWELL

JOSE BLINKED AT US. "So you're her *stepbrother?*"

"That's right. Well, I *was* her stepbrother. For a few years."

"And eight years later, you were her *escort?* Do I have that right?"

"That's right. Lowell hired me after that incident with the police. For damage control," Kyle said.

I gritted my teeth. It had been my idea to tell the truth, but it was still an ugly truth. I noticed that Lucas's PR woman had gone from looking grim and tapping into her phone to watching raptly with her mouth wide open.

"And then you two… fell in love?" Jose asked.

"Correct."

"And got engaged?" He sounded incredulous.

"That is also correct," Kyle said.

"And it's *real?*" Jose leaned forward on the couch, his hands clasped together. "You can tell me the truth, you know. America wants to know."

"It's real." Kyle smiled at him and pulled me close. "Are you married, Jose?"

Jose nodded.

Kyle gave him a long look. "So when you proposed, you knew it was real, right? Like you *had* to marry your wife? That you had to make it official and show the world that she was yours?"

Jose smiled and nodded again. "It's been six years, but yeah, I remember. That's how it felt."

I rubbed Kyle's back. What he'd said gave me the chills. It was exactly how I felt.

"For us," I said, jumping in, "it should have been a difficult decision. In some ways, it was. I had some feelings for him in the beginning, but I didn't act on them. There were just so many obstacles."

Kyle tucked my hair behind my ear, and I squeezed him again.

"But then I realized that the only obstacles were the things I let stand in my way. I was worried about my career, about our parents... and I still worry about them," I said. "But I wanted to do the right thing for me. Because you only get one life, right? And when you finally meet the person you want to spend that one life with, you have to be brave and go for it."

"Wow," Jose said. "Kyle, you're a lucky guy."

Kyle beamed "I'm fully aware of that."

Jose turned back to me. "What about the fact that he was… an escort? Was that difficult for you?"

I shrugged. "Lots of people screw other people for money. What Kyle was doing was just more… direct, I guess."

"If I could go back and change the past, of course I would," Kyle said. "But I was in a place where I felt that I had very limited options. So I did what I had to do to survive, and I don't regret that. I actually quit a week ago. I didn't even tell Lowell. I just… had to be with her for the right reasons. There were lots of them."

Jose nodded as if we were actually making sense to someone other than ourselves. I could only hope that our parents, my fans, and the people in the industry felt the same way.

"What do you think is going to happen now?" Jose asked me. "With your career? The director of your latest film's been pretty vocal since your run-in with the police."

I nodded. "I have no idea what's going to happen. I can only hope that my fans know how much I love them and appreciate them. I want to keep working, that's for sure. But will that be possible?" I shook my head. "I don't know. Plus, my director's still on me to lose another ten pounds, so—"

Jenny, Lucas's PR girl, stood and stamped her feet. "Enough! That's a wrap! Not another word, Barton!"

Jose raised his eyebrows.

"I'm not taking orders from you. Or anyone else," I snapped at her.

Jenny stood there, fuming with her arms crossed.

I squeezed Kyle's hand and looked back at Jose. "We're doing this interview to tell the truth. The truth is this is the man I love. I also love my work. While I'm at it, I want to add that I really hate starving myself just so I can do my job. I guess my point is that I can't keep living a lie just to save face. To pretend I'm perfect when I'm not. I just want to be who I am. And be a good person. And do good things. I hope you all can accept that."

I looked up and saw Jenny glaring at me while Gigi gave me the thumbs-up. So my performance was already getting mixed reviews, but I didn't regret it.

I looked at Kyle, who was beaming at me, and I felt sure.

Doing the right thing really *was* always a good idea.

JOSE WAS THANKING us for what he said was the best interview of his career when we heard a commotion out front.

Kyle and I jostled past the crew to the door.

"What's going on?" he asked as I peered out the window.

I groaned and leaned against the door, wishing I could un-see the scene outside.

"What? Tell me," he said, his voice urgent.

"It's my mother. It looks like she's holding a press conference, chock full of fist-waving and screeches."

Kyle blew out a deep breath. "You wanna just ignore her?"

I shook my head. "Let's go out the back door and sneak around." We hustled past Jose, and I jerked my thumb toward the front of the house. "You're missing a story out there. My mom's holding an impromptu press conference."

Jose let out a low whistle. "You two are exciting." He grinned. "My wife and I just binge-watch cable shows for excitement. We're boring."

"Boring is good," Kyle called, pulling me toward the back. "We're striving for boring as soon as this is all done."

"I highly recommend *Game of Thrones*," Jose called. "A little something for everyone. Even has dragons."

Kyle gave him a thumbs-up then headed into the kitchen.

"You did a fantastic job with that interview," Shirley said when she saw him. "Seriously, we listened from in here. I might have to hire you, Kyle. Public relations in this town isn't for the faint of heart, but you're a natural."

"Thank you—if my dad decides to fire me again, I might just take you up on that." He grinned. "But right now we have a situation. Lo's mom is out front, having a hissy fit in front of the press. You might wanna come watch."

Tori looked at me in sympathy as Shirley grabbed the vodka. Gigi joined us and they followed us out.

"I can't keep up this pace," Shirley said, huffing behind us. "I might have to retire after this, Lowell. You might be my last client."

"Nah," I said, "you're too good at what you do. Plus, you'd get bored."

We rounded the corner to find my mother standing on my steps, her face fully made up. She was wearing a cashmere T-shirt that had probably cost a thousand dollars and was gesticulating wildly.

Shirley let out a low whistle. "Bored sounds pretty good to me right now."

"Me too," I whispered as I watched in dread.

"My daughter has been taken *hostage* from me," my mother said. "This new boyfriend of hers, this *Kyle*, has emotionally blackmailed her. He's turned her away from me. He has Lowell under his control—like a puppet. I fear for my daughter's safety."

"Do you have any evidence of abuse, Mrs. Barton?" one of the reporters called. "Because that's a pretty harsh claim."

My mother was the picture of righteous indignation and unnaturally smooth skin. "I knew him when he was growing up. He was a bad boy then—*very* irresponsible. I don't know what sort of trouble he's dragging my daughter into now."

I took a deep breath and gathered what was left of my strength.

"I think she's been *brainwashed*," she said. "If anyone wants an exclusive interview with me, for all the gory details, I'm accepting bids now."

"Okay! That's enough," I said, coming around the corner. I looked at my mother accusingly, but she just squared her shoulders and stood her ground, as if daring me to contradict her. I pointed at my mother and faced the press. "This woman is my mother, and I love her. But she's having a temper tantrum right now because I've chosen to be with Kyle against her wishes. What she's telling you is a lie." I turned back to my mother. "It's time to get off the podium, Mother. Your mascara's running."

She quickly ran her fingers underneath her eyes. "Is it better now?" she whispered. I just blew out a deep sigh and nodded.

"If you guys want to know the real truth about my relationship with Kyle, make sure to tune into the Entertainment network tonight at seven. Jose said it was the interview of a lifetime. He got the real scoop." I looked at my mother, though I was still addressing the press. "All of it."

She paled beneath her makeup.

"Ladies, gentlemen, we're going in now, but I'll be back this afternoon if you want to take some pictures then. Anybody thirsty or hungry?"

Some of them yelled yes.

"I'll send out lemonade and cookies." I waved to the photographers, and they waved back. Then I grabbed my mother's elbow and hustled her into the house.

"You're quite the actress." She sniffed.

I just rolled my eyes at her, finally loosening my hold when we got inside. "You've got some nerve. I'd say I was surprised, but I know by now there's no bottom to how low you'll go."

She shot a look at Kyle. "You either, apparently."

He smiled at her and winked, which made her flush a deep, angry red.

"I won't have you ruin my daughter's life—"

"That's enough," I said, cutting her off. I wanted to tell her the specifics of the interview that was going to air tonight, just to rub her face in it, but I couldn't. I couldn't risk her running out the door and selling the story to the highest bidder.

She had to stay. Here. For now. As if she were... a prisoner.

"Tori... Shirley... Gigi... my mother needs to stay here. Probably locked up. At least until the interview airs."

"Locked *up?*" My mother whirled around. "You've gone completely crazy. Under no circumstances will I stay in this house. Not until you apologize to me and do something about *him.*" She jerked her thumb toward Kyle.

I crossed my arms and smiled at her, my real smile. "But I'm *not* sorry, Mother. So I don't actually owe you an apology. I love Kyle, and we're getting married, and I'm not supporting your bony ass anymore. So when you're done being locked up here, go get a job. Or a husband."

I thought I saw Tori and Shirley high five in the

background, but I was so focused on my mother that I couldn't be sure.

"I don't know why you're here anyway—I thought Pierce had you on salary."

"He does. But this goes further than the pittance he's offered me, dear. You're ruining everything. I figured if you were going to blow up your career, I might as well try to get some long-term security out of this debacle. I'm the one who helped you build your career. But you don't seem to remember that, or to care."

"You came out here to extort me. To sell my story to the highest bidder. To make a profit from my mistakes. I don't owe you anything—I've already paid. I'm done."

She was shaking, she was so livid. Then she started to cry. "I can't believe you're turning your back on me like this. I've done everything for you. I was the one who believed in you and your career. I drove you to all those auditions… sacrificed money for your acting lessons and your braces…"

"That wasn't your money! And what else did you have to do? Play tennis? It's not like you were out curing cancer or even waiting tables, for Christ's sake!"

She looked as if I'd slapped her. "You've changed, and I don't think it's a good change, young lady. You're flushing your career down the toilet because of a man—

no, a *boy*. He can't even support you. You know that, right? Pierce cut him off cold."

"I don't need a man to support me. I can take care of myself, thank you. And if my acting career's over, so be it. I can get some other sort of job. I'm not afraid to start over. The only thing I'm afraid of is missing out on the chance to love Kyle. A chance to really be happy." A traitorous tear crept down my face, and I roughly wiped it away. I needed to say this, but even after everything she'd done, it still hurt me to hurt her.

"I love Kyle." I reached for him, and he moved beside me, letting me have my say with my mother. "We're meant to be together. I love him more than I love my career. If I have to choose between the two—and I hope I don't, but if I do—I choose him. Because a life without him would be an empty life."

She shook her head. "You are making an impertinent, lust-based decision that's going to ruin your life."

"Just because Dad left you doesn't mean it'll happen to me! Or to you again!" I yelled. "I know you were hurt when that happened. I know you never got over it! But you've just pushed everyone aside. You treat people like they don't matter. All you care about is things. I don't want to be like that. I don't want to be *you*."

I was crying for real now, my nose running, and I didn't care. I'd never called my mother out on her feelings for my father and on what that abandonment had done to her. It was as if she'd become an ice princess after he left. No one could get to her heart, make it warm and loving again, full of life and vulnerability.

"Don't you dare speak about your father. You don't know anything about it." Her voice was hoarse.

"I'm sorry that happened to you. To us." I wiped my face and was grateful to feel Kyle still at my side, strong and supportive. "But you never gave anyone else a chance after that. It was like you were playing a game with your husbands: How much money could you get? How cold could you be?"

Caroline straightened her shoulders and dried her eyes, looking at me levelly. "Did it ever occur to you that it's less humiliating that way? That it's more dignified to be angry than sad?"

For better or for worse, I felt my heart soften. "No, Mom. It didn't."

"Well, of course it didn't." She sniffed. "You're not the only one in the family who's a great actress. Now"—she turned to Gigi—"if I'm being held prisoner for the rest of the afternoon, I have a couple of requests: Kleenex, a stiff drink, and magazines." She sniffed again then sashayed off to the living room.

"Don't let her out of your sight," I whispered to Tori, Shirley, and Gigi.

Tori nodded solemnly and handed me a tissue. "I'm proud of you." She gave me a quick hug.

I blew my nose loudly and grimaced. "Ugh. I'm not done yet. I gotta go see Lucas. Please don't let my mother drink all the booze. I'm pretty sure I'm going to need some when I get back."

KYLE

"I'm proud of you too," I said.

Lowell was looking in the visor mirror, fixing her makeup, as I drove us to the studio.

"Thank you," she mumbled. "I only had the courage to say that to her because of you though."

"Don't undo it." I put my hand on her knee and squeezed. "You did that yourself. It took lady balls, and you did it."

She smiled and put on some more lipstick. "I'm going to need even bigger lady balls to deal with Lucas."

"Well, I have my man balls. For backup."

She laughed, and I suddenly knew that everything would be all right.

"You've got a lot of nerve," Lucas's assistant said to Lowell when we walked in. "Jenny wants you dead. Lucas is off-the-wall right now."

Lowell just smiled tightly at her. "I'm sure he is. Is he available?"

"For about two seconds, which is all it's going to take to fire you," the assistant quipped.

We went into his office, and Lucas shook his head at Lowell. "Jenny told me everything. That was fucking unbelievable. You have royally fucked me. You know you're fired, right?"

Lowell dealt him a tight smile too. "Actually, Lucas, I quit. I don't think this movie supports a healthy body type, and I no longer want to be associated with it."

"Are you fucking kidding me?" He stood, red and livid.

"Nope. And that's the interview I'm giving *tomorrow*. No need to send Jenny. You're no longer affiliated with my brand."

She tossed her hair, and I followed her out. Lucas didn't even have the chance to speak. We walked back through the office, and his assistant was sitting at her desk, clearly stunned. She must have been listening in.

Lowell smiled at her again, but this time it was genuine. "See ya, Cristina. He's all yours. Good luck with that."

A NEW MERCEDES SUV was parked outside Lo's house when we got back.

"I've never seen that one before. It doesn't look like one of the photographer's cars." I glanced at Lowell.

"I don't recognize it either," she said.

We smiled, held hands, and kissed for the photographers on our way in. Katie was back, scowling at us. I winked at her and blew her a kiss. She frowned sourly, but I no longer cared.

That was a nice feeling.

Lowell grabbed my hand and checked her watch. "It's almost time. Are you ready?"

I nodded and pulled her to me after we went through the door. "I'm only ready because you've given me the strength to be ready."

"Nah," she said, beaming at me. "We were already both strong. We just gave each other another really good reason to be."

I kissed her forehead and wrapped her in my arms. "Thank you for being my reason."

Shirley interrupted us. "We've got company."

I raised my eyebrow at her.

"More company," she insisted.

We followed her into the living room. Seated on the couch next to Caroline Barton was my father.

"Hey, Dad," I said, surprised and wary. "Are you here to yell at me like Lowell's mom?"

He stood and shook my hand, a gesture that stunned me. "No, son. I came out to show my support." He nodded at Lowell. "I'd like to rescind our previous conversation, if that's okay with you. I was… pretty upset."

"Okay," Lowell said, wary as well.

"Congratulations on your engagement," he told her. "I know you'll make my son very happy."

"Th-thank you, Pierce. Isn't that nice, Kyle?" She elbowed me.

I opened my mouth then closed it. I just looked at my dad. "Do you mean it?"

"I do actually." He dropped back down into his seat next to Caroline.

I blew out a deep breath. "But… do you know we taped a major interview that's going to premiere tonight?"

"Caroline filled me in," he said.

"Did she tell you it's a *tell-all* interview?" I asked, bracing for the worst.

"She mentioned that, yes."

I couldn't believe how calm he was. I sat across from

him. "Do you know what that means?" My father was brilliant, but he had probably never watched the Entertainment network in his life.

He shrugged. "It means that you're going to tell everyone Lowell hired you as an escort. They already know that I was married to her mother."

"That's right," I said cautiously, watching his face. "We told them everything. We want a fresh start, Dad. We don't want to start our lives together pretending."

"I think… I think that's very mature, Kyle." He looked at me. "I'm *proud* of you."

"Huh?" I asked. "I did the opposite of what you asked me—no, what you *begged* me—to do. I ruined your launch too."

"My launch *is* inherently compromised. But at least my *Forbes* piece will be entertaining." Pierce nodded thoughtfully, his eyes twinkling. "When I spoke to Lowell yesterday and she told me about the truth coming out, I lost it. After that, I sat in my office for a while, fuming… and I realized it didn't matter. If you two really love each other enough to risk your privacy and your reputations, then who am I to stand in the way?"

"My father," I reminded him. "Who has a vested interest in the situation."

"I know you went against my wishes, son. But I also

know that you did it for the right reasons. And you used good judgment. Which, I might add, I've never seen you do before. So this is sort of a big deal."

I felt the pinpricks of tears in my eyes, but I willed them away. "So you don't... *hate* me?" Lowell clutched my arm, giving me the strength I needed to hold back the tears.

My father's face softened. "You're my son. I could never hate you. Even when I cut you off, I was angry, but I didn't hate you. That's not possible." He gave me a long look. "This isn't how I would plan things, but I've never seen you this happy. I've never seen you this together. I feel like, for the first time since you were a kid, since before things went... wrong with us, I feel like you've been honest with me. And I *like* you when you're honest and together." He grinned at me. "I actually like you, son. Between worrying that you were going to kill yourself and wanting to kill you myself for so many years, I didn't know that was possible."

"Gee, thanks, Dad," I said, grinning.

"You're welcome, son."

Lowell leaned forward. "And you forgive *her?*" She jutted her chin at her mother.

Pierce patted Caroline's knee. "Don't be so hard on your mother. She's been through quite a shock."

I might have imagined it, but I thought I saw a small smile pass over Caroline's lips.

Here we go again. For better or for worse.

WE WERE HEADED to the *Hearts Wide Open* premiere.

"I'm nervous," I said as I adjusted the bow tie on my tuxedo for the thousandth time. "And I don't get nervous."

"Yes, you do, you big lug," Lowell said and swatted my hands away from my neck. She fixed my tie and blew me a kiss. "You look gorgeous, though. Nothing to worry about."

"Everybody knows I was an escort. They're probably all going to be thinking about *this*." I motioned to my cock.

Lowell burst out laughing then clapped her hand over her mouth. "Sorry." Her shoulders were still shaking. "But are you really worried that people are going to be focused on your *penis*?"

I shrugged defensively. "Maybe. Probably. Usually."

"I'll be thinking about it. That's for sure." She grinned wickedly.

"Don't make me mess up your pretty dress," I growled and chased her around the room.

Squealing, she ran until I had her in a corner.

"Kyle, don't!" she yelled, laughing hard. "I just had my makeup done!"

"Then you better behave," I said, fake-menacingly. "And stop looking at my dick."

She was laughing so hard, her mascara was going to start running. "I love you, babe," she said when she could catch her breath.

"I love you too. And I'm looking forward to messing up your pretty dress later, when you can feel free to look at my dick."

ON THE RED CARPET, we saw a lot of our normal photographer friends but also a lot of new faces.

"Lowell! Kyle! Over here!"

"Show us the ring again!"

"How does it feel to have everything out in the open?"

"It feels great," I called.

"Do you two have any regrets?"

I looked at her, and she looked at me.

"I wish we'd slept together sooner," she said so only I could hear.

"I wish we were getting married sooner," I said.

We'd decided to get married six months from today, on the beach. Then we were going to Hawaii for our honeymoon. I was finally going to teach my girl to surf. I couldn't wait to see her catch her first wave.

It would be awesome. All of it, from now on.

What seemed like a thousand flashes went off.

"I'm pretty sure they're all looking at your dick," she said, under her breath.

"Of course they are, babe. I told you so. It's my not-so-secret weapon."

"Bang bang," she said, laughing and holding me close.

"So do you?" the reporter called again. "Have any regrets?"

We turned back to him, both of us flashing our best megawatt smiles.

"None," we said in unison and moved on to the next question.

EPILOGUE

LOWELL

"You can do it, Lo. This is it. This is it!" Kyle called as we paddled our boards toward the gathering wave. He watched me for second, looking excited, then he turned back to the water rising behind us. "It's gonna be a good one. Do you remember what we practiced?"

I snorted. "We've been practicing non-stop! Of course I remember!"

I watched the water rise, fear and elation mixing in my chest. I was going to catch this wave. This *was* it. I knew it.

"Get ready!" Kyle called, and he turned his board around in the clear, aqua water.

I tore my eyes off his muscled form and watched the

wave get higher and higher. I paddled around so that I was facing the beach, ready for it to carry me to shore.

"Start paddling!" Kyle hollered.

I did, panicking that I would mess up my timing and get too far in front or too far behind. Kyle had taught me all of the important safety precautions, and I knew how to clutch my board and roll under the wave if it crashed above me, but I was still afraid. I paddled, holding my breath, feeling the water gathering strength behind me.

"Go, go, go!" Kyle yelled.

I made long strokes with my arms. I felt the power of the water behind me starting to push me forward. I paddled harder. It was almost time.

"You got this, Lo! Stand up! I'll meet you on the beach!"

I got onto my feet as he'd taught me, finding my balance quickly. I wasn't a coordinated person, but Kyle had been so patient, so determined to get my body to know what to do. I crouched low, a thrill surging through me as the turquoise water rose around me. This was it.

This was it.

I stood and maneuvered the board along the crest of the wave. Everything rushed past me as I rode forward. *I've caught a wave.*

I rode it all the way in, relishing the freedom and

power. I hopped off my board just as I reached the shallow water; I felt the enormous smile plastered across my face.

Kyle rode the next one in, his smile matching mine. "You did it! I knew you could."

"I knew I could because you knew I could," I said, grinning. "Let's do it again!"

I didn't have to ask him twice. He turned his board around, and we headed back out, together, ready to catch the next wave.

IT WAS our last night on the Big Island. Tomorrow we were heading back to reality.

Everything was turning out better than I'd hoped. Pierce had opened up a West Coast office so Kyle could work as his director of PR and we could live together in LA, now that we were married.

Married. Just the thought of it gave me tingles. The press had pushed us for wedding details. In the end, I invited all of them, even Katie from *XYZ*, so that nobody had to sneak around.

I was enjoying my clear conscience, and I intended to keep it that way.

But in our day-to-day life, Kyle and I were no

longer big news. The press had moved on to a married reality star who was pregnant with someone else's baby and a pop star who'd checked into rehab for sex addiction. No one camped out on my front walk anymore. If I met a photographer on the street, I always gave them a big hug and a bigger smile for the picture.

I'd learned that if you couldn't beat them, you could at least play nice. They only ran pictures of me looking good now, which was a bonus.

Tori was dating Kyle's friend, a reformed bad boy rocker named Trent. He was perfect for her—he had a house in desperate need of organization, and he loved her sunny disposition and curls. They were so cute together I could hardly stand it, but in what I considered a very hypocritical twist, Tori wouldn't let me constantly pester her about the status of her relationship.

Elena had told Kyle that even though he'd quit, her business was booming. She was looking for new male escorts to add to the squad. Kyle's notoriety and good looks had created a new market of women looking to hire men for dating, companionship, and...stuff.

Lucas had hired a newer, thinner actress for *Renegades Forever* but the film had done nothing at the box office. He'd actually called me, asking if I wanted to meet for lunch to discuss new projects, but I'd told him I was booked.

Police Officer Deborah had gotten a promotion and started a leadership program for women within the LAPD. She even taught a class about how to appropriately deal with mansplainers.

Police Officer Scott had shown the video of me throwing up on Officer Deborah to his teenaged daughters many times as a warning to not abuse alcohol.

Shirley Feener's business was booming. She'd recently bought a lovely new Mercedes and paid cash for her perfect little bungalow in the Valley. Gigi was still working with her, swishing her ponytail and somehow earning her fifteen-percent commission.

I'd started my own production company and was currently writing a script based on *Little Women,* adapted to the modern day. I intended to include actresses of all colors, shapes and sizes. We were going to have kick-ass food at craft services.

I'd bought Ellie a new headset and hired her to help me run my company.

Kyle and I still went to the gym every day. I hadn't lost any weight, but I'd never felt better. I loved working out, and I loved eating—I thoroughly enjoyed eating snacks with my husband every night while we binge-watched *Game of Thrones.*

Pierce's app launch went better than expected, netting him a hefty bonus from his backers. He put it into Kyle's trust, mentioning something about grandchildren. Several somethings.

The issue of *Forbes* that ran his interview was its best-selling issue of all time.

Caroline had moved up to Cambridge with Pierce. They'd agreed to never get married again, and Pierce gave Caroline a very robust shopping allowance. She sent me pictures of them together sometimes, eating caviar in their pajamas and watching the Entertainment network. We'd never spoken about the fight we'd had, but things seemed better between us. Good, even.

She had also mentioned something about grandchildren. Several somethings.

On the last night of our trip, Kyle and I went to a traditional luau for dinner. I was wearing a dress I knew he'd like—short and strapless, showing off my newly acquired tan. We sat next to each other at a long table, feasting on Hawaiian barbecue chicken, coconut-and-cashew rice, grilled-pineapple-and-shrimp kebabs, and a mysterious blue drink that was so yummy we asked our server for the recipe.

He linked his hands through mind, running his thumb over the enormous diamond ring on my left hand. He'd found a new ring we both thought was perfect, and he'd paid for it with his salary, a fact he was very proud of. He smiled at me, looking so handsome in the fading light it made my heart stop.

"Remember that time I showed up as your escort? And you tried to kick me out?" he asked.

"Yes," I said, laughing.

"Most awkward family reunion *ever*."

"I know, right?"

"I've known you for a long time. But it seems like it took us a long time to get here," he said, still touching the ring.

"That's because it did."

"I hope this next part takes a lot longer. I hope it takes forever." He's stroked my cheek tenderly, sending shivers through me.

I kissed the man I loved, the man I never thought could be mine. "It will," I promised. "It'll be our own personal forever."

USA Today Bestselling Author Leigh James is currently sitting on a white-sand beach, nursing a Mojito, dreaming up her next billionaire.

Get ready, he's going to be a HOT one!

Full disclosure: Leigh is actually freezing her butt off in New Hampshire, driving her kids to baseball practice and going grocery shopping because her three boys eat non-stop. But she promises that billionaire is REALLY going to be something!

Visit her website at www.leighjamesauthor.com to learn more. Thanks for reading!

Printed in Great Britain
by Amazon